CHERISHED

THE PLAYGROUND CLUB
BOOK 3

SHANNON ELLIOT

Cherished

The Playground Club Series

By Shannon Elliot

To request permission or for more information, contact the publisher at pa@authorshannonelliot.com.

Paperback ISBN 978-1-964117-20-1

Ebook ASIN B0FDP69CMK

Second edition December 2025

Edited by Bookcase Media

Proofed by Bookcase Media

Cover Art by Eve Graphic Designs

Formatting by Creative Shannonigans

www.authorshannonelliot.com

CONTENT AWARENESS

Please take the following under advisement before reading.

Your mental health matters.
<u>Hate, Discrimination & Oppression</u>
Fatphobia & body-shaming (Past), Workplace harassment (Past)
<u>Alcohol and Drugs</u>
Alcohol consumption
<u>Pregnancy and Childbirth</u>
Childbirth (Supporting character, not on-page)
<u>Blood, Injury and Medical</u>
Body modifications (Tattooing), Chronic illness (Type 2 Diabetes),
Hospitalization, Medical treatment, Sterilization (Tubal ligation)
<u>Kink Related</u>
Exhibitionism, Fisting, Rope, Use of Adult Toys

This book contains "spice", or graphic sexual content, and is intended for persons of legal age. The content of this work should not be used as a manual or a realistic depiction of kink, fetish, or BDSM activities, and all characters are of legal age. This novel is intended for entertainment purposes only.

RESOURCES

Your mental health and safety matters to me.

Please make note of the resources below if any content in this book is triggering for you:

Dial 988 for the Suicide & Crisis Helpline or visit their website for more resources. (https://988lifeline.org)

For support after losing a loved one to suicide, call 1-800-646-7322 or visit the Friends for Survival website. (https://findahelpline.com/organizations/friends-for-survival-suicide-loss-helpline)

Call 1-800-662-HELP (4357) for SAMHSA'S national helpline (Substance Abuse and Mental Health Services Administration) or visit the website for more resources. (http://www.samhsa.gov/find-help/national-helpline)

For all the people who want to be worshipped, but can't take a compliment to save their life.
And for the friendships whose love is ever expanding and never ending like the universe.

WELCOME TO THE...

Playground
Club

1

SELENE

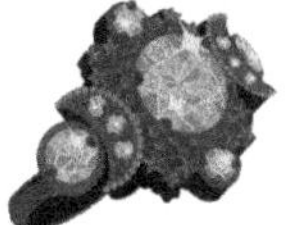

January 11—Capricorn New Moon

Most people assume I've had my wedding planned since I was a little girl, but that couldn't be further from the truth.

For a long time, I had no idea what my future would look like. There was no reason to think that far ahead. Everything was about being in the moment, just letting the stresses and pleasures of life flow through me as I navigated their waters.

The thing about water is it's not to be trusted. It may be vital to life, but it will drown you if you're not careful.

Right now, with a massive binder before me full of decisions I need to make, ones Gunnar insists I should make without him, about this wedding, I feel like I'm nearly underwater.

"I know it's intimidating," Ivy le Fleur, my good friend and the resident event planner for The Playground, says while holding my hand. "But I promise it will fly by. We'll make it fun for you, and I'll do the heavy lifting."

When I look away from the binder and at Ivy, her patient expression makes my nerves mount.

With her blonde hair and icy eyes, Ivy seems to float through life without a care. She carries herself with the grace of a mythical being. But something about people being so certain of things puts me on edge.

No one can guarantee anything, so why even make promises in the first place?

"Right," I reply, taking a deep breath to calm my racing heart. "Where do we need to start?"

"Well... is Gunnar joining us?" she asks, curiosity lighting up her expression.

I shake my head, knowing he'd come up with any excuse under the sun to avoid something like wedding planning, even though I specifically asked him to make time for this meeting.

He keeps telling me this wedding is about me and what I want. He wants me to have everything I envision for this wedding, but there's a lot of pressure that comes with making all these decisions alone. It feels wrong not having him with me here. There's only so much I can do to strong-arm a man a foot taller than me into something he doesn't want to do.

"Okay. What do you already know you want for your wedding?" She pauses, looking at me to fill in a blank without context. "I'm assuming we're having the wedding here at the resort."

"I mean, yeah. That's why I'm here, talking with you," I chuckle.

There's nowhere else I could imagine having this moment with Gunnar.

The club has been such an integral part of our journey and our relationship with each other, and it's where we've built the relationships we will treasure forever.

Gunnar and I have found our real family here—the family we *chose*.

So, it only makes sense to bring everyone together here.

Plus, our blood relations know enough about The Playground and our loyalty to it not to ask too many questions, making hosting our big day at the resort that much easier.

"Okay, perfect. Venue is checked off the list. Do you have a date in mind?" she asks.

This is something I had actually prepared for.

For a woman working in tech, some people think it's unusual for me to believe in astrology. My profession relies on finite solutions and knowing the correct way to do things, but the rest of the world doesn't always follow a neat little pattern or path. For me, my spirituality gives me the flexibility to believe in the Universe's own form of order.

I pull up the list of dates I made on my phone and hand it to Ivy. "I already looked up their astrological significance. So, I'd like to choose from these dates, depending on what you think is a reasonable timeline for planning everything."

She looks at the list skeptically. "We might have to add onto this list to give ourselves more time to plan. In my experience, grand weddings like I think you're wanting take a year or more to plan."

"A year?" I choke out.

I had hoped this wouldn't take more than a year to plan. The idea of being engaged for even longer than that has my breath shortening.

Gunnar told me to marry him, and at my core I know saying yes was the right decision.

But giving us over a year to plan the wedding also gives me over a year to spiral into a full-blown panic as well.

"Let me text this to myself," she continues while sending herself the note from my phone. "And I'll look at what we have available on our calendar later." When she looks up at me she's all smiles, completely oblivious to the thoughts already swirling in my mind. "Next, is there a specific color palette you love? A favorite flower? Have you looked at dresses yet?"

"Amélie Sartre," I jump in, thankful she asked the one question I actually have an answer for.

Ivy's demeanor lights up at the mention of the renowned designer, known for her whimsical and ethereal gowns—and her commitment to size inclusivity.

"Oh, excellent. I love where your head is at. Her dresses are to die for," Ivy says with a broad smile and a gleam in her eye.

"Right?" I exclaim, tightly latching onto the subject. "Ever since I got an inkling that Gunnar was going to propose, I started trying to figure out what I want for the wedding. I found her on some social media site, but I've been obsessed ever since."

"Okay. That's good! That's really good," Ivy says, scribbling quickly in her notebook. "It might take a while to get an appointment, though. She's typically booked out several years in advance for custom designs." My heart drops into my stomach at the mention of the extended timeline once again. "I'll check on that immediately to see if we can get an appointment. But she has a vibe to her stuff, which I think is perfect for you. This is a great direction for us to move forward in."

"Really?" I ask, pulling myself from my thoughts while the unsure part of myself looks for validation.

"Yeah! Of course. Really, this isn't going to be as hard as you think it will be. Plus, you have me to help," she says, pulling out a sparkly notebook and bright pink pen with a puffball at the end. "Now, have you and Gunnar talked about budgets and such?"

"I asked him last night when I reminded him about our meeting, and he just laughed at me." I shrug. Gunnar seems to think that by letting me plan this all myself, that I'll end up with the wedding of my dreams, but really it's just left me feeling alone and overwhelmed. "I'm not sure if that means there is a budget?"

She nods thoughtfully, writing something down in her note-book before looking up at me with a stern expression.

"Okay. An unlimited budget isn't realistic. So, why don't we go through some of the big-ticket items to get an idea of what we're looking at? Then we can go through the different sections I've put together for you in here," she says, dragging the cursed binder over to us.

The following two hours are spent poring over the pages in the binder, with Ivy taking meticulous notes throughout. When we reach the last section of the binder, all related to the honeymoon, I want to throw a temper tantrum like a child who needs a nap.

"Ivy," I interrupt her mid-sentence with my most authoritative tone. "I need to stop."

"Oh!" she says brightly, which only grates on my nerves despite knowing she's well-intentioned. "Okay. That's fine. We can pick this up later."

"Thanks. I need to get back to work," I tell her, grabbing my things and rising to get out of the cafe where we chose to meet. "I'll call you later?"

"Yeah, of course," she says with an elegant smile.

Ivy seemed perfectly comfortable the entire time we talked. She was totally in her element. Meanwhile, I want to crawl out of my skin just thinking about sitting here for even one more minute.

This isn't my world.

I love all the people in my life. I adore bringing people together and helping them make connections they might not have otherwise made. I'm the ideas girl—the one tossing out wild themes and color palettes at brunch. However, the large-scale party planning has typically been left to the rest of our friend group, including Ivy.

Quite frankly, my Pisces energy can't handle the logistics of everything.

Which is curious considering my career in technology.

Tech is different, though. Computers make sense. There's a system and framework where my creativity can fully express itself.

Well, almost fully.

I may find myself at home in my office, working on whatever project my team is currently tackling, but I find true freedom in another part of my life.

The Playground Club, a venue where people from all walks of life gather to find a way to free themselves from the shackles of society, is truly my home.

My childhood friend, Griffin Reyes, started the business several years ago with his polycule. They went through hell and back to build their empire, but now the entire venture is thriving.

I've been honored to see its growth and how it's changed since it opened.

Though I'm most grateful for the people this place has brought into my life.

Including my fiancé, Gunnar.

The night The Playground Club opened was the first chapter of a love story that would be told for generations.

Gunnar says he knew I was meant to be his when he saw me across the room.

It took me longer to accept the idea. For a year, we played a classic game of cat and mouse, each toying with the other, and then one day, it all clicked.

Running into people I knew from my vanilla life wasn't something that happened often, but there was a silent understanding between parties that what happened at The Playground stayed there.

Because of that, there had never been a time when I'd worried about my safety.

I knew Gunnar watched me.

It was never creepy; if anything, it made me feel protected.

It's a feeling that has stuck with me since I first met him at the club's opening night.

Somehow, I knew in the marrow of my bones that this man would do anything for me. He'd sacrifice everything he has for my safety, my happiness.

I think it was that feeling that scared me in the beginning and kept me at arm's length.

It wasn't until one night, long before I met Elsie and started working with her, that the feeling of safety at the club was threatened by a man I'd never expected to see there.

The moment I spotted him in the club, I started frantically searching for safety with Gunnar.

"I need your help," I tell Gunnar urgently as I approach him.

Gunnar's voice seems to catch at my appearance, but I can't have him hesitating.

"Gunnar," I say, snapping in front of his face. "Help, please."

"Yes."

"You haven't even heard what I need help with," I snark.

"The answer is still yes, Selene," he says, his expression filled with awe.

"Okay," I say skeptically. "Um. I need you to be yourself, okay."

"And that would be?" he smirks.

"Be... yourself. I don't know. Grumpy. Protective," I rush out, glancing over my shoulder at the man approaching us. "Be you. Got it?"

"Yes. Understood." Gunnar schools his features into a less pathetic puppy dog look, and a serious, unfeeling mask slips on.

"Fuck. Here he comes," I say, glancing over my shoulder again.

"Here, who comes?" Gunnar asks, scanning the crowd behind me.

I can tell when he spots my boss, Joseph—a fit older man in his late 50s—approaching us with long strides.

"Fuck. Shit. Fuck." My language seems to take Gunnar aback, even though he's heard me curse a million times before. "I should have left when I spotted him."

"Selene?" Gunnar finally asks. "Why is that man stalking toward you like a lion on the hunt?"

"Because he thinks he has a shot with me now that he's seen me here." I sigh. "He's my boss. He's so fucking creepy. I didn't know he was in the lifestyle. Though that makes his behavior at work make so much more sense now."

"And he doesn't," Gunnar says coolly, a murderous look in his gaze. "Have a chance with you, I mean."

"No. No way," I reply, shaking my head.

"Good." Gunnar's eyebrows furrow. "Then tell him that."

"There's no way I'm telling my boss that he can fuck off," I say quickly, feeling Joseph staring at my ass as he approaches.

"Why not?"

"Because... Because I don't want to make a big deal out of it. If he outs me as being in the lifestyle, then I'm screwed. I'll lose my job."

"If he does, then he exposes himself, too." I look at him with surprise. "He wouldn't harm his position just to hurt you. No one is that stupid."

"Maybe not stupid, but if I slighted him like that, he might be vindictive enough. I can't risk it," I say quickly, my shoulders dropping in defeat. "He'd figure out how to make it happen and still keep his nose clean. He plays dirty like that."

"You don't owe him anything, Selene. Not your time, your attention, and especially not your body," Gunnar says, his frustration clearly building.

"I know that. I never said I owed him anything... I just..."

Gunnar reaches for me, and the small connection of his hand cupping my elbow sparks a fire under my skin.

"Selene..." he starts.

"Hello, Selene," the smarmy man's voice interrupts us over the hum of the club's music. "Lovely seeing you again, here of all places."

"Mr. Harrow." My smile is disingenuous, but I can't give a single fuck. "Good to see you." I lie.

"*No need for formalities, Selene,*" *he says hungrily.* "*Joseph is better out of the office.*" *He pauses.* "*I was wondering if you might want to spend some time together tonight. Get to know each other a bit better outside of the office?*"

The only things grounding me are Gunnar's gentle hold on my arm and his warmth at my back.

"*I would,*" *I say, my voice overly sweet.* "*But my boyfriend and I are actually leaving here in a bit.*"

I can feel Gunnar freeze behind me, but he doesn't say anything to contradict the lie I'm forming.

"*Oh. I didn't realize you two were together,*" *Joseph says.*

"*Yeah. Well, it's recent.*" *My fake smile tightens.*

"*Well, surely he won't mind us spending some time together... alone,*" *Joseph pushes.* "*Especially considering where we are.*"

Joseph is really laying it on thick, and with each word he utters, the urge to strangle him until he can no longer speak grows.

"*Yes. I would,*" *Gunnar bites out.* "*I would mind a lot.*"

Gunnar's arm circles around my waist, pulling me closer into his body so I'm now fully cradled between his legs.

I sink into Gunnar's hold, relaxing in the safety of his arms, and I feel him straighten behind me.

My boss laughs in a way that freezes me up again, and immediately, Gunnar's free hand skims up and down my arm to soothe me.

"*Seems like you found a possessive one, Selene,*" *Joseph says, a smarmy smirk sliding onto his lips.* "*Good luck with him.*"

"*Thank you,*" *I turn to Gunnar, feeling more honesty in my next words than I thought I could admit.* "*I'm thoroughly enjoying it.*"

"*Alright. Well, another time maybe. Once you've settled in a bit,*" *Joseph says before turning from us.* "*I'll leave you two to it then.*"

Joseph stalks away, his shoulders rigid in a form of angry defeat.

I watch him as he retreats, and my body relaxes further into Gunnar's.

But even in his arms, his deep voice startles me when he speaks.

"Selene?" he says, getting my attention and turning me to him. "Don't ever do that to me again."

"What?" I ask, my eyes widening as I turn to face him, still encircled by his strong arms.

"I won't be your fake boyfriend. You can't use me like that," Gunnar says, and my heart unexpectedly drops into my stomach, and my throat begins to close.

Guilt, with an unexpected dose of devastation, overwhelms me, and I drop my eyes from his face. "Sorry. I didn't think... No. It doesn't matter. I shouldn't have done that to you."

"No. You misunderstand." With a finger under my chin, he lifts my gaze to meet his once more. "If I'm going to be your boyfriend, then I want it to be real. I want to be yours, little Goddess."

It wasn't a lightning bolt moment—our whole dynamic was more like a slow, sexy burn I'd been too stubborn to name.

The stars had aligned, and it felt inevitable.

Gunnar was always the quiet support I needed to balance out my whirlwind of chaos. Even when we weren't officially together, he was always a soft place for me to land.

With his job in security, Gunnar has always been physically fit. He has physically carried me away from more than a couple of altercations where I admit I lost my composure. But his tall, muscular build has always made me feel safe and protected in his arms. That night, though, I knew I could trust his strength in a new way.

In that moment, I felt *seen*. That's when I knew I was screwed. And maybe just a little bit in love.

It's his icy eyes framed by high cheekbones and blonde hair that make my body alert every time we are in the same room. It's the way he's always looked at me—as if I'm the center of his universe. There's nothing quite like the feeling of someone's happiness revolving around your own, but the way Gunnar has always watched me gives me that exact feeling. And maybe I shouldn't like it, but I do—that I'm the calm in his storm, the one thing that softens the sharp edges he never shows anyone else.

Arriving back at the office, I'm greeted in the break room by Oliver, assistant to my friend and boss Elsie Snow, who's making coffee, probably her third or fourth cup of the day.

"Where were *you* all morning?" he teases with a wink. "Hope you and your *fiancé* were doing something fun."

"Oh, stop," I smile back at him, grateful for the lightheartedness he brings to the day. "I was meeting with Ivy about wedding stuff. Nothing *fun* about it at all."

"That bad?" he asks genuinely. "This is why I eloped."

The twinkle in Oliver's eyes whenever he talks about his partner, Chandler, always makes me a little jealous. It's something about the reverence and tenderness with which he speaks about xem and the calm that settles on his shoulders.

"By the way, Elsie asked me to let you know she needs you in her office when you get a chance," Oliver continues, taking the coffee out from under the machine and preparing it the way she likes.

My brow furrows. "You know you don't have to do that, right?"

Oliver turns to me with another dazzling smile. "I know. Today just seems to be a harder day than normal."

"You're too good for us," I tell him, giving him a pat on the hand as I pass him to go into the fridge for my can of caffeinated beverage.

"I really am. I deserve a raise for it," he grins and chuckles.

"I'll tell Elsie," I say as I close the fridge and head out of the break room toward the boss's office.

Walking down the hall to Elsie's corner office, I smile and say hello to the staff I pass, checking in with each of them as I go.

One of the benefits of working at an organization like Coral Crude, a leading consulting and technology resource for environmentally friendly oil companies—if that's even possible—is its size. You get to know the people you work with and avoid feeling like a minnow floundering in the ocean all alone.

Walking into Elsie's office without knocking, I find her engrossed in thought, looking over a stack of reports on her desk.

"Morning!" I chime, making her look up in my direction.

She glances over to the old school clock on her desk with a frown. "It's after lunch."

Despite being nicknamed the ice queen of the oil and gas industry, Elsie is genuinely one of the kindest people. She just takes some time to warm up to others.

We met two years ago at The Playground. I had seen her around a few times, but she mostly stuck to herself those nights.

There was something in me, though, that felt as though she needed us, the family I've cultivated at the club. So, I invited her to join us one night, and since then, we've become business partners and the closest of friends.

"Well, then that totally explains the uneaten lunch sitting on your desk, now doesn't it?" I tell her with a wink, which earns me an eye roll.

"I've been hyper-focused all morning trying to get this situation with our latest contract wrapped up," she continues.

"They're still giving you trouble?" I ask, leaning forward in the chair I've taken in front of her desk.

"Yeah," she sighs, her head dropping back onto her shoulders, letting her auburn waves fan out around her. "They're giving legal a bitch of a time."

"Gross."

"Exactly," she says, the smallest of smiles creeping on her face.

"So, Oliver is getting you coffee just because of the contract, right? Nothing else is happening?" I ask, which causes her to snap her head up and face me with a raised eyebrow.

"I didn't..." she starts.

"He only does that when something is wrong," I point out. "That man has the patience of a saint to stick it out with you for this long, but if he's bringing you coffee *multiple times* a day? It's more than a contract, Señora Presidenta." *Madam President.*

Elsie scowls at me, knowing I'm right.

"I'm not ready to talk about it," she says, more vulnerable than I've heard her in a while.

I study her for a minute, trying to gauge how much I should push her right now. But with how close her emotions seem to be to the surface, I set aside my curiosity and let her keep things under wraps a little longer.

"How'd wedding planning go this morning with Ivy?" Elsie finally asks, changing the subject away from herself.

"Ugh," I slump back in the chair and take a sip of my drink. "Brutal."

My friend cringes just as Oliver walks into the room carrying Elsie's coffee, a pastry, and apple slices on a plate.

"Hello, lovelies," he chimes. "I'd say sorry for interrupting..."

"But you aren't," Elsie and I chorus.

"Coffee and a snack for the boss. Eat it on your own, or I'll watch to make sure you do," Oliver says in his stern parenting voice.

I give Elsie a look as she reaches for the chocolate croissant and rolls her eyes at me.

"What were we talking about?" Oliver says as he moves to sit in the other chair next to me.

"Wedding planning," Elsie says, taking a bite and finally relaxing for the first time since I stepped into her office.

"Oof. I have a feeling that's gonna come up a lot now, isn't it?" Oliver asks.

"Probably," I admit.

"Well, have fun with that," Oliver says, turning to Elsie excitedly. "What I want to hear about is the engagement party this weekend."

"What?" Elsie says, crumbs falling from her lips that she wipes away with a napkin.

"Oh, please. Like you, Bex, and the rest of the girls haven't been conspiring since the engagement to make this happen," I tease her.

"And I demand details!" Oliver announces.

"Honestly, me too. No one will tell me anything," I cross my arms. "The only reason I know Nay is coming is because that woman can't keep a secret to save her life."

"I don't know what you're talking about," Elsie says, shrugging as she picks up her coffee. "This is just a normal weekend at the club. No one has anything planned, really."

"Right. Totally normal night," Oliver says conspiratorially, rolling his eyes in solidarity with me. "You know, we couldn't team up against you like this if you'd never told me about the club."

"But it's so much more fun now that you know," I laugh.

"Pretty sure it's a major HR violation," Elsie grumbles, which makes both Oliver and me burst into laughter.

"Y'all are the worst," Elsie sighs, but there's a lightness in her voice that wasn't there before and a small smile on her face. "Now get out of my office. Don't y'all have work to do?"

"Fine," Oliver acquiesces as he rises from his chair.

"Goddess, our boss is such a bitch," I groan, standing up from my seat and grabbing my bags before stepping out the door.

"Actually, Selene?" Elsie interrupts my exit. "Why don't you stay a minute?"

"Oooh. Somebody's in trouble," Oliver chuckles.

Elsie rolls her eyes, and I can't help but laugh at the exchange between the two.

Oliver gently closes the door behind him as he exits Elsie's office, leaving us alone.

"You seem stressed," Elsie says. "More than normal."

"Girl, I'm planning a wedding," I chuckle.

"It's not that, though," she continues. "Spill."

"It just feels big. You know?" I say, confiding in her. "This is like, life-altering."

"I can relate to that," she confesses, a tightness in her eyes which unsettles me.

I raise my eyebrow at her, but she doesn't elaborate.

"I love Gunnar with all my heart," I continue, saving us both from the silence that threatens to hang between us. "But..."

"But?" she asks.

"I can't help but feel like this is going to change everything," I tell her.

"Well, it is," her voice is sure. "You're entering a new phase of life."

"Yes! Exactly," I sigh.

"You're acting just like you did when Gunnar asked you to be his girlfriend," she smirks at me knowingly.

"What do you mean?" I ask.

"You don't like change, Selene. You like predictability and consistency," she explains, leaning over the desk to make sure she has my attention. "I'm sure it's part of why you love Gunnar. He shows up for you in a way that comforts you."

"Well, yeah. Doesn't everyone need that in a relationship? Isn't that like a basic expectation?" I tilt my head in question.

"It can be," Elsie explains. "You just need it in a different way. It's like when Gunnar officially asked you to be his partner. You freaked out then, too."

"I did not *freak out*," I say defensively.

Elsie lets out a full laugh, one I normally love hearing from my friend.

"Oh, you absolutely did," she says, her smile wide. "I'm pretty sure it was all we heard about for months. You were *convinced* that dating officially would be the beginning of the end, even though you were already acting like a couple with the way you spent all your time together. But you did it."

"Yes. I did," I say, thinking of the PowerPoint I put together with my concerns and Gunnar's patience as he addressed all twenty-seven slides.

"You said no to him three times before you said yes to being his girlfriend. Even giving you Beef Cake on his second try didn't work," Elsie goes on. "Still, for months after you said yes, you were convinced the earth was going to fall out from beneath you. So, what was it that changed between then and now?"

"I don't know. We just... found our routine at some point," I explain.

"Exactly. You gave it time, and the fear started to die down." Her expression is open and understanding, but the confidence Elsie is known for is there just the same. "Understand?"

"I think so."

"Good," she says with a smile.

"I'm gonna get back to work if that's okay," I say, standing to grab my things and head out of her office.

When I reach the doorway, her voice has me turning back to my friend.

"Selene? Change is inevitable. There's a lot of it coming our way. And it's fucking scary," she says, a little bit of fear creeping into her voice. "But... whatever is going on, it will be okay. I know it."

I try to give Elsie an encouraging smile. "Love you, Señora Presidenta." *Madam President.*

A giggle escapes my friend, and I know she'll be okay.

We both will.

All morning, I've only been thinking of myself and how hectic this year is going to be, with the wedding planning, work, and life in general.

But it is for all of us.

We're all going through our own things.

We just have to remember to lean on each other.

To ask for help.

To show up for each other, even with the fear of the unknown.

2

GUNNAR

January 12—Mars sextile Saturn

When people discuss their partners, most say that their spouses are their best friends or their other half.

I understand the sentiment, the feeling of connecting with someone on such a deep level that your lives are closely intertwined. However, for me, my relationship with Selene goes far beyond mere friendship or the sense of being complete, whole.

My relationship with Selene is a spiritual experience.

Entering her orbit and existing in her life is a privilege like no other I've ever experienced. It took time, but I've been honored to be a part of her life, her day-to-day.

Selene is like a Goddess.

Her state of being is far superior to anything I could ever aspire to, and the fact that she tolerates having me around, with all my imperfections, is a miracle unto itself.

The first time I saw her from across the club's lobby, I knew this tiny woman would have me wrapped around her finger for the rest of eternity.

I smile, remembering the moment in vivid detail.

It was the night The Playground Club opened. I was standing with my friends, Cy and Ember, and the other members of their future family when she walked through the club doors. One scan of the crowd had her gracefully striding toward us with the confidence of a woman who'd never doubted herself or her value.

The way her hair was styled that night, with her dark hair in waves around her face and adornments sprinkled throughout, made her look like the Goddess I always claimed her to be. Despite the dim lighting, I could see the bright gold flecks in her hazel eyes, which I've come to love so dearly.

Her beauty is a marvel of nature, and her bright smile a gift from the Gods.

In that moment, all the air in my lungs suddenly dissipated as she approached. I thought she was coming straight to me, but my heart plummeted when she started speaking in rapid Spanish and wrapped herself around Griffin, who stood a few feet away.

One day, that woman will be mine.

I turned to my friends, Cy and Ember, and asked them the most important question I've ever needed an answer to.

"What's her name?" I asked breathlessly.

Ember gave me a knowing look, but Cy just scowled at me with a protective gleam in his eye.

"Selene," Ember answered with a grin.

The single word became the center of my evening. The simple gravity of her nearness stirred waves of feeling in me like the moon Goddess she is.

Juliana was masterful in her matchmaking maneuvers. She had me stand near the entrance of the club, where everyone would enter for the evening. I didn't even hear the words Juliana said to the crowd gathered that night; all of my senses were focused on *her.*

I never let Selene out of my sight the whole night, even if she didn't quite know it.

All I know is that the moment I was close enough to feel the heat of her body near mine, I knew I never wanted to leave her side. For the rest of the evening, I kept a watchful eye on her as she flitted through the club, meeting and greeting everyone with a warm smile.

Near the end of the evening, when people started trickling out of the club, I found her on the dance floor by herself. She was having the time of her life with only herself for company. It was the first time all evening that I had found her alone, and I knew it was the best opportunity I was going to get with her.

I went up to her, coming near enough to have her turn to me, and held out my hand as the DJ transitioned to a slower country song, with a captivating bass-line.

The moment her soft hand was in mine, the whole world stopped.

"I'm Gunnar," I told her, stepping into position to lead her in a two-step.

"I know," she replied with a smirk.

The shock that went through my system was like being struck by lightning.

"Do you?" I asked, trying to gather my composure.

"Yes." The satisfied glint in her eye told me she knew more than just my name. "You've been watching me all night long. I asked around about you."

"Oh? And what did you learn, little Goddess?"

Laughter burst from her lips, and the musical sound heated my whole body.

"I know that you are friends with the owners. You're some kind of security specialist if my sources are correct," she says.

"I am."

"You must be pretty good at it if you are on the same level as Griffin's metas, Cy, and Ember." She eyes me skeptically. "Which means you're trouble."

"Oh?"

"Trouble isn't a bad thing, though." She smiles wickedly. "I like trouble."

I pull her closer, leaning down to whisper in her ear.

"And what kind of trouble do you like, little Goddess?" I murmur before pulling back to look into her brilliant eyes.

"The dangerous kind."

In that moment, I knew she was it for me.

There wasn't anything in this universe that was going to keep me from her.

That night marked what ended up being the hardest year of my life. I spent a full year watching Selene, hoping she would notice me and *want* me.

Before meeting Selene, my world was dull and lifeless.

Sure, I was moving through my day, but it had no true purpose.

All of my accomplishments, including several gold medals from international shooting competitions, turned out to be meaningless. All the training, education, degrees, and even starting a business with my close friend, Emir, proved insignificant in comparison.

Before Selene, I was merely the CEO of a security firm, an accomplishment that felt empty like the barrel of a gun before you load your first shot. Everything in my life centered around work because there was nothing else keeping me grounded on this plane.

Then I met her.

It was the most magical, spiritual moment I've ever had in my life.

The moment she appeared in the lobby of The Playground was like experiencing sunlight for the first time.

Nothing compares to the light she shines into this world.

She is the center of my universe.

The Goddess I worship daily.

My everything.

Even when she's yelling at me.

"Gunnar!" Selene's voice rings out through the house. "Gunnar, what the hell is up with this email?"

I close the door leading to our garage behind me and drop off my bags in the mudroom, only to be greeted by a steaming Selene when I walk into the kitchen.

Her frown is deeper than the Mariana Trench, an expression I feel compelled to wipe away.

"Speak, Viking," she snaps, holding her phone out in front of me.

Slowly, I take the phone out of her hand and skim through the email she has open on her screen.

"I replied to Ivy," I explain. "She had questions, and I figured I'd handle it since I knew you had a busy day today."

"And you didn't think I might want to have input on any of this?" she growls, snatching the phone out of my hand and turning to pace the kitchen. "This is our *wedding,* and I am the fucking *bride.* Did you ever pause to think I might want some input on these things?"

Tentatively, I take a few steps towards her.

I explain, "I thought you would want a break. You were complaining last night about how overwhelming your meeting with Ivy was. I thought I was helping."

I can't help but grin internally at the pout that takes over her expression; it's adorable.

"Well, you weren't," she sighs, dropping her head back. "And you were. I just... I'm just overwhelmed."

"I know," I say, reaching for her hand. "It's a lot, but you don't have to do it alone."

Her fingers curl around mine without hesitation, like her heart already knew what her mind's still catching up to. For a beat, the world shrinks to just this—her warmth in my palm, and the promise we're not facing any of it alone.

"But the *date*?" she whines. "You didn't think we should make that decision together?"

I pause, trying to collect my words before I step on a landmine.

Because I know what I've done, and *why*.

If I hadn't responded to that email with a decision, Selene would have dragged her feet picking a date for the wedding for as long as possible.

"You gave Ivy a list of dates you would prefer. She returned with what was feasible. I chose from those," I say carefully. "Isn't that deciding together? Plus, I think the Spring Equinox is a great day to get married."

Selene mutters something unintelligible to herself.

"Though any day is the perfect day to marry my Goddess," I say smoothly, hoping flattery will get me somewhere with her.

"Fine," she huffs. "You're right. It would have been the one I chose, too."

I can't help the smile that spreads across my face at the small victory.

"How about I start on dinner, and we talk through some of her other questions?" I suggest, knowing that Selene is likely close to her Hangry Hour at this time of day.

"Fine," she caves with another sigh. "I want noodles with nuggies."

"As you wish," I reply, squeezing her hand before letting go to prep everything we need for the meal.

Selene leaves me to do my prep work for a minute, but quickly comes back to the kitchen with her laptop in hand.

"What are our tasks for tonight, Luna?" I ask as she settles onto a stool at our central island.

"Ivy suggested we work on our guest list and figure out our wedding party," Selene begins, probably pulling up the spreadsheet she started to keep track of all our wedding details. "That might be the easiest thing to tackle right now."

"Sure," I smile, grabbing the ingredients for the vermicelli noodle and tofu nugget curry dish Selene loves. "Tell me what you need."

"Okay. Let's start with our wedding party, then family and friends?" she suggests, her body relaxing as she settles into her comfort zone at the keyboard.

"How many bridesmaids are you planning to have?" I ask, starting the burners on the stove and placing my pans on top to warm up.

"Bex, Naomi, and Elsie for sure," she begins, thinking deeply about the question as she starts adding names to her spreadsheet. "But there are a few other people I might want to include. I guess it depends on how many people you have in your groom's party?"

"If you tell me you need ten groomsmen, I'll make that list. If you only need three, I'll give you that list too."

"Gunnar," she says, disappointment in her tone. "I need you to be serious about this."

"I am." I chuckle softly.

"I know you have opinions, though," she pushes on. "I'd like to hear them so we can incorporate them."

"Selene, any dream I have is about what you want and what will make you happy." I pause, looking up from chopping tofu to watch her eyes go wide at my statement.

Selene, always the chatterbox, is struck silent for a moment before she shakes herself out of her stupor.

"Okay," she says softly. Turning back to her computer, her brow furrows as she concentrates on the task at hand. "Let's just start adding names, and we can figure out which ones will be a part of what later."

By the time dinner is served, we have over 300 people on the wedding invite list. While I thought addressing this item on the to-do list might mitigate Selene's stress, the look on her face tells me it's done quite the opposite.

"Eat, Luna," I tell her, taking the computer away and pushing her food in her direction.

When I look at the computer, I see a color-coded spreadsheet with columns for everyone's information. There's a space for notes for each person we include on the list, as well as formulas to track the total number of individuals on the list compared to the parties attending. There's even a dreaded column for prioritizing who must be at the wedding and who would just be nice to have there.

"This looks so good," I praise as Selene takes her first bite of her food. "You did an excellent job, Luna."

"I do love a good spreadsheet," she jokes through another bite. "It's just a lot. I worry..."

"We have plenty of time to figure it out," I interrupt as I close and set down the computer. "Plus, not everyone will RSVP 'Yes' to the wedding. There's plenty of time to narrow things down."

She frowns, but doesn't say anything.

"March 21st is a long way off, Luna," I reassure her.

"And yet it feels like it's right around the corner," she mumbles, looking down at her dinner with defeat. "Can't we just run away?"

I chuckle, knowing this will probably be a topic that comes up a lot in the next few months. "We could."

Her eyes widen.

"You'd be okay with that?" she asks earnestly.

"I would. I want what you want, Luna. This is your day." I reach out, taking her hand in mine. "I want to give you everything you want, Luna. I want to give you everything."

A silent understanding wraps around us.

"Is that really what you want, Selene?" I ask her earnestly. "We can elope if you want to, but..."

"I don't," she cuts in. "I want everything—the wedding and the dress. I want to be surrounded by our family and friends. I want it all with you."

"Then that's what we do." I smile at her. "I'll make your dreams happen, Luna. I promise."

3

SELENE

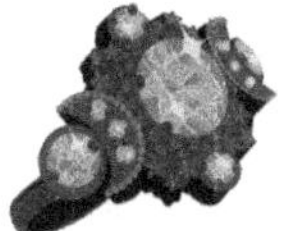

January 13—Moon in Pisces, Sun trine Uranus

Since its inception, The Playground Club and Resort has been an oasis for those who live alternative lifestyles. It provides a safe space for people to come, express themselves freely, and live in alignment with their values.

All of this exists outside the scrutiny of society and its harsh judgment of people's life choices.

Gunnar and I met at the club's opening, and since then, it's become a home to us. It's where we've found our community, our family—the people who mean the world to us and stand by us through life.

Tonight, that family has gathered at the club to celebrate Gunnar and me for our recent engagement.

"To the happy couple!" someone shouts over the music blaring through the speakers on the first floor of the club.

"To Selene and Gunnar!" everyone cheers, the sound ringing through the space.

Alcohol has been flowing freely all night, and everyone is in high spirits. I'm celebrating the man I love, surrounded by the people I love.

Looking around at my friends, I realize how lucky I am to have found them, my people.

Everyone always talks about how magical it is to find the person you want to spend the rest of your life with. Tonight is very much a celebration of that part of my life.

And when I catch Gunnar across the room, watching me with that ridiculous soft smile—the one he reserves just for me—I feel it: that thing everyone talks about. The buzz in my chest. The warm, safe knowing that he's mine and I'm his.

I raise my glass to him in a quiet little toast no one else sees. He winks, because of course he does.

Still, I can't help but think...

There was a time my friends were my whole world—chosen family, ride or die, no question. But this next step? It changes everything. Gunnar's not just part of my life anymore—he's the center of it. Figuring out how to hold that truth without dropping the rest of what matters... it's harder than I thought.

"Lena!" Naomi cries as she weaves her way through the throng of people.

Naomi, my closest friend in the world, walks over to me with her blonde curls bouncing. As she moves, the club lights flicker across her body, emphasizing the curves that are so similar to mine. However, she stands several inches taller than my 5'4" frame.

"Nay!" I reply in kind, throwing my arms wide for my bestie.

"I'm so happy for you," she says, wrapping me in a hug when she gets close enough. "You deserve all the happiness in the world."

"How drunk are you, Nay?" I giggle into her hair.

"Only a lot," she laughs.

Naomi and I have known each other for over a year, but as

long-distance besties, this is the first time we've met in person. It's made me feel the warmest feelings to have her so close.

Tonight, though, is the first time I've heard her so carefree in a long time, despite all the stress she's been under at school.

I know endorphins are running through her after doing her first ever impact scene with Alvie on the St. Andrews Cross upstairs, but I can tell the alcohol is getting to her more than the flogging.

"Nay, I think you need to sit down and drink some water," I chuckle.

"Booo," she whines, swaying alongside me where we stand in place. "You're not much better than me."

"Yeah, well, this is my engagement party. I'm allowed to get wasted," I raise my cup, filled with my favorite soda and locally made vodka. "I'm celebrating! Remember?"

"Because you're getting *married*!" Naomi squeals, her baby giraffe impression growing more exaggerated with her excitement.

Dragging us over to a set of couches, we collapse next to Zuri and Elsie, who are engaged in a deep conversation.

On the couch, Elsie, who's technically my boss but will always be my friend first, sits with her ankles crossed in a deep blue lingerie bodysuit that contrasts with her auburn hair. Next to her, Zuri—the founder of an adult toy company focused on promoting products for all body types—sits in a bright yellow bra and panties set that has more straps than lace, contrasting against her deep brown skin.

"Wha'cha talkin' 'bout?" Naomi sings to them.

"Marshall has been following Elsie around like a puppy all night and making eyes at her," Zuri chuckles.

"And I'm just horny enough to want to do something about it," Elsie says softly, but all three of us hear her and burst into laughter.

The sudden sound draws the attention of the very man Zuri

and Elsie were speaking of, along with several other people, including my fiancé.

"Girl. I would have jumped on that train a long time ago if he were interested," Zuri laughs.

"He's very pretty," Naomi says with a slight slur.

"That's the thing, though," Elsie says with a frown. "I know he's pan."

"Which makes him all the hotter," I joke, and Elsie smiles, agreeing with me.

Then her smile falls. "But it seems like he's been with *everyone*."

"So? Just proves that he's good in bed," Naomi says with a shrug before her eyes go wide and her hand shoots up.

A look is exchanged between Zuri, Elsie, and me before I call on her, just like in one of Naomi's classes.

"Yes, Nay?" I laugh.

Her hand lowers, but her excitement doesn't.

"Does that mean he has a really big cock? Or does he know how to use what he has?" she whispers conspiratorially, sending the three of us into fits of laughter.

"Sounds like I need to go find out," Elsie says matter-of-factly. "For science."

My best friend is vigorously nodding her head, and since I agree with her, I join in with the same enthusiasm.

"Do it," Zuri says confidently, with a quick salute. "Ride that man like the dragon he is. Go have magical sex, Madame Unicorn."

Elsie looks between us and makes her decision with a level of conviction and determination I think only she is capable of having.

She gets up, adjusts her dress slightly, and strolls over to where Marshall stands, tapping him on the shoulder when she wants his attention.

Marshall turns around, and his eyes go wide. Elsie crooks her finger, telling him to lean in close to hear her.

I'm not sure what she says, but suddenly, Marshall's face shows pure lust and desire. He takes her by the hand and tugs her along to head upstairs without hesitation.

Only slightly off balance from the sudden jolt, Elsie gives us a small wave as she gets dragged through the club, and our group hoots and hollers after her, turning heads from all around the club toward our little trio.

"Let's talk about other things," Zuri says when Elsie's exit is complete. "Have you thought about any plans for the wedding yet?"

"Well, Naomi is going to be my maid of honor," I say, turning around to find Naomi slumped on the arm of the couch, fast asleep. "Whenever she's awake enough to ask. And I'm going to ask Bex to be my matron of honor."

"Oh, she'll love that," Zuri coos.

"Of course, y'all are all invited," I continue. "But beyond that, I haven't really gotten that far. Ivy is handling a lot of it."

"Oh, yeah! She just got hired on full-time, didn't she?" Zuri asks, pushing her dark brown braids away from her face.

"Yup!" I say cheerfully. "About time she got hired on. She's been volunteering here since the beginning, right?"

"I think so," Zuri replies before her gaze moves around the room as though she's looking for someone or someones.

"I think you should go dance," I announce, grabbing Zuri by the hand and pulling her to her feet. "I'm gonna stay with Nay and make sure she gets some water."

"Lena," Zuri protests. "It's your engagement party. You should go have fun!"

"I'm having so much fun. I just need a little rest," I tell her honestly. "Go. Have fun. I'll chill with Nay for a bit."

Zuri looks at me skeptically, but eventually gets up and moves over to some of our friends who are shaking their asses off on the dance floor.

I watch my friends enjoy themselves, happiness floating in my chest as I see them smiling and dancing together.

Nay shifts, cuddling herself up to me, so I wrap my arms around her to lean into the comfort of her touch.

AFTER WAKING up from a quick nap with Naomi in our cozy corner of the club, there are several more toasts to Gunnar and me as everyone joins in our excitement for the night.

Alas, after far too many drinks, Semisonic's "Closing Time" plays through the club speakers, telling everyone it's time to go home.

Everything's a little fuzzy, but the second I feel Gunnar's arms wrap around me, I slump into his comforting hold.

"Let's get you home, Luna," he says in his deep voice.

"Mhmm," I reply as I soak up his warmth. "Hotel room, home? Or home, home?"

"Hotel room," he chuckles, running his hands through my now-destroyed curls.

I vaguely hear Gunnar going back and forth with what sounds like Bex and Alvie before we start moving toward the doors.

"Wait!" I shout, causing Gunnar to come to a startled halt. "What about Nay?"

My eyes go wide, and soberness returns as concern filters in.

Gunnar chuckles at me, and my brow furrows. "Bex and Alvie are taking her back to her villa. She's taken care of."

"But I wanted to say goodbye," I pout. "She's my bestie."

"I know that, Luna," he replies patiently. "She's still going to be here tomorrow. You can drag her out of bed in the morning for some brunch. How does that sound?"

I ponder his suggestion for a minute before responding.

"I do like brunch." That earns me another one of his deep, rumbling chuckles. "Deal."

Walking back to the villa with my hand in Gunnar's feels like a dreamy haze.

The whole way back, my mind drifts through memories of the night—the feelings of joy and pleasure, the beauty of being surrounded by people you love and who love you in return.

When we get to the room, I go to the bathroom to get ready for bed while Gunnar immediately sits down to take off his shoes.

Walking into the bathroom, I grab my skincare products and start my routine. The ritual calms me, but it also gives me too much time to think.

Tonight marks a change in my relationship with the man in the other room.

I've agreed to marry the man of my dreams, but that comes with its own consequences, including the reactions from my family back home in Puerto Rico, who are staunchly Catholic. There's a heaviness to that decision that is only now starting to settle in, heavier than anything Gunnar and I have faced so far.

It's easy to say yes to things. Drinks, parties, you name it—it's all easy.

That's how getting engaged felt: easy.

Like it was the right thing to do, the easy thing to do.

It's the next step. It's the journey we're on, right?

With a sigh, I finish my nighttime routine and walk back into the bedroom, where Gunnar is fast asleep under the covers, resting peacefully.

Already dressed in lingerie, I crawl over to the man.

I curl up against my fiancé and let the world fade away as I drift off to sleep.

4

SELENE

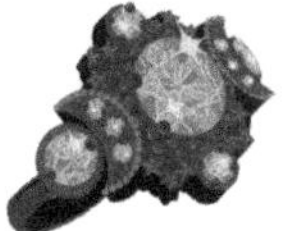

January 16—Mars enters Capricorn, Supportive Mercury aspects

Today has been an absolute shitshow, and I'm ready for it to be over. Everything seems to annoy me, and nothing is helping, not even my favorite snacks.

This morning, I had a follow-up appointment with my doctor regarding my tubal ligation back in December, which went fine, except for the results of my blood tests, which I'm deliberately ignoring for the time being.

It was frustrating to deal with, but the true travesty of the day was the text from Ivy that now haunts me.

> IVY
>
> She doesn't have availability for anything custom until two years out.
>
> I'm so sorry, love.

A few months ago, if you had asked me if I would have a full-blown breakdown over not being able to have my dream wedding dress, I would have said no.

Today?

Since the message came in, I've been crying nonstop. It's bad enough that Elsie made an executive decision at work and sent me home two hours early for the day.

I've been sitting on the couch in the den, numb to the world, since I got home. Tear- and snot-soaked tissues surround me like a nest of sorrow, and I'm wrapped in a blanket, snacks strewn around me that don't seem appetizing at all.

Which is exactly how Gunnar finds me when he gets home from work.

"Selene?" I hear his voice cut through my haze from somewhere else in the house. "Luna?"

The concern in his voice makes the tears that had only recently dried up reappear.

"Oh, Luna," Gunnar says softly as he comes into the den and kneels before me, concern etched on his face. "What's wrong? What happened?"

"I..." I hiccup. "I just..."

"Whatever it is, we'll figure it out," he keeps his voice gentle, but everything that comes out of his mouth right now is like sandpaper on my delicate emotional state. "It's okay, Luna. It will be okay."

"It is absolutely not okay," I snap, scooting away from him on the couch and standing to pace the room. "It was the *only* thing I wanted for this wedding. Everything else could go to shit, but this was the *thing*."

"What, Luna? What's so important about the wedding that it has you this upset?" he asks earnestly.

"The dress!" I shout, my voice echoing through our living room. "I've never had a dream wedding. There's no set plan that must be followed, but I was *really hoping* I would be able to have a dress made by a specific designer."

Gunnar stares at me blankly.

"This is because of a dress?" he asks, confused.

"Yes!" I snap, my frustration mounting with every dumb-ass word that escapes his lips.

"It's a dress," Gunnar states as neutrally as he can.

"This is my *wedding dress*. It's kind of fucking important," I growl, pushing down the temptation to throw the box of tissues in my hand at him.

Smartly, Gunnar stays silent as I process my anger at the situation, but instead of calming me down, his silence only fans the flames of my passionate rage.

"Say something!" I snap.

"I don't know what you want me to say, Luna," he starts gently. "It's a dress."

It's like a blow directly to the chest, and all the air in my lungs escapes in one exhale. Tears gather at the edges of my eyes, and I don't even try to stop them from falling.

"You don't get it," I sniffle.

"I don't," he says softly, reaching for my hand, but I bat him away.

"It's fine," I say, standing with my blanket and turning to walk down the hallway as my heart breaks once more.

Gunnar is my person; he's supposed to understand and accept me as I am, but this feels far from that dream.

"Luna," he calls after me from the doorway to the den, and I turn to look at him. "I'm sorry about the dress. We'll figure something out."

I blink back at him, this perfect specimen of a human whom I adore with every fiber of my being.

"Okay," I mumble, turning away from my Viking again.

"I love you," he says.

I'm grateful he can't see my expression as I roll my eyes at his words.

It's not that I don't believe them; instead, they seem like a small bandage on a gaping wound—useless.

"Love you too," I mumble back.

Fed up with Gunnar and his lack of sympathy for my plight, I leave him to live with himself while I spend time with the true love of my life.

Walking past my office, I stop to gather my computer and then continue down the hall to Beef Cake's cat den.

Walking in, I see my furry man curled up in the corner chair, which I usually sit in when we hang out here together.

"Hey, boy," I say, sitting on the edge of the chair and giving him some scratches behind his ears.

Beef Cake's eyes flutter open, and, despite his eternally grumpy expression, I can tell he's excited to see me.

Rolling over, he gives me his belly, and I give him pets as I work to slow my breathing to a normal pace.

"I don't understand how he doesn't get it," I tell the feline. "This is important, isn't it?"

I look down, but Beef Cake is blissfully in his own world as I pet him.

Picking up the massive Maine Coon and setting him aside, I pull a blanket off the back of the chair and scoot back to get comfortable.

As I open my computer to distract myself with my favorite game, a notification pops up telling me Naomi just messaged me.

MINDFUCKMASTER

Checking in.

I stare at the message for a moment.

How does she always *know*?

OVERTHEMOON

I need you to come down for Spring Break.

> OVERTHEMOON
>
> No arguments.

MINDFUCKMASTER

Okaaaay.

Taking a deep breath, I hold back the emotions that threaten to overflow.

> OVERTHEMOON
>
> We have to go dress shopping. 😭

MINDFUCKMASTER

Oh. Lena.

I'm guessing based on your emoji usage that she isn't available. What happened?

> OVERTHEMOON
>
> She doesn't have availability for *TWO YEARS*
>
> So now I have to figure something else out.

MINDFUCKMASTER

I'm so sorry, girl. I know you had your heart set on that designer. You must be heartbroken.

> OVERTHEMOON
>
> I am! And Gunnar is making it sound like I'm overreacting!

MINDFUCKMASTER

Oh no.

> OVERTHEMOON
>
> I swear to the Goddess, that man *does not* know when to shut up.

MINDFUCKMASTER

Pretty sure that's you, babe.

> OVERTHEMOON
>
> Whose side are you on here, Nay?

MINDFUCKMASTER

Yours obviously.

OVERTHEMOON

Better be. I was going to ask you to be my maid
of honor.

MINDFUCKMASTER

LENA

OVERTHEMOON

Well, duh.

And if you'd been sober this past weekend, then
you'd have known this when I told Zuri. lol

MINDFUCKMASTER

I was a little... distracted?

OVERTHEMOON

YEAH YOU WERE

TELL ME EVERYTHING

Naomi and I fall into our usual banter as she catches me up on
everything that happened with Bex over the weekend. She even
checks in about my doctor's appointment, and I admit that I have a
bunch of tests in my patient portal that I need to review—but have
been avoiding.

By the time we finish catching up, I feel miles better. Still irritated with my fiancé, but not enough to lash out at him like earlier.

I should probably apologize for that.

Unfortunately, it's late, and Gunnar is already asleep. So, that
will have to wait for another time...

Or.

Or I could wake him up with an 'I'm sorry' blowjob? I mean,
who wouldn't like to be woken up to a little 2 a.m. fellatio? It is on
our 'Yes' list, after all, and I really *didn't* mean to fly off into a fit.

The dysregulation of everything crashing around me was a little too much to handle.

And I'll be happy to tell him that... after.

Gunnar's leg sticks out from under the blanket, and the scrap of covers draped across him barely covers his body. It's a sign from the universe that I need to creep up onto the bed, gingerly placing myself between his legs.

I rest my head on his thigh, with my lip between my teeth as I stroke him gently and slowly through his boxers, hoping to keep him from waking up just yet. He shifts, mumbling in his sleep, and the way his face looks right now—the softness, sweetness, and unguarded expression—sends a wave of butterflies through my stomach.

This man is really going to be my husband.

The love of my hopefully very long life.

The tenderness feels at odds with how quickly his cock grows against my palm. I smile, pulling the top of his boxers down just enough to free his length. The heat of him in my hand, the weight of him, makes something in me shake as I lift my head. I place a small kiss at the base, in the middle, and on the tip.

As I open my mouth and position myself over him, I look up just in time to see his eyes half-lidded with sleep. His lips are parted as he watches me. I blush slightly, heat rising on my skin, overwhelming me.

"Please don't stop on my account."

My stomach drops at that. I know he loves me more than I can possibly fathom. It's clear in his eyes, in the way they darken just at the sight of me.

"We aren't married yet." I lick at the tip, earning a hiss, making his hips buck up, telling me he's already on the brink of release.

"Doesn't matter," he smirks, that same damn smirk that had the nerve to *tell* me to marry him in the middle of a crowded room.

"You've always been mine. I knew where this was going to end, even if you didn't."

I don't want to admit he's right, but I also don't want to tell him that he's wrong either. Instead, I open wide and relax my throat. I let his entire length slip inside me.

Not once do I look away from him.

He groans, his head falling back. His hands find my hair. They curl between the strands and move me up and down his length. I let him direct me. I let him take what he wants because it feels so fucking good to touch him like this and just *be* with him without thinking of anything outside this bed. Outside of him and me.

"Fuck, little Goddess. Fuck," he pants.

My eyes water and my jaw burns, but I push myself further down his length. I push myself down until he's cursing and groaning. I come up with a gasp, licking at the mess I've made. Before I can continue, Gunnar pulls my chin up as he leans down.

He kisses me like a drowning man tasting fresh air on my lips. He pulls me towards him, gripping my body until I'm moving up, shifting into the crook of his arm.

"Don't you want to finish?" I ask.

He shakes his head, kissing every inch of my face—my temples, even the top of my head. "I just want you."

His words melt my heart, and my body becomes putty in his embrace.

So yeah, maybe he gets on my nerves.

That's a good thing, though. Right?

Relationships take work, but they shouldn't be hard.

They're about supporting each other.

Through thick and thin.

Good times and bad.

You love, comfort, and honor them.

In sickness and in health.

And whatever else those vows say.
I'm already doing all that—for him... maybe.
Right?

5

GUNNAR

February 11—Moon in Pisces conjunct Venus & Neptune

Selene said that a trip to Dallas to visit Naomi was essential.

To me, it just looked like a shopping trip.

Plus, I couldn't sleep for shit without Selene last night since she spent the evening at Naomi's place, but I know how much both she and Naomi needed time together.

When I pursued Selene, I understood how vital her friendships were and saw how she prioritized them in her life.

It wasn't until we officially started dating that I realized just how meaningful those relationships really were. It caused a bit of friction initially, but eventually the people she holds close to her became just as much a part of my daily routine as hers.

So, when she told me she was going to spend the night with Naomi, she did offer to let me stay too, but I chose the hotel, knowing I couldn't say no and that they needed their time.

I can't deny that woman anything.

I don't need to be the center of her universe; I'm just lucky enough to be in her orbit.

Picking her up and watching her say goodbye to Naomi was

both heartbreaking and heartwarming. Their goodbye hug was so tight and long, I thought they would both pass out from lack of oxygen.

Finally, they let go of each other, and Selene took a dramatic step back like she was being torn away from the other half of her heart.

I gave Naomi a quick side hug goodbye, and she whispered "thank you" to me as Selene started walking to my SUV, likely holding back tears.

"Call if you need us. Anytime," I tell Naomi before letting her go.

She nods and follows me out to the car, waving goodbye to Selene while I get into the vehicle. Selene returns her wave as I back out of my parking spot and turn away from her friend to exit the garage.

The cab of the SUV is quiet for a while, which is highly uncommon for Selene, but I merely reach out to take her hand and start to drag my thumb slowly across the back of it. I let her sit with whatever she's feeling while I do my best to support her silently.

"I swear, there's something about sleeping in a different bed that hits different," Selene finally says with a watery smile as we head up the on-ramp to the highway home.

"I'm glad y'all were able to spend time together, though," I tell her honestly.

"Yeah. Me too," Selene's voice is small, a sound I'm not used to hearing from my fiancée.

Her hand stays in mine, steady and sure. Selene turns to stare out the window as I drive, lost in thought.

After a few too many heavy sighs, I break the quiet that surrounds us.

"You want to talk about wedding planning, maybe?" I ask, knowing what I'm getting myself into, but offering anyway.

Selene finally tears her gaze away from the empty farmland around us and looks at me, mild shock in her expression.

"You have me trapped in here for at least another three hours. Might as well use that to your advantage," I shrug, chuckling internally and already dreading whatever torture she's about to come up with.

Not that it matters—as far as my heart's concerned, we're already married. The wedding is her chance to be celebrated the way she deserves.

"I..." she fumbles for words. "We could narrow the guest list? That might be the easiest thing to tackle right now."

"Sure," I smile, glad to see her coming out of whatever funk she was settling into.

We spend the rest of the drive to our halfway pit stop going through the list of who we would invite to the wedding.

By the time I pull into the parking lot of a Buc-ee's, we have fewer than 200 people on the wedding list, and instead of her formerly lost and forlorn look, Selene now looks *stressed*.

"Luna. We will figure it out," I tell her as I open my door to fill us up on gas. "Remember, not everyone will end up attending."

"Yeah. It just all sounds important," she says, looking at me with her brow furrowed and her lips pressed into a tight line.

"We'll figure it out," I say. "Now go inside and stock up on snacks and drinks."

"Aye aye, Captain," she replies with a little mocking salute. "Energy drink for you?"

"Yes. And a water, please."

Shifting her cozy car cocoon around, Selene manages to get out of the SUV in one piece and makes her way into the building.

When I'm finished filling the car up with gas, I move it into a regular parking space and journey into the store.

I'm immediately hit with the smell of BBQ and baked goods

when I enter, but when I search the snack section, Selene is nowhere to be found.

Turning around, I face off with the section of these stores that I dread, the home goods section.

I swear, you could decorate a whole house from this store; it's overwhelming.

After a few minutes of searching, I find Selene looking at a display of dish-ware designs along the back wall.

"Planning on registering us here?" I ask from behind her, making her jump at my sudden appearance.

She spins around to me with a basket full of drinks, snacks, and knick-knacks.

"Of course not," she turns back to the display. "But it does get me thinking."

"About what, Luna?" I say, pulling her into me by her hips.

"Like, do we even need all this stuff? The registry and what-not?" She pauses. "I just... We have a good life, you know? We're happy and healthy. We have a home we love and probably more stuff than we need. Plus, jobs that are fulfilling and pay us well." She pauses, thinking. "I just don't know that there's anything we *need*."

"Then we don't do a registry. We encourage people to donate to a cause or something," I tell her.

"Oh. That's smart," her face lights up. "Maybe the rescue where I got Beef Cake from?"

"We can absolutely do that," I smile down at her, then lean down to kiss her on the forehead.

Selene beams up at me, and I know I've said the right thing this time.

"Come on. Let's check out and get back on the road," I say, taking the basket from her and guiding her to the register with a hand on her back. "Let's go home."

"Yeah. I like that," she smirks. "I miss my favorite man."

"I think I'll always come in second place to that fur ball, won't I?" I chuckle as the clerk rings up our items.

Selene shrugs, "Probably."

"I think I can live with that," I reply, scanning my card on the PIN pad. "So long as I get to spend the rest of my life with you, I can handle a few more years with Beef Cake outranking me."

"Oh, but don't you know?" Selene looks up at me with a devious glee in her expression. "Beef Cake is immortal. He will forever outrank you."

My eyes practically roll into the back of my head, but internally, I'm just grateful to have my Selene back being herself.

She doesn't always believe me when I say it, but I genuinely mean it when I say I will love her long after my last breath.

She's my everything.

My heart. My soul. My reason for breath.

Her happiness is paramount.

Even if that means I'm outranked by a cat.

6

GUNNAR

Usually, returning from a weekend trip means laundry and curling up with Selene, watching her favorite baking show to decompress.

Instead, my phone is going wild as I try to unpack and repack my go-bag.

Caving to the insanity that is the buzzing of my phone on the nightstand, I pick it up just as the screen flashes again with another message.

EMIR

Bad news.

The contract we just signed?

They're not happy.

They want us in DC this week.

GUNNAR

Of course they do.

Valentine's Day is this week.

EMIR

I'm honestly shocked we didn't get called away
for your engagement.

They always call at the least convenient time.

GUNNAR

Sure do.

Have we considered telling them to fuck off?

EMIR

Pack your bag, asshole. Our flight leaves first
thing in the morning.

The details should be in your inbox.

Sure enough, a few emails with my flight and hotel information are waiting for me in my email inbox.

With a groan, I sit on the bed and glance at the clock.

It's only 6 p.m.

This means there's plenty of time to put together something special to celebrate Selene and my first Valentine's Day as an engaged couple.

I throw my final items into my go-bag and grab the suit I'll need this week while I'm on The Hill, then I pull out my phone to start calling in favors.

Within thirty minutes, I have a fully fleshed-out plan and reservations to boot.

"Selene! We're leaving in an hour," I announce as I walk through the house to find her.

After looking everywhere else in the house, I find her in Beef Cake's room, where I can only presume she's been working for a while, given the way she's snuggled in her chair.

"What? Why? Where?" she replies, confusion furrowing her brow.

"I'm taking you to a Valentine's Day dinner," I tell her.

"But Valentine's Day isn't until like... Wednesday," she says, putting her computer down to stand up from where she was previously curled up.

"Yeah, but I just found out I am being called out of town this week, so I'm going to miss the actual day," I explain.

A pout forms on her face as the news settles in.

"You're leaving me?" she says, her voice pitching up in a dramatic whine. "You're gonna leave me all alone on Valentine's Day?"

Taking a few steps toward her, I reach for her hand and tug on it until she fits snugly against my chest.

"I promise I'll make up for it," I tell her softly. "Come on, let's get you ready. Our reservation is in forty-five minutes."

"Forty-five?" she shrieks. "That's not nearly enough time!"

"It is if I help," I tell her, smoothing back a strand of hair that's escaped her messy bun.

I love how she melts into my touch, how the simplest of connections between us has her relaxing in a way I don't often see her do.

"Come on. You focus on makeup. I'll pick out clothes and curl your hair," I say softly, prompting her toward the door with a hand on her shoulder.

Playfully, I chase her up the stairs into the bedroom, and while she starts on her makeup, I go into the closet to pull out clothes for us to wear to dinner.

When I come back, Selene has stripped down to nothing, and I stop in my tracks.

My gaze follows every curve of her body as I study her in the mirror.

Handing over the undergarments I picked for her to wear under the dress I chose, I let my hands rest on her arms.

"Fuck," I breathe out. "You're stunning."

Selene glances up at me over her shoulder.

"I know," she says with an adorable smirk.

7

SELENE

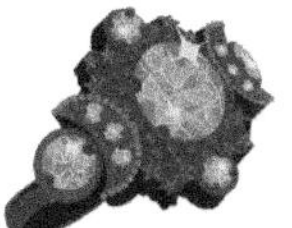

The ritual Gunnar and I have developed when getting ready for events—the time he spends meticulously placing my hair in curlers while I focus on perfecting my makeup—is one I love.

Every time it happens, it reminds us how connected we are.

How *right* we are for each other.

It took me less than 30 minutes to get ready, which is a miracle, all things considered. We were out the door just in time to make our reservation.

Though I'm not sure how Gunnar managed to get us a reservation at such a nice restaurant at the last minute.

The place is packed with people when we arrive, and I'm grateful when they lead us to a table along one of the back walls, tucked away from the others, even if only a little.

We sit down and make ourselves comfortable as one of the staff members comes over with menus and wine lists.

"Thank you," Gunnar says with a nod to the waitstaff before turning to me. "I have a present for you," he tells me softly, pulling out a box and pushing it in my direction. "But you'll need to go into the restroom to open it up for yourself. Just a little something special for tonight."

I give him a look of suspicion, but my curiosity gets the best of me, and I rise to go in search of the restroom.

With the bathroom stall door securely locked behind me, I pull the small box out of my purse and tear into the red wrapping paper, which reveals the gift inside. My cheeks are already aching from grinning as I grab my phone—because yeah, he's definitely getting a text about this.

SELENE

A toy?

GUNNAR

Yes.

A butt plug.

SELENE

And you want me to wear it tonight?

GUNNAR

I was hoping you would.

I thought we could play a little game tonight.

I stare at the box in my hand, turning it around to find where it opens. The seal has clearly already been opened, and when I lift the lid, I find both the plug and its remote, along with a few small packets of lube inside.

Selene: You thought of everything, didn't you?

GUNNAR

I try to be prepared.

SELENE

Fine.

You win.

GUNNAR

Not yet, Luna. The game hasn't even begun.

I put the box and my phone back into my bag before pulling down my panties and shoving them into a deep corner of the tote.

I hike up my dress, tucking the skirt into the waistband to keep it out of the way. Then I sit on the toilet and reach for my bag and the toy.

Gunnar and I have done and played before, but never anything like this. We've played with fingers, mouths, small dildos, and plugs, but never a plug that's quite this big or has a remote.

Ripping open one of the packets of lube with my teeth, I hold the butt plug in one hand while I slather it with lube from the packet.

Taking the excess on my fingers, I reach around and play with my puckered hole. A shiver rolls through my body at the cold feeling of the lube against my ass.

Once the lube warms up a little, I press a single finger into my hole to gauge how ready I am.

Feeling that I am prepared enough to use the plug on myself, I reach around with the hand holding it and place the tip at my back entrance.

I press in slowly, pushing the plug in and out of my puckered entrance, allowing myself time to adjust to its girth. I can feel that it's about halfway in when I meet more resistance than I'm used to.

With my free hand, I reach around my front to stroke my clit. The small nub is already pert and pulsing with need.

As I circle my clit, my body begins to relax, and I'm able to press the plug further into my ass. The rhythm of my fingers against my clit grows faster, just as the pulsing of the plug in my other hand gains speed.

I can hear people coming and going outside of the stall I have locked myself in, and it reminds me that I need to contain my sounds of pleasure.

My fingers move more rapidly against my clitoris, and I can feel my body reaching to take in the broadest part of the plug now.

My breath is shallow as I pant through the pleasure that's ricocheting through my body.

Every nerve stands on end... ready for the crashing wave of bliss that awaits me.

Only, I know how Gunnar likes to play his games, and he'll want to witness my pleasure for himself.

The thought of having Gunnar watch as I career over the edge —wild, unguarded, and entirely his—allows my body to relax to insert the plug in fully, and my hips twist as I adjust to the fullness in my ass.

I'm so close to the edge and my body is in desperate need of release, but instead of finishing myself off, I wipe my lubed fingers off before putting on my panties and grab my bag to go, wash my hands, straighten my dress, and then head back into the dining room.

"How are you enjoying my gift, my Goddess?" Gunnar asks me softly when I get back to the table.

"It's very... fulfilling," I tell him.

I sit down next to my fiancé, squirming slightly as I get used to the feeling of the butt plug in my ass.

"So, what's this game you want to play?" I ask.

"You will see," Gunnar replies while looking around the room for our waiter. "Hand me the remote."

The command in his voice sends a thrill through me. Whatever this game is going to be, I imagine it will be one hell of a time.

I hand over the remote just as our waiter appears at our table.

Gunnar takes my hand in his own, and there's a silent pass of the small remote.

Pleasantries are exchanged, and the waiter begins going through their evening specials.

I try my best to pay attention, but a soft vibration ricochets through my body just as the waiter lists the dishes.

I glare at Gunnar, who would otherwise appear completely oblivious to my current state if not for the smirk on his face. He is as heated as the ovens in this restaurant's kitchen.

I can't help but squirm in my seat as conversation buzzes around me.

Each time I open my mouth to speak, Gunnar clicks on the remote, and the vibration grows more intense, quickly shutting me up once again.

I can only focus on the tingling vibrations running through my body.

With each second that passes, my mind sinks further and further into its own world that consists only of pleasure and bliss.

I squirm in my seat, trying to find some semblance of relief from the overwhelming sensations coursing through my body, but each movement only shifts the focus on the sensation.

I barely notice when the waiter leaves our table, and glasses of wine appear in front of us out of thin air.

"Gunnar," I pant, my breath coming out as fast as my heart is racing.

"Yes, my Goddess?" Gunnar's gaze is molten with heat. "Is there something you desire? Something I can help you with?"

"You know damned well what you're doing right now and what you can 'help' with," I growl through the tremors that wrack my body.

"But how could I?" he asks, a dangerous gleam in his eyes. "Even a Goddess such as yourself must tell her disciples how she wishes to be worshipped."

I stuff down the whimper that threatens to escape my lips and redirect that energy toward glaring at the man beside me.

"How can I serve you tonight, my Goddess?" he purrs. "Tell me what you need, and it's yours."

I'm gripping the table for dear life, clinging to reality with every fiber of my being.

"I need to fucking come," I whisper through clenched teeth.

The vibrator in my ass, as delightful as it feels, isn't enough to bring me to the edge of orgasm quite like I need it to. It seems to edge me for every minute that Gunnar leaves it on.

When the vibration stops, my whole body slumps with relief, only to have it start back up again in a less consistent pattern this time.

"Fuck!" I gasp, a little too loudly.

The attention of others dining around us is drawn in our direction by my outburst.

"Fuck," I murmur, adjusting to the new pattern that vibrates through my body.

I feel both full and empty at the same time. With every clench around the plug in my ass, my pussy aches to be filled, and my clit longs to be touched.

They feel left out, ignored.

"I need you to touch me," I demand, fighting through the fog of pleasure that threatens to engulf me. "You're going to reach under this tablecloth and between my legs. Then you're going to use those skilled hands of yours to get me off at this table."

Gunnar chuckles, "Yes, Goddess."

"And after," I continue, causing him to raise a brow in question. "After you make me come at this table in front of all these people, you're going to find somewhere in this building where you can pin me against a wall and make me come again on your tongue and fingers."

"And my cock?" Gunnar asks lowly.

"Your cock stays where it is tonight for all this torture you're putting me through," I growl.

Immediately, Gunnar pulls my chair closer to his. He drapes one arm around my shoulders, bringing me close to his body, while the other gently slides up my leg toward my center.

I'm grateful for how my dress splits to the side, perfect to allow him easy access to my pussy without having to push up my dress entirely.

Another shiver of delight rolls through me when he pushes my panties aside and his fingertips brush against the curls at my center.

"Oh, such a good girl. Already wet and waiting for me," he purrs into my ear.

To those around us, it appears as though we are a couple having an intimate conversation in the dim light of the dining room.

To me, however, it feels like a spotlight is being shone on my cunt with the way he touches me.

Electricity sparks at the first brush of his fingertips against my clit, sending a humming throughout my body.

"That's good," Gunnar whispers into my ear. "You're so fucking needy, aren't you?"

"Yes," I breathe out as Gunnar's fingers slip between my folds to graze my entrance.

My hips subtly rock against his fingertips, silently pleading for him to slip them inside me.

"So wet for me. Ready for anything I give you," he pulls back just enough to look me in the eyes. "You want to come, Goddess? Then take it. Use me for your pleasure."

I snap my hand around his wrist suddenly, making Gunnar's eyes grow wide at my sudden movement. But then I move him so he's thrusting his fingers inside of me, making my whole body relax now that it has what it needs.

A chuckle escapes Gunnar's lips as he sees me relax into my chair, and he leans in to place a kiss under my ear.

Slowly, he rocks his fingers inside of me, finding that perfect pressure point that drives me wild.

He strokes the spot, stoking the ember of my desire into a raging fire.

Every touch of his hand on my shoulder, his lips on my neck, and his fingers in my pussy drives me closer to my peak.

Out of nowhere, my wave of pleasure crashes down from the heights Gunnar drove me to.

Biting down on my lip, I force myself to retain the cry that wants to escape as I ride the river of bliss that flows through my body. I let my head fall onto Gunnar's shoulder as I take deep breaths, trying to steady myself just as the vibrator in my ass turns off.

My cunt clutches Gunnar's fingers desperately, practically begging for another round. But I don't think my racing heart can handle another orgasm like that right now.

My eyes clamp shut, focusing on the sensations swirling through me, and though we're surrounded by people, it feels like Gunnar and I are completely alone.

I'm surrounded by him. Protected by him.

Slowly, I come back to myself as Gunnar retreats away from me.

My body is limp in the chair, and my vision is fuzzy. Everything swirls around me in random energy, color, and light patterns.

When the waiter heads in our direction, Gunnar raises his hand—the same one that was just forcing an orgasm out of me—to usher them over.

"I'm so sorry," he says in his typical gruff way. "I think my fiancée had too much to drink before we came tonight. Could we get our food wrapped up to go? I think it's best to get her home."

Without a word, the waiter nods and walks off, presumably to get our food to go.

Turning back to me, Gunnar slides one of the fingers that was coaxing an orgasm from me into his mouth, and he groans.

"Much better than anything on the menu," he says with a twinkle in his eye.

Gathering myself, I push myself up straighter in my chair.

"What about the second half I asked for?"

Gunnar raises an eyebrow at me.

"Would you rather have me give you one more orgasm in the hallway here? Or..." His gaze narrows on my lips. "Would you rather I take you home and ravish you where you can scream my name like I know you want to?"

Well, that answers that.

8

SELENE

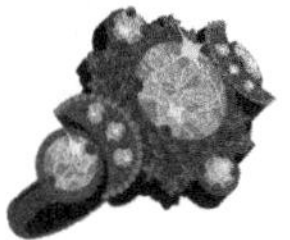

February 14—Mars conjunct Pluto in Aquarius, Moon in Capricorn

It's Valentine's Day, but with Gunnar out of town for work, it's just me and Beef Cake in the house.

It's too quiet.

So, to distract myself, I grab a snack and go into the cat cave with my laptop, opening the server chat I have with Naomi.

OVERTHEMOON

This sucks.

It doesn't take more than a few seconds for her reply to come through.

MINDFUCKMASTER

Valentine's Day without Gunnar?

OVERTHEMOON

Maybe…

The house is just really empty without him.

And everyone else in the group has plans.

MINDFUCKMASTER

You miss him. It's natural.

OVERTHEMOON

Yup. So, it's just me and Beef Cake tonight.

MINDFUCKMASTER

Awe! Valentine's Day with the true love of your life.
How sweet!

OVERTHEMOON

lol yeah

MINDFUCKMASTER

BTW… when did you get Beef Cake? In all the
time we've been friends, he's just been around.
But I've never heard the meet-cute story.

OVERTHEMOON

Really?

Gunnar got him for me.

MINDFUCKMASTER

WHAT?

OVERTHEMOON

Yeah. It was the second time he asked me to be
his girlfriend.

MINDFUCKMASTER

Second time? He had to ask twice?

OMG WAS BEEF CAKE A BRIBE?

OVERTHEMOON

Beef Cake was 1,000% a bribe.

But no, Gunnar had to ask three times. Beef Cake
was a gift on attempt number two.

MINDFUCKMASTER

AND YOU SAID NO?

OVERTHEMOON

Well, yeah. I told him he couldn't bribe me like that.

MINDFUCKMASTER

And you kept the cat?

Diabolical!!! 😅

Memories flood back to me of the night I came home to my condo to find that Gunnar had prepared an entire candlelit dinner.

"Hey," he says softly as I come into the dining room.

"Hey?" I reply with curiosity in my voice. "What's going on here?"

"I made dinner," he continues. "Come. Sit."

Warily, I slip off my work heels and make my way over to the table to sit in the chair Gunnar pulls out.

He's dressed in a full suit, tie, and everything, which is odd for him on what should be a regular Thursday date night.

"How was your day?" Gunnar asks as he slips into his own chair and reaches to serve us both from the dishes on the table.

"Good," I say skeptically.

"Good. Good." He nods.

"Gunnar. What the fuck is going on? Why are you being so weird?" I ask.

Gunnar continues to serve us both our cuts of steak and sides of mashed potatoes and asparagus without a word, which only heightens my frustration.

"Gunnar!" I demand a little too loudly, my voice echoing in the empty apartment.

Just then, there's a loud sound that fills my home, which can only be described as a yowl.

"Gunnar?" I ask as I rise from my seat and head in the direction of the sound, which grows louder with each step. "What is that noise?"

"Selene!" Gunnar calls after me.

I storm down the hallway and into the guest bedroom, where I find a kennel, containing a massive orange and white cat.

I gasp, turning to Gunnar, who's come to stand behind me. "Is that?"

"Surprise," Gunnar says with a sheepish grin as he runs his fingers through his blonde hair.

"Did you get me a cat?" I squeal, already opening the cage and pulling out the massive Maine Coon.

"Yeah. I had this whole plan that involved him, but the little asshole kinda ruined it," Gunnar explains.

"Don't you dare speak to my son like that," I snap, shifting my scowl away from Gunnar before beaming lovingly at my new furry companion. "He's not an asshole at all. Are you, boy? You're just as sweet as can be!"

Gunnar chuckles.

"So, what was the plan?" I ask after a few moments of cuddling with the new love of my life.

"Well, I was going to feed you dinner. Then the plan was to bring out this big guy and have him give you the note around his collar," Gunnar says, gesturing to the cat's collar.

I reach for the small note buried among the cat's dense fur and pull it off.

Opening the note, I see the chicken scratch of Gunnar's handwriting.

The words "Will you be my human?" with a paw print beside it are just above "Will you be my girlfriend?" and Gunnar's initials, GH.

My heart stops at the sight.

"Gunnar," I say softly, guilt already swarming my chest.

"I was hoping there'd be more time to talk about it before we got to this part," he admits.

Looking up at my handsome Viking, I can see the passion and fear in his gaze.

He's worried I'll say no again.

"*I didn't want to blindside you, though,*" *he rushes out, more nervous than I've ever heard him before.* "*That's not my intention at all.*"

"*Gunnar,*" *my voice cracks.*

"*You don't...*" *He pauses, fortifying himself.* "*You don't have to say yes. I know...*"

There's genuine heartbreak evident in every part of his body and expression.

"*I can't agree to be your girlfriend, Gunnar,*" *I say softly.* "*I'm not... I can't commit to that.*"

"*I love you, Selene.*"

All the air in my lungs suddenly disappears.

It's not the first time he's said it, but the way he's speaking right now is with such conviction that I can't help but feel the full force of the words.

"*I can't help but love you,*" *he continues earnestly.* "*And I know you love me too. I don't understand why it's not possible for us to make that official. To announce it to the world.*"

"*Gunnar...*"

"*Selene...*" *His expression grows serious as he fortifies himself.* "*Everyone knows we're together, so what's the harm in labeling things?*"

"*I just...*" *My words are trapped among my swirling thoughts—all the fears I've had spinning through my mind for the past year as we've grown close.*

"*Are you ashamed of this? Of me?*"

"*What? No!*" *I say quickly, clutching my feline companion lightly like my sanity depends on it.* "*Of course not.*"

"*Then why?*"

When he doesn't say anything more, I can't help but admit, "*What we have right now is good. It works. I don't want to ruin that.*"

"*It won't ruin anything, Selene. I promise.*" *Gunnar reaches for my hand, and I let him draw me over to the bed so we can sit.*

"*You can't make those kinds of promises, Gunnar,*" *I say softly,* looking down at the furry beast, who's happy as can be cradled in my arms. "Being your girlfriend... everyone's going to start to expect things. Big things. And I can't do that. I can't promise you forever."

"I'm not asking you to." He reaches to cup my face and draws my attention to his own soft expression. "This is me advocating for myself, Selene. For what I want. I love you. Every day, I choose to love you. Everything I am is devoted to showing you how much. I can't help it. You're the center of my universe, and I'm lost without you."

"I know, Gunnar. I know," I choke out.

"Selene, we're not committing to be together forever. Not right now. We're not saying this is going to be perfect," he says confidently. "We're committing to try and be our best selves for each other."

Something about his words makes my tender heart melt, and tears form at the edges of my vision.

"Say it. Please," he says breathlessly. "Tell me how you feel about me. I'm begging."

"I..." My words catch in my throat.

It's not that I don't want to say them, nor that I don't feel them. Rather, the feeling is too big, too heavy, too dangerous to utter out loud.

But the way he's looking at me, so open and honest, has me caving.

"I love you too," I murmur, and a huge grin spreads across Gunnar's face.

"You love me," he breathes out.

I nod, unable to repeat the words I know in my heart are true.

"Selene Aracely Solis de Estrella loves me."

His eyes gleam with the same light he accuses me of shining constantly, and the openness of his expression has me leaning in to kiss him.

"I love you," I repeat, my words more confident this time. "But I can't be your girlfriend. Not now. Not yet."

"Okay, I can live with that," Gunnar smiles, leaning in to kiss me gently before pulling away. "I've lived a thousand lifetimes just to experience your love, Selene. I can wait a thousand more to make you mine."

The cat in my arms shifts and breaks the tension between Gunnar and me.

"Girlfriend or not, I'm keeping the cat. And I can agree to shared custody," I reason, which draws a deep chuckle from Gunnar's throat. "He can spend the week with me, and he'll come over to your place whenever I spend the night."

Beef Cake was totally worth it, though.

So is Gunnar.

I know he is.

Another ding comes from my computer, alerting me to another message from Naomi.

MINDFUCKMASTER

I should be done with this study session in about an hour if you want to have a Galantine's Day together.

OVERTHEMOON

That sounds perfect. Just let me know when you're done.

MINDFUCKMASTER

And to think, it took him three tries to get you to say yes to dating him.

OVERTHEMOON

Shut up! Whose side are you on?

MINDFUCKMASTER

Yours obvi

OVERTHEMOON

Good. Otherwise, Beef Cake privileges would be revoked.

MINDFUCKMASTER

YOU WOULD NEVER!

OVERTHEMOON

I wouldn't, but it's good to keep you on your best behavior.

MINDFUCKMASTER

Like you know what "best behavior" is…

OVERTHEMOON

You're right. 🤭

MINDFUCKMASTER

I'll message you after I'm done. Love you.

OVERTHEMOON

Love you too.

9

SELENE

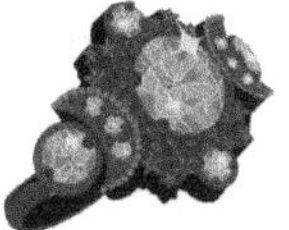

February 15—Venus sextile Neptune, Moon in Taurus

When people talk about getting into shape for their wedding so they can walk down the aisle in their perfect dress, I used to laugh. Now, after a flurry of texts from Ivy about a cancellation that led to me racing out of a meeting at eight in the morning, I'm standing in the main workshop of my favorite designer's atelier, having tried on at least twenty different gowns so far today. I understand what they meant.

It's not the *wedding dress* they're preparing for; it's the wedding dress *shopping*.

Ivy and I have been here for hours, and I've tried on enough dresses that they're starting to blur together. However, that might actually be my vision and not just my mind playing tricks on me.

"Selene?" my friend's bright voice comes through the door of the dressing room I've locked myself in. "Honey, can I come in?"

I let my head fall back onto my shoulders and take in a steadying breath.

It's not that I don't love and appreciate Ivy for dropping everything to come out and do this with me, but the overwhelm has set in, and I feel like I'm underwater.

"Lena?" The door creaks open slightly, and Ivy pops her head in. "It's been a while now that you've been hiding out. Everything okay?"

Looking at her in the mirror, my eyes start to well up with tears.

"Oh no. Nope. Those are not good tears," she rushes out as she steps into the dressing room. "Talk to me, Selene."

"I just..." I take a deep breath, trying to collect myself. "I feel like shit, and this is taking forever, but I feel like I'm no closer to finding something I love than when we walked in here. But this is my *dream designer* for my dress we're talking about. You pulled a miracle getting me in here, and I feel like I've ruined it."

"Okay," she says in a calm tone. "That's valid. Weddings are an overwhelming process, and I imagine it feels like there's a lot of pressure here to make the *right* decision."

Ivy skirts around the edge of the room, stepping carefully to ensure she doesn't trip on the hem of the oversized ball gown I'm wearing.

"Let's check in," she says softly, reaching for my hand. "I'm guessing you didn't have breakfast this morning because you were too excited. I know I handed you a granola bar, but I'm not sure you ate it. It's probably been at least five hours since you last had anything to eat or drink, other than the champagne they keep handing us."

I cringe internally at her reminder, thinking about the blood test results I've pointedly been avoiding in my patient portal and knowing it's probably more than just not eating for a few hours and having one too many glasses of bubbly.

"Why don't we get you out of this monstrosity and let the staff know we will need to come back another day?" Ivy's voice is gentle as can be.

"But we *can't* come back." The tears start falling in earnest now. "Isn't that the whole point of having a last-minute appointment? They're booked out for *two years*, Ivy."

"I know, honey. But this isn't the end; it's just the beginning. We can ask about another appointment, and in the meantime, we can look around at other designers and boutiques." She squeezes my hand, slowing the tears a little and allowing me to give her a slight nod. "Okay. I'm going to find someone to get you out of this cupcake of a dress."

"It's too much, isn't it?" I ask, looking at myself in the mirror once more. "It swallows me whole."

"Kinda like you did with those Jell-O shots at the club," Ivy giggles. "But yeah, kinda. And wedding dresses are supposed to highlight the bride, not hide her."

"You make an excellent point." A shiver rolls down my spine. "Someone get me out of this nightmare of a dress."

A light rap comes through the door, followed by a new voice.

"Selene?" Amélie's voice can be heard from beyond the door. "I know it's been a long day, but I have one more dress for you to try on."

Ivy begins making her way around the edge of the room once more and opens the door slightly to let Amé in.

"Okay. This is the only dress of its design, but it is one of those 'hear me out' moments. I want you to keep an open mind. Got it?" She looks nervous, an expression I'm not used to seeing on the designer's normally confident face.

Then she sweeps into the room, bringing the dress into view.

"It's... blue," Ivy says inquisitively.

My eyes struggle to take in the dress displayed before me, my vision blurring slightly at the edges. It's nothing like a wedding dress *should* be, but it feels like it's everything to me.

The dress is made of a soft blue fabric that folds over itself in a Grecian style on the bodice. The skirt is like the aurora borealis, and each layer of the fabric has adornments that make it look like the layers of the cosmos.

It resonates with a part of me that none of the other garments I've worn today have even dared to touch.

"It's perfect," I breathe out.

Ivy's face breaks into a broad smile, highlighting her high cheekbones and bright, twinkling eyes.

"How much is it?" I ask.

"Doesn't matter," Ivy says quickly. "If you love it, then we'll make it work."

"Ivy..." I warn. "I need to know how much I'm dropping on this dress."

Amé looks between us with confusion. "I thought..."

"Ivy!" I cry, interrupting her. "Ivy Andrea le Fleur, cuanto cuesta el maldito traje?" *How much is the fucking dress?*

"Don't think about the cost, lovely. Just try it on." Ivy backs into the room to allow Amélie space to make her way over to the hooks on the far wall, where several other dresses hang, discarded like last season's castoffs.

When Amé hangs it up, she fluffs the bottom of the dress, sending light sparkling through the room as small gems reflect their brilliance around us.

"It's truly breathtaking. It will be perfect for you. I can't believe I didn't think of it sooner," Amé says, her confident tone hits straight where it was intended to.

"It is," I breathe out, grounding myself before I let things get out of control. "Fine." I glare at Ivy. "I'll try it on, but I make no promises."

A complete lie.

Ivy's burst of laughter leaves me unsteady on my feet, and I sway a little.

"Selene?" Ivy's voice grows serious. "Are you okay?"

"Yeah," I pant, my breath growing more rapid. "Just a little woozy, that's all. Too much champagne."

No one in the room looks convinced, least of all Ivy, who is already reaching out to steady me.

"Maybe we should come back another time to try this one on," she says gently.

"Really, I'm fine. I think I just need to get out of this dress I'm in," I rush out, trying to cajole the women around me. "I want to try it on now. Please."

The look of skepticism exchanged between the two is doubtful, but they don't push me too far before my heels truly dig in.

"Okay. Out of the cupcake we come," Amé says with a giggle, clearly having overheard Ivy and me's earlier quip about the dress. "I'll grab my assistant to help you get into this new one."

Ivy and Amé quickly vacate the room, leaving me alone with the most beautiful dress in the universe.

Reaching over to feel the dress, I pick up the light fabric of the outermost layer of its skirt and rub it between my fingers. The fabric slides effortlessly against itself, making the softest of rustling noises.

I don't even fully process the experience as I get out of the itchy cupcake dress. I'm too focused on the blue wedding gown and how it slides over my body.

Once it is settled in place, I lift the outer layer of the fabric again, absorbing the soft rustle and scratching sounds it makes against itself.

"Miss?" the low voice of Amé's assistant filters through my hazy thoughts. "Miss Selene, would you like to show your friend?"

"My friend?" I ask, my brow furrowed in confusion.

"Yes? Ms. Ivy is waiting for you in the main room of the atelier." The assistant looks at me curiously with their head cocked to the side.

"Right. My friend. Ivy." I pause, trying to conjure the face of the woman I brought with me. "Yes. I'll show her now, if that's alright."

"Of course." The assistant smiles. "Same way as before."

"Right." I step through the doorway, looking left and then right.

It takes me a moment before I remember which direction to head.

With each step down the hallway, my breathing seems to grow more shallow, and my heart rate increases.

She's going to love it, right? My friends will too, I'm sure.

I turn the corner into the main workshop, but the blinding lights from above have me reaching for the wall beside me to steady myself.

A shrill squeal comes from across the room, but I can't concentrate on what everyone is saying. It sounds like they're excited, right?

My free hand trembles when I reach up to place it over my racing heart, and it feels like my lungs are incapable of taking in enough air.

"No me siento bien," I mumble—*I don't feel good*—but I don't think I can be heard over the voices chattering around me.

Someone takes me by the hand and leads me onto the pedestal in the center of a half-moon of mirrors. Looking up at my reflection, what little air remaining in my lungs whooshes out.

"I look ethereal," I whisper.

"What was that?" a voice comes from behind me.

"I said, I look ethereal." Only the words don't sound right as they come out of my mouth.

"Lovely, you're not sounding right," someone chuckles. "She's literally speechless!"

Every bounce of light against the dress reflected in the mirror is more disorienting than the overhead fluorescent bulbs shining down on us.

But I do look beautiful.

Even if I feel like crap.

"Does anyone have something I can drink?" I pant out, my mouth drier than the Texas desert.

"Mhmm!" someone replies before a glass is placed in my hand.

I down the liquid greedily, but it doesn't quench the thirst I'm feeling.

Something is wrong.

A familiar face comes around in front of me and smiles.

I know them. I swear I do. But the name won't come.

"Honey?" The person reaches forward, and a warmth radiates from where their hand lands on my shoulder. "Selene, I think you should sit down."

I want to nod; I think I do, but everything feels so heavy.

I know someone is holding my hands, prompting me to move down from the podium, but I can't bring myself to take the step down.

"Selene?" a melodic voice permeates the fog that surrounds me. "Take a step forward, lovely."

It feels like a gargantuan effort to move my body. Suddenly, I'm so tired; I only want to lie down and rest.

My eyes are heavy, and my head is swimming, but my heart races faster than a Formula One car.

Everything seems to happen in slow motion, yet it all happens simultaneously.

The step down feels like it takes an eternity, but when my foot connects with the ground, my body gives up, or rather, it goes down.

Gasps filter in around me, and I'm aware of the presence of concern surrounding my body, but I'm not really there.

Darkness creeps in at the edges of my vision like one of those old photographs with grayed edges.

A small prick of light filters through my vision, but there's nothing to see beyond that.

The chaos around me is far and distant. I'm too disconnected from my own body to process how *I* feel, much less what's happening.

Fatigue takes over, and my body goes limp just as the dark closes in.

A nap sounds really good right now.

10

GUNNAR

February 16—Sun conjunct Saturn, Moon in Gemini

Getting a call that my fiancée is in the hospital was not on my schedule while I was in DC, but yesterday afternoon, I got the call that Selene had collapsed. Ivy told me they were on their way to the Medical Center after Selene passed out trying on wedding dresses, of all things.

I was in a meeting with one of our largest clients when I got that call. For all I cared, they could fuck off.

Within seconds of hanging up the phone, I was out of my chair and headed to my hotel. Then, I went straight to the airport to catch the next flight home.

Thankfully, Emir, my business partner, could smooth down the ruffled feathers I left in my wake. Whatever excuses he made for me deserve a nice bottle of scotch.

We started Tartarus Guardians Security (TGS) ten years ago with an investment from a generous benefactor who believed in Emir and me, even though we had only been in the national security sector for five years.

That said, the handful of gold medals framed in our lobby for my years on the International Shooting Sport Federation (ISSF) and a few turns around the Olympic circuits do tend to give some public weight to our firm's credibility, even if most people don't look beneath the surface to see what made me such a sharp shooter.

Though it's truly Emir's knowledge of technology and infrastructure that keeps us miles ahead of our competitors, the way his mind works and how he's able to see problems before they even arise is incredible.

Sometimes, when I'm bored with beating my employees into the ground in the training facility, I'll go to his office and watch his screens for a while before he finally notices anyone is in the room with him.

Now, a decade later, we're the largest firm in Texas, primarily handling private security contracts for international corporations and individual security contracts with high-profile clients.

But nothing matters more to me than the love of my life.

So, when I arrived at the hospital in record time, the helpful person at the front desk was kind enough to direct me to where they had placed Selene after a single, albeit barked, request.

I'm a rather large man at 6'2", often referred to as a Viking because of my size and blonde hair—a nickname Selene gave me early on in our flirtations.

I'm not used to people telling me no or getting in my way, but when I got to Selene's floor, this nurse stood firm in her orthopedic work shoes and refused to let me pass.

Honestly, I'd hire her in a heartbeat over many of the guys employed at my firm based on how she handled a standoff face-to-face. As a bonus, she has a medical background as well.

I should tell Emir we need to start looking at recruiting nurses for our teams.

After a few polite words, I was able to charm the nurse enough that she let me by, albeit begrudgingly.

But by the time I was able to see Selene with my own eyes, my body was coiled tight and ready to fight the next person who looked at me wrong.

Entering the room, I take in the visage of my fiancée.

She seems to be resting. Her eyes are closed, and her head is resting on a pillow, where her brown hair sprawls out, framing her face like the Goddess she is. Part of me almost anticipated walking in to see Selene still dressed in an expensive wedding gown, but instead, she's clothed in a basic hospital gown, which she will hate when she's up.

Walking over to her bedside, I take her hand in mine, which rouses her from her dozing state.

"Hey, Luna," I say softly with a smile, pushing down the lump of distress that's formed in my throat.

The smile that forms around Selene's eyes lightens the weight trying to settle on my chest, and I take a full breath for the first time since Ivy's call.

"Hey there, Viking," she says, her voice thick with sleep.

"How are you?" I ask, letting my gaze catalogue her body as my eyes travel up and down her curves.

"I'm okay. Just got a bit lightheaded or something," she says with a shrug, adjusting herself on the hospital bed to get more comfortable.

"Or something?" I ask, my brow furrowing at how flippant she's being.

"Yeah. I'm not sure. One minute I was fine and trying on the dress of my dreams, and the next, I was in the ambulance," she tells me blandly. "They're running a bunch of tests right now, I think. They took blood draws and everything."

"Have you heard anything from the doctors yet?" I press, trying to gather more information to assess the situation.

"Gunnar, I just told you I haven't heard from them yet," Selene says, annoyance lacing her tone. "Nunca escucha." *Never fucking listening.*

Just then, a knock sounds at the door, and a petite woman pokes her head into the room.

"Hello! Ms. Solis de Estrella, right?" the woman says as she takes a few steps into the room until she's at the foot of Selene's bed.

"Please call me Selene. The full thing is long as fuck." Selene chuckles, and the woman smiles back at her.

"Hello, Selene. I'm Dr. Stone, and I'm taking over your case," She explains. "I was going over your chart, and it looks like you had blood drawn a few months ago after your tubal ligation, correct?"

"Yes," Selene says with a tilt of her head.

"Did they ever talk to you about those results?" the doctor continues.

"Maybe? I'm not entirely sure," she replies evenly, but I can see through the facade.

"Selene?" I ask.

"Yes, probably? I know they wanted me to follow up with my primary care, but I just... never did?" My fiancée, the strongest woman I know, hunches in on herself.

"Alright. That's okay," the doctor says, flipping through the pages of Selene's chart until she finds what she's looking for. "So basically, what they would have talked about with you is some of your lab results that they got back post-surgery."

I give the doctor a hard look, silently willing her to get to the fucking point, but she continues without paying any attention to me.

"It appears that your A1C levels came back quite high after surgery. Your test then came back close to 6.9%, and when we reran the test today, it was a little over 7.2%, which is not ideal," Dr. Stone continues, looking at Selene for understanding.

On the other hand, my fiancée looks confused, as though everything the doctor is telling her is a foreign language she's never heard before.

"What does that mean, exactly?" I clarify.

The doctor's tight smile presses into a hard line as though she's trying to bite her tongue before turning back to speak with Selene.

"As I was saying, A1C is the test we run to check your blood sugar levels over the past 2-3 months. Basically, it's how we check to see where people fall within the ranges to determine if a patient is normal, pre-diabetic, or diabetic. And yours is coming back rather high." The doctor delves into explaining the minutiae of the tests, but I'm no longer paying attention.

My person is sick.

She's sick—and I didn't even know.

I *knew* letting her go to that surgery alone, with no one to watch out for her, was a bad idea.

Twenty- to thirty-minute procedure, my ass.

Sure, I dropped her off and picked her up from the hospital, but it's not the same as being there to support her the whole time.

I don't even remember what bullshit meeting was happening that I felt I had to skip the ordeal.

And because I wasn't there, I missed it.

I missed the information that could have prevented today from happening.

"So what?" I interject, my voice a little too loud and startling the doctor and Selene, who were clearly deep in their conversation. "What does all this mean?"

"As I was explaining to Ms. Selene, her tests indicate that she has diabetes," the doctor says shortly, turning her attention back to Selene once again. "It's likely that the combination of your blood sugar levels and the stress of your day contributed to you ending up in the hospital."

"I thought diabetes was something people have since child-hood?" I ask, my voice still too harsh.

Dr. Stone turns to me slowly. "Type 2 diabetes is more likely to be diagnosed in adults than Type 1. Though Type 1 can be diagnosed at any point in someone's life, it just happens to pop up earlier for most people, depending on the level of care they are provided as children. But either can develop at any point in a person's life."

This doctor's look grates on my nerves, but I grit my jaw and hold back the biting remarks I want to tell this woman.

"So, the appointment they wanted me to schedule?" Selene asks the doctor.

"It would have been to talk about your condition, treatment options, and lifestyle changes that will need to be made," the doctor says sweetly to Selene, giving me a stern glare from the corner of her eyes. "I can talk you through things and prescribe some temporary supplies. Though ultimately, to get everything truly underway and start managing your condition, you'll need to coordinate with your primary care provider, who will then refer you to the specialists you will need."

"Specialists?" I ask.

"Yes. Ultimately, depending on how your case progresses, you'll end up working with an endocrinologist, nutritionist, ophthalmologist, and a few others."

The fact that the doctor won't answer me directly only aggravates me more, but Selene grabs my hand, a silent signal not to do or say anything out of line to this woman.

I focus on her warm hand in mine as the two women continue to converse.

At 5'4", Selene is significantly shorter than I am, and seeing her small hand engulfed in my massive, rough one is grounding. I study the way my calluses graze roughly against the softness of her palm.

She adjusts her hand in mine so she can run soothing circles on my skin with her thumb, further dampening my frustration as I melt into her touch.

Selene is my everything, my sun and stars. She's my entire universe.

And I could have lost her.

Something worse could have happened, and I could have lost her.

I always thought I would be the one to face the most danger in our relationship.

Working in security exposes you to all kinds of threats.

Sometimes, there are... favors. Ones where no one asks questions, but you sign on because you know it's the right thing to do.

I've risked life and limb for people I care about and saved countless lives with my skill.

But how do you save someone from themselves?

What do you do when there's a silent battle being fought internally?

How do you prepare for that? How do you fight it?

How do you win when you can't even see your opponent?

I'm finally drawn out of my spiral when I hear the retreating squeak of the doctor's shoes.

"Gunnar?" Selene looks up at me with concern in her expression. "Are *you* okay?"

"Yeah. Just..." I shake my head of the dark thoughts creeping into the periphery.

This definitely wasn't how I was expecting all of this to go.

"How are you feeling, though?" I ask.

Selene shrugs. "Annoyed mostly. It feels like just one more thing to deal with on top of everything else. A little betrayed. Like..." She glances down at her body. "Body? How dare you?"

She looks up at me once again with that bright light in her eyes that's always drawn me toward her.

I lean down, placing my free hand against the curve of her cheek, and place a kiss on her forehead.

"How dare," I sigh into her hair.

Selene lets me linger there, just breathing in her floral scent. When I pull back, Selene looks at me with a concern in her gaze that I want to wipe away.

"Did she say when you could leave?" I ask softly, still gripping her hand like a lifeline.

"I've just been waiting for the doctor to make rounds and go over the test results. They had me eat and checked my blood sugar. Now that's all done, they'll discharge me," Selene says, still gripping my hand like a lifeline. Selene's eyes go wide, glancing over at me. "*Please* tell me you brought me clothes."

Looking down at her hospital gown, I scowl, realizing for the first time that she probably has nothing to change into since they brought her in wearing a, now ruined, wedding dress.

"I have my gym bag in the truck," I tell her, leading to her wrinkling her nose at me. "It's clean, Selene. I've been traveling. It's just sitting in my truck."

The relief she expresses is a full-body reaction as she flops back onto the bed.

"Okay. I can do that," she sighs.

"I'll be right back," I tell her, giving her a quick kiss. "Love you, little Goddess."

11

SELENE

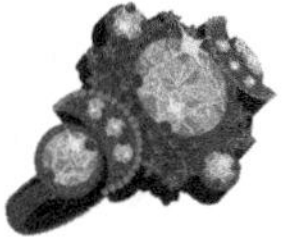

Thankfully, Gunnar decided to pack sweats and a *normal* T-shirt for his workout instead of the awful, cut-up shirts he usually wears to the gym. Otherwise, the stares I get leaving the hospital would have been for my side boob instead of my current combo of workout clothes and sky-high, red-bottomed shoes.

"So, what happened to the dress?" Gunnar asks as we finally settle into the car, taking my hand as always.

I can't help the groan that escapes my throat.

Finding that dress, the perfect dress, was a magical moment. Knowing who I wanted to design my dress was one of the few decisions I really felt I could commit to in this whole wedding dress process.

Now, the certainty of finding the perfect dress is shattered.

And with it, some of my certainty about the wedding planning process.

"Oh, no," he chuckles.

Dropping my head back on the headrest, I think back to the most mortifying moment of my life.

It really was so sweet of Amé to follow us to the hospital, though I feel like it was more to get the dress back than anything.

But when I saw her face fall when she entered my room, finding the gown discarded onto the cucking chair in the corner?

It was clear that the heartbreak hit her hard. I've never seen someone's expression crumble that fast.

She tried to hide it well, but the way the medical team had butchered the dress in order to get me out of it makes me mourn its beauty. I can't even imagine how she felt.

I apologized profusely, and even offered to pay for the ruined dress, but Amé silently shook her head and went about packing up the gown.

Witnessing the entire process was like watching a royal funeral, and all three of us—Amé, Ivy, and I—grieved with every fiber of our being.

"The designer took it back to her studio with her," I tell Gunnar, keeping the details to myself this time. "I'll pay for it, of course. But I don't think that automatically heals that kind of hurt."

At this point, I wouldn't be surprised if Amé never let me back into her studio ever again. I think she broke a little bit in that moment, and I will always be the one to blame for that.

"I mean, it's just a dress. We can afford the damages," Gunnar says nonchalantly, making my gaze snap to his face.

"Just a dress?" I ask, my voice getting higher with every word. "Did you? I can't believe..."

"Selene. It's a dress. It's nothing compared to your well-being." He shrugs, glancing over at me but clearly disregarding the pure fury I'm emanating from every pore.

I try to control my breathing as silence settles around us in Gunnar's SUV.

Gunnar has always had an enviable ability to focus, which makes him an excellent sharpshooter and even better lover.

However, his focus is also his downfall on occasion, giving him tunnel vision that he can't escape, and he misses the bigger picture at hand.

A few minutes into the drive home—thankfully with my heels kicked off—Gunnar decides to break the silence.

"Selene?" he asks.

"Hmm."

"Why didn't you tell me?" Gunnar's voice is soft, but there's a hurt in it, too.

"About the tests?" I ask, unsure why such a little thing would hurt him.

"Yeah. Why didn't you tell me about it?" he says, his voice too small for his big presence. "I could have done something to help."

"Gunnar," I sigh, collecting myself. "I don't know. It just didn't feel like that big of a deal."

"But it is a big deal. One that landed you in the hospital because you weren't taking care of yourself," he says a little too harshly.

"Gunnar. I'm fine," I reply, my body tensing at his tone. "It's not like I was keeping this from you. Hell, I barely remembered myself. I just... wasn't thinking."

"I should have gone with you," he says with conviction. "I could have handled it for you."

I chuckle at his statement. "Much like you *handled* the doctor in there today?"

"She was being a total bitch," he grumbles.

"She was doing her job and talking to her patient. And you know it," I snap at him. "And I am perfectly capable of handling my health."

"Clearly not," he replies under his breath.

"Gunnar, be very careful here," I tell him, my voice hard as the stones on my left hand.

"Do you know how scary it was to get that phone call from

Ivy?" There's a shake in his voice that softens me a bit. "And I was so far away. Totally helpless to do anything."

"I was in excellent hands, though. They took very good care of me," I say, trying to soothe him.

"It's *my* job to take care of you, Luna," he replies.

"No, it's your job to support me, Gunnar," I huff, trying to control the frustration that's building in my chest. "I'm perfectly capable of taking care of myself."

"I'll call and make your follow-up appointments for next week."

"Gunnar. I can do that myself," I sigh.

"Well, you didn't last time. You had months, and you never did," he shoots.

"Yes. And you haven't seen your eye doctor in over a year," I laugh, trying to ease the tension in the car.

"My eyesight is fine. That's not what we're talking about here," he says with a frown.

"Well, what the hell is it that we're talking about? Because this seems like a foolish argument if you ask me," I sigh, trying to release the tension from my body.

"It's not. We're not arguing. There's nothing to argue about," Gunnar says adamantly.

I roll my eyes.

"I'd prefer not to see you in the hospital again." His voice is so earnest that my hard exterior softens for him, like it always does. "So, since you won't take your well-being seriously and look after your health, I will."

I understand Gunnar's desire to care for me; it's an innate part of his personality, one that I love dearly under normal circumstances.

I've always loved him for his protective nature, and the way he makes me feel safe no matter what is going on around us. He's always had this uncanny ability to ground me even in the middle of my most chaotic spiral.

There's no other person in the world I would want to have care for me like he does. It all comes from a place of love and respect. "There's going to be a lot of changes we need to make," he says as we pull into our garage. "I'll make your PCP appointment for next week, and we can find out more then, but I'll start doing research tonight so we know more."

"Gunnar."

"Selene."

"You're being really excessive. It's really not that big of a deal."

"Everything with you is a big deal. I don't know why this would be any different," he says before getting out of the car and leaving me alone, dumbstruck.

Motherfucker.

February 26—Waning Gibbous Moon in Cancer

I feel like a child.

Gunnar scheduled me an appointment with my primary care physician as soon as he was able to get on the phone with the practice and even managed to have them squeeze me in this week.

Which means I'm now stuck in the waiting room of my doctor's office, waiting to be called back for my appointment.

Only instead of being by myself for the appointment, I have a keeper with me.

Gunnar.

He insisted on coming with me today because he had "questions for your doctor," which turned out to consist of three printed pages.

I'm already on edge just from being in the office. There's an inherent anxiety as a fat person that comes with visiting doctors, since you never know what kind of treatment you'll receive until you've finished the appointment. All of that is more than enough to keep me on edge, but Gunnar's bouncing knee next to me might be my final straw.

"Will you quit?" I snap, putting my hand over his knee in an attempt to get him to stop moving.

He stills but gives me an irritated look nonetheless.

Though his annoyance doesn't even come close to my frustration with him.

This morning, he replaced my usual breakfast of eggs and bacon with yogurt and berries, even though I hate them. It's a routine he's adopted over the past few days, and it might actually be what drives me to murder.

"Ms. Estrella?" a nurse calls out through the room.

"Oh, thank Goddess," I murmur under my breath as I stand and walk toward the door the nurse holds open.

I follow her back, but freeze when she directs me to stand on a scale.

I whip around to face Gunnar. "Turn around," I demand.

He looks both startled and confused.

"I don't even like seeing my weight. So, I'm sure as hell not going to let you either," I explain. Meanwhile, the nurse is waiting with an expression that clearly displays her discomfort at Gunnar and my exchange.

"Okay," he says slowly, turning around to face the door we just walked through.

I sigh and hop on the scale.

Thankfully, the portion of the appointment with the nurse—getting vitals and going over current medications—goes quickly, even with Gunnar jotting down his own notes and hovering the entire time.

When the doctor finally arrives, I'm well and truly done with his antics.

"Hello, Ms. Solis de Estrella?" the doctor asks as they enter the room.

"Yes, Selene is fine," I tell them. "Less of a mouthful."

"Of course." They glance over at Gunnar, who stands by the window. "And who do we have with us today?"

I sigh. "This is my fiancé, Gunnar." The doctor raises an eyebrow at me in question. "Yes. It's fine that he's here."

"Alright," they say skeptically. "My name is Dr. Byrd. Your former physician moved practices. So, I will be looking after you going forward."

"That's fine," I say with a shrug.

They nod. "It looks like the last time we saw you was about six months ago?"

"Yes," I affirm.

"Any changes in your health since then? Surgeries or hospitalizations?"

"I mean, I had a tubal ligation back in December," I tell them. "It should be in my chart."

"She was in the hospital last week," Gunnar interjects, earning a stern look from the doctor. "She passed out and was taken to the emergency room. They said it was a result of her fluctuating blood sugar levels."

"Will you let me talk?" I snap, turning around to look at Gunnar directly.

He takes a step back, but I can tell he's on edge already.

"Last week, I went into the ER after passing out while trying on wedding dresses." The doctor's lips quirk as though they're suppressing a chuckle. "Yeah. Very embarrassing. Anyway, it was because my blood sugar dropped, and I needed to be checked out."

"They kept her overnight," Gunnar starts.

I glare over my shoulder, which shuts him up for a minute.

"After I got my tubes tied, they told me my A1C levels were off and I should come in to get checked out. My overnight adventure was related." The doctor nods along as I explain myself.

"They said she has diabetes," Gunnar interjects.

"Okay. Can we kick him out?" I snarl, turning in place to look at Gunnar again. "Love you, but I can't handle you interjecting every other sentence."

Gunnar raises his hands in placation, but it does nothing to dampen my frustration.

"Sir, I'm going to have to insist. If Selene isn't comfortable with you being here, then I will speak with her alone," the doctor says, saving me from pushing back against him.

"At least ask them my questions," he says, his shoulders hunched as he steps toward the door.

Taking the papers he offers me, I give him a reassuring nod, though I have no intention of going through every question on his list.

When the door shuts behind Gunnar, I turn back to my doctor, who looks concerned.

"Do I need to be concerned about his presence today?" they ask.

"What?" I ask, surprised by the question.

"Are you safe? With him, I mean," they continue.

"Oh, Goddess. Yes," I laugh uncomfortably. "Sorry. He's a mother hen and has been really worried since last week, but there's nothing to be worried about other than maybe my sanity."

Looking reassured, the doctor and I review my lab results together and begin discussing the next steps.

By the time I leave the patient room to head back to the lobby, I have a folder of reference papers and notes, along with the promise of referrals to several specialists I will need to start seeing.

When I reach the lobby, Gunnar stands immediately upon spotting me.

His expression is one of pure concern, but I can see how tense his body is, coiled and ready for anything.

I approach him, clutching the folder of papers in my hands.

Stopping in front of him, I look him straight in the eye.

"You should know I'm mad at you," I whisper before turning to head out of the building.

"What?" His voice comes from several steps behind me, but his long strides have him right behind me before I can take another step. "Mad? Why are you mad at me? What'd I do?"

His innocent tone almost makes me laugh, but my anger simmers too much right now to allow it.

"You embarrassed me," I growl. "Just now. You kept interjecting."

Gunnar speeds around me and begins walking backward through the hall leading to the parking garage.

"I was just trying to fill in the blanks. You weren't telling them everything," he says defensively.

"Yes. And in doing so, you treated me like a child in there." I stop and pinch my forehead at the temples. "It was humiliating. To be talked over like that? I'm a fucking adult, Gunnar. I don't need you doing stuff like that."

I try to push past him, but he stops me with a gentle hand on my shoulder.

"I wasn't trying to do any of that, Luna," he says softly. "I was just..."

"Just what? I'd love to hear your reasoning for this," I huff.

"Is it so wrong for me to worry about you and your health? To have questions for your doctor?" he asks exasperatedly.

"It's not wrong. It's belittling," I sigh, taking a deep breath to calm my racing heart. "I can handle this. I don't need you hovering and inserting yourself like this in my life."

We stand in the hallway like that for a beat while he tries to understand my words and meaning.

"Okay," he says. "I'll stay out of your doctor's appointments and stuff."

"And stuff?" I ask.

"I don't know. I just..." he exhales. "I'll do better."

"Good," I say, relaxing a little.

Taking him by the hand, I turn us to head out of the building.

"Take me home, Viking," I say softly, leaning into him as we walk to the garage.

"Yeah. Of course," he murmurs in his deep rumble.

Ever the gentleman, Gunnar opens the passenger door for me when we get to the car and helps me inside.

When he has me buckled in, he leans over and places a kiss on my forehead.

"Love you, Luna," he whispers as he backs away.

I smile back at him, knowing how true that statement is.

"Love you too, Viking."

12

———

GUNNAR

February 27—Moon in Cancer opposite Pluto in Capricorn

Selene has been sleeping like a baby for hours, but after sitting in bed for about an hour, I realized there was no hope for sleep tonight.

There's too much going on in my head, too many worries, thoughts, and fears.

I make my way into the kitchen to grab a water, but when I do, I spot the folder from Selene's doctor's appointment on the island.

Just seeing the folder taunts me.

Sure, I promised Selene I wouldn't involve myself in her doctors' appointments anymore, but that didn't mean I couldn't do some light reading on the realities she now faces.

Grabbing a water from the fridge, I turn to face my temptation.

My curiosity and concern quickly win out, and I pick up the folder.

Like a thief in the night, I make my way to my office with the stolen goods.

In my office chair, I lay the folder on my desk and stare at it for a minute.

This feels like an invasion somehow. Like I'm overstepping. Selene said she could handle this by herself.

I believe her, truly I do.

But my mama taught me that you do anything for the people you love, that you protect them the best way you know how.

This is how I know I can take care of her, protect her.

So, curiosity gets the best of me, and I open the folder.

It only takes me a few minutes to review all the papers Selene was given, but they've only raised more questions, not provided answers.

This is how, after several hours of research in my office, I find myself in the kitchen surrounded by trash bags.

It's still dark outside when I hear our alarm go off, but the connection between the sound and the fact that Selene is getting up for the day doesn't register.

I'm too deep into my project, lost in the manic chaos I've taken on in the middle of the night.

It's not until Selene actually appears in the kitchen, beautifully disheveled from sleep, and flicks on the kitchen light that I fully realize how far things have gone.

"Gunnar?" she asks groggily.

"Hey," I say, turning to face her sheepishly.

"What are you doing?" she asks, glancing around at the war zone that is our kitchen.

"I'm cleaning," I say hesitantly. "And I placed a grocery order?"

"Why?" Her head tilts to the side.

"Well, the cleaning kind of necessitated the grocery order," I shrug.

"We just got groceries this past weekend. Why would we need more?" she says, rounding the island to where I stand, surrounded by several black trash bags.

"Gunnar," she gasps. "What did you do?"

I laugh awkwardly. "So, I kind of read through the papers the doctor gave you. Many of them had to do with changes to your diet and what foods you should and shouldn't be eating."

"So, you decided to throw out all our food?" she shrieks, clearly having sobered from her sleep.

"Not all of it," I say in an attempt to defend myself. "Just... a lot of it."

Selene opens the bag closest to her and pulls out a box.

"These are my favorite chips," she says, her voice tinged with a slight whine.

"Yes, but HEB has an alternative that sounds similar," I explain, going over to my laptop where I still have the grocery order pulled up. "Only it's made with chickpeas instead of potatoes. So, it's not as much starch."

She's going through the whole bag, and her face drops even more with each item she pulls out.

"Gunnar. You can't just get rid of all of this," she sighs.

"It's kinda too late." I shrug. "And it's for the best."

"For the best?" she asks, warning in her tone. "For the best... for *who*, exactly?"

"For you, of course," I tell her, putting items back in the bag she just undid before grabbing all the trash bags to haul them to the garage.

"Gunnar, we talked about this! I'm perfectly capable of making decisions on my own," she says, frustration lacing her voice. "I don't need you making executive decisions about my well-being."

"It's better this way," I say with conviction.

"Ugh! I'm done with this," she growls, then stomps off.

I hear each of her footfalls as she makes her way upstairs, her steps echoing through the kitchen.

I've seen Selene mad before, but never quite like this, and I don't think I like it.

But it really is for her own good.

I have to believe that.

I need her to be healthy in order to be happy.

Selene means everything to me, and I won't let anything get in the way of her happiness, even if it's herself.

March 1—Venus square Uranus, Pisces season

The rest of the week passed by tensely.

Selene stood in the kitchen, glaring at the bags of food, while I finished putting away all the groceries after I picked them up from the store. Then, for the rest of the week, she would sigh or pout every time she walked to the kitchen for a snack, and as part of her protesting, she completely refused to contribute to cooking any meals.

By the time Friday rolls around, I'm convinced Selene will continue to ignore me all weekend while we're at the club to celebrate her birthday.

I'm packing up for the weekend in the bedroom when Selene storms in like a hurricane.

She stands in the doorway for a minute, watching me put things into bags, before she speaks.

"Look. It's my birthday party tonight," she says with a sigh. "I don't want things to be tense between us like this for the whole weekend."

Pausing my task, I turn to face her while she goes on.

"Truce? Can we just let this go for now?" she asks, a slight pout in her voice.

"I don't really know what we're calling a truce over, Selene," I answer her honestly. "All I know is you've been pouting all week."

I sit down on the edge of the bed and pat next to me for her to join.

"I can understand being resistant to change, but this isn't

something you can continue to ignore, Luna." She settles beside me, and I take her much smaller hand in mine. "I'm just trying to protect you."

Selene softens, and for a minute, I think I've really gotten through to her.

When she sighs heavily, I know that's not the case.

"You don't need to protect me, Gunnar," she says, her voice a little softer and more patient than earlier. "You're an excellent Viking. 'See, came, conquered.' doesn't work here. There's nothing to fight."

"But..." I start.

"But nothing." Selene's shoulders slump in defeat. "Look, when you bulldoze like this, you're taking away my opportunity to grow. When you try to protect me by doing things for me, you keep me from becoming a better version of myself. I need to do this on my own."

It's on the tip of my tongue to tell her that she doesn't.

She doesn't have to do this on her own at all.

She has me.

I'm right here.

But I don't do that.

Instead, I squeeze her hand and help her up from the bed.

"Okay, Luna. I get it," I lie, guilt weighing heavily on my chest. "Let's get all this stuff into the car and head to The Playground so we're on time for your party."

A brief smile breaks out on her face for the first time since she found me in the kitchen surrounded by trash bags, a sight which I've sorely missed.

It's as if the clouds of her misery have been blown away, and in their place, I can now see a galaxy of light shining from her soul.

"Okay," she says, rising from the bed. "Though, I swear if you got me some bullshit sugar-free cake, I will scream until your eardrums bleed."

13

SELENE

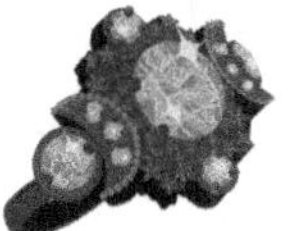

Birthdays are a big deal in my family, and by some miracle, I managed to snag the entire month of March for my own birthday celebrations.

So, when the opportunity presented itself to kick off the festivities at the club with all my friends on the first of the month, I grabbed it.

Everyone has gathered in high spirits tonight.

Drinks are flowing.

Friends are laughing and dancing.

It's been a great night overall.

Only I haven't received a single birthday orgasm yet.

And that seems like such a shame.

"Where's my fiancé?" I call out among my friends, causing heads to turn in my direction.

Finally, I realize they're not looking at me but *behind* me.

"Oh! Good. There you are!" I exclaim as I spot Gunnar behind me, sitting in our usual spot in the party room.

"Here I am," He chuckles, pulling me into his firm body as I approach him.

"I need something from you," I tell him as seriously as I can.

The warmth of his body against mine is the connection I've craved.

Everything has been so messed up recently and I need this with him, a moment of intimacy between us.

"A water maybe?" he jokes, drawing me out of my emotional swirl of thoughts.

His smile is radiant and captivating. If I weren't on such a mission tonight, I'd definitely let myself get lost in his golden grin.

"No. No water," I tell him emphatically.

"You sure about that?" he asks, already reaching for the cooler next to him filled with iced mixers and water bottles.

When he cracks open a water and hands it to me, I take it on instinct and down it in a few gulps.

"'Attagirl," he purrs. "Now what did you want, Luna?"

"An orgasm," I tell him, matter-of-factly. "Or several, if I have my way."

The initial shock of my statement quickly fades, and Gunnar's expression quickly shifts to one of amusement.

"And what kind of orgasm would you like, Luna?" he asks, a smug smirk on his lips.

"A good one. Duh." I roll my eyes and shift so I'm sitting in his lap versus straddling him. "Oof. So much comfier. You've got big hips, man."

Gunnar lets out a full laugh at my antics.

"Not the only thing that's big, darlin'," he jokes back at me.

"Mhmm. You definitely are a big boy," I say with a wink. "I think you should put those big-boy hands of yours to work and get this birthday girl off tonight."

I nuzzle up to him, running one hand along his chest and the other through his hair.

"Oh? Is that right?" he says slyly.

"Yes," my voice is matter-of-fact. "I think I deserve birthday orgasms. Immediately."

"Ah. I see," Gunnar smirks before lifting me into his arms and standing up.

"Well then, it sounds like I should get on that," he says suavely.

With a bounce, Gunnar shifts me so I'm hanging over his shoulder, my dress riding up to expose my bare pussy to everyone in the club.

"Gunnar!" I giggle as I cry out, loving how he manhandles me while he strides through the quickly parting crowd.

He carries me up the stairs to the second-floor playrooms and, when he reaches the voyeur bed, plops me down on the mattress with a bounce.

I can barely breathe from laughing at his antics, and his grin stretches wide when I look up at his gorgeous face.

"How would you like to enjoy yourself tonight?" he asks, his low voice permeating through the music surrounding us. "How would my Goddess like to be worshipped?"

I shift back so I'm further toward the center of the bed, but Gunnar follows me. His body cages me in, and he crawls on the bed with me, hovering close enough to touch but still too far to do anything for the lust burning in my veins.

"I want you to fill me, stuff me full of your cock," I tell him, my pussy already throbbing at the thought of being filled so completely by him. "But I don't want you to come. I want this to be about me."

"There's no way I can have your cunt strangling my cock without coming inside you, Luna," he purrs into my ear. "But I can fill you with the big hands you admired earlier. How does that sound?"

Electricity shoots through my body at the idea of him filling me with his fist.

"Oh, yes. You want that, don't you?" he chuckles as he searches my gaze. "You want me to stuff you full, one finger at a time, until I'm wrist deep in your pussy, don't you?"

My breath quickens with each word he utters, my pussy clenching at the picture of pleasure he paints.

"Yes," I pant. "Yes, I want that."

"Spread your legs wide for me, then, Luna. Show me the heaven between your legs."

His words run over me like warm honey, sweet and decadent.

When he steps back and leaves me alone on the bed, I pout at his absence, but soon he's back with a bottle of lube in his hand and a wicked grin on his face.

"You ready for me, Goddess?" he says, kneeling back down on the mattress between my legs. "Are you ready to have your pussy destroyed by a mere mortal like me?"

"Yes," I breathe out on a sigh.

The sharp snick of the bottle of lube opening up has my attention snapping to Gunnar's hand, which now glistens with the thick liquid.

He trails his clean hand up my inner thigh and spreads the lips of my pussy to reveal my center. Then, with his other hand, he reaches to coat my pussy in lube.

"Be a good girl and relax for me."

I try, but it seems my efforts aren't enough, and he uses my moment of hesitation to land a sharp smack on my pussy lips.

"Fuck!" I cry out before shooting him a glare worthy of a brat. "That was uncalled for."

Gunnar raises an eyebrow at me, challenging me to fight back, but I decide it's not worth it and lean back on my elbows to watch him.

When his slick fingers first make contact with my aching cunt, I shiver at the pleasure such a simple touch brings me.

One finger slips into my pussy easily, and he uses it to test my body, see how relaxed and ready I am. Whatever he feels must satisfy him because before I can even ask for him to give me another, he's already pulled out the first so he can ease back into my pussy with two fingers.

The slight stretch is incredible; he takes his time to press against my walls and open me up to take more.

The third finger that slides in is pure bliss, but the fourth has me squirming and panting for breath.

With all four fingers inside me, he spreads them open, encouraging my walls to expand.

He strokes against them in a circular pattern, coaxing me with each caress to relax further into the sensation.

My mind can't keep up with the amount of pleasure ricocheting through my body.

Slowly, he starts pumping in and out of me, adding lube and pressing a little deeper each time he thrusts into my cunt.

"That's it," he coos. "Take all of me like a good little whore. So stretched out and ready for my fist."

I whimper at the smooth words he utters as he continues to press further and deeper into my pussy.

On his next push in, my body tenses and forces him out.

"Oh, you can do better than that," he teases, adding more lube. "Relax and take all of me."

Lightning shoots through me when his thumb next comes in contact with my clit, and as I ride the wave of electricity running through my body, I slowly relax.

Slow circles on my clit match the pace at which he fills me with his fist. Everything moves slowly at first, at an agonizing pace, with me tossing and turning on the bed.

I want to beg for more, but I'm too breathless even to speak.

The room swirls around me, a mix of color and sound, as I'm lost to the sensations wracking my body.

Pressure builds in my core as he works me over. Every stroke against my upper wall, combined with the zaps of electricity thrumming through my clit, has me right on the edge.

It feels so close and yet so far.

Gunnar slows his pace, focusing on filling me with his whole hand.

"'Attagirl," he says, his voice as soft as velvet. "Relax for me. Take everything."

I'm gasping for air, sinking beneath the ocean of pleasure and pain that has overtaken every nerve in my body.

We've done this before, but there's still a pinch of pain as his hand sinks deep into me and my walls stretch around him.

I know the moment when he's fully seated inside me by the look of pure pride and satisfaction that spreads across his gorgeous golden features.

Gunnar looks like someone who's truly seen a Goddess.

The sight of him, so utterly wrapped up in the moment and focused on my pleasure, has me speeding toward my release.

He shifts his position on the bed and continues to work me over until I'm screaming, finally begging to come.

"Come for me, little Goddess. Come all over me. Give me your pleasure," he says, and his words send me over the edge.

The pressure that had been building in my abdomen releases, and there's a gushing sensation between my legs as Gunnar presses up into my most sensitive wall and down on my clit at the same time.

The pressure causes a combination of sharp pains and waves of euphoria to overwhelm every nerve in my already exhausted body.

Without hesitation, Gunnar dives in headfirst, his tongue replacing his thumb on my clit. He ravages me like a man desperate for water, which my pussy is more than happy to supply.

He drinks me down, smiling the whole time, as I come down from the peak of my orgasm.

Small shockwaves roll through my body with every shift of him inside me. The small crashes of sensation force a tremor through me, which only continues the cycle of perpetual pleasure.

When I begin to still, utterly exhausted from my fall from heaven, Gunnar works his hand free from my pussy with slow strokes in and out.

My greedy cunt is reluctant to let him go, though, and clenches tightly around his hand with each retreat he tries.

"Greedy Goddess," he chuckles, looking at me with stars in his eyes as I lie limp on the bed.

Finally, his hand is free of my pussy, and I'm left feeling sated, yet empty all at the same time.

Limp as a rag doll, Gunnar pulls me up into his chest and holds me tightly. I let my head fall to his shoulder, sucking in lungs full of his cologne and natural musk as I try to breathe normally.

"Such a good girl," he says soothingly into my ear. "Let's get you comfy, okay?"

A small whimper escapes my lips, despite my every intention to stuff down the sound.

"It's okay, Luna. I've got you," he murmurs.

Gunnar settles me on a nearby couch, and someone brings me a blanket while he gets me my water and snacks.

Upon his return, Gunnar pulls me into his lap and wraps us both in the blanket, cocooning us in its plushness.

Gunnar makes sure I sip my water and nibble on my fruit gummies while I float among the clouds of my bliss.

"That was such a beautiful thing to witness," a patron says as they pass us on the couches. "Thank you."

Internally, I can't help but chuckle. And from the expression on Gunnar's face, he agrees.

When the couple is far enough from us, Gunnar leans in to whisper in my ear.

"Seems odd to thank me for something that's such an honor."
His smile is genuine, and a storm stirs in my stomach.

This man is truly a blessing.

He calls me his Goddess, saying it's an honor to serve me.

But he might just be my God.

14

GUNNAR

March 10—Moon in Capricorn conjunct Pluto, Square North Node

The training facility is finally blissfully quiet now that most everyone else is done for the day.

I've already exhausted my trainees, but the usual satisfaction that comes with the end of those sessions isn't there.

Instead, a hum under my skin won't escape me, no matter how many rounds I go on the mat or reps I lift at the machines.

So, I run.

The pace I've set for myself on the treadmill is brutal, but it's the only thing keeping me from putting my hand through the wall.

Selene and I had another fight, or "disagreement," according to her, this morning. Evidently, I loaded the dishwasher incorrectly, so the load I ran last night didn't actually get cleaned, though it all looked fine to me.

Usually, she does it every night after we've finished dinner, but yesterday she was complaining about work. I told her to go to bed and that I would handle it before joining her.

The whole interaction has my head spinning.

I don't know when I became the villain in this situation.

I didn't do anything worth the kind of frustration she was openly experiencing.

By the time I was done with the trainees this morning, I needed to get out of my head.

Hence, the running.

Only, it's not really working.

That's why I barely notice Emir when he enters the room and suddenly appears in front of where I'm running on the treadmill.

"You good?" Emir asks, his hand reaching to slow the pace of my run to barely a jog. "You've been at this for at least..." He glances at the screen that shows my lap time. "For an hour. Are you planning to run a marathon today?"

I gradually slow the treadmill further until I'm walking at a normal pace.

"Wasn't planning on it," I grumble, grabbing the towel from the handlebar and wiping the sweat off my face and neck. "Just kinda headed that direction."

He waits patiently as I cool down for a minute or two at a walk.

I know he's waiting for me to tell him what's going on, but I'm not ready.

When the treadmill comes to a stop, I grab a water bottle to take a few gulps before grabbing the cleaning supplies from nearby to wipe down the machine.

"Wanna tell me what's going on?" Emir finally asks while I'm facing away from him.

My shoulders slump, and I turn back to him. My posture is evidence of the defeat I feel.

"Selene and I had another fight this morning," I admit, spraying and wiping down the machine to avoid looking at him directly.

"That's been happening a lot more recently." He doesn't ask; he simply states what he knows to be true.

"Yeah."

"What was it this time?" he asks gently.

"Does it matter?" I reply a little too harshly before sighing. "Dishwasher."

Emir shakes his head and gives me a slight chuckle.

"It's not funny, man," I say defensively. "It became a whole thing this morning."

Emir stares at me with a questioning expression. "Was the fight really about the dishwasher?"

"What?"

"Was it about the dishwasher or something else?" he asks patiently.

I can't help but stare at him blankly. "Of course it was about the dishwasher, right?"

The look he's giving me tells me I'm way off base here.

"Look, Derek and I have been married for 4 years now," he says with a raised eyebrow. "It's never about the dishwasher. Or the smelly workout clothes he tosses on the floor. Or that he forgot to fill up the car with gas."

"I don't understand," I say blankly.

"Walk with me. I'll save you the therapy bill, but I need your help with something in my office," he replies, heading toward the doors that lead to the offices.

We walk through the hall and to the elevator in silence, but once inside, Emir breaks the quiet.

"So, the dishwasher. You were trying to be helpful, right?" he asks, but it's more of a statement than a question.

"Well, yeah." I shrug as we step off the elevator onto the executive floor.

"You've been helping a lot?" This time, his question is genuine.

"Of course. She's going through a lot with wedding planning and all of her recent health stuff. I just want to support her," I reply.

I give my assistant a nod as we pass their desk on our way to Emir's office.

Once inside, Emir continues his inquisition.

"And I'm guessing that's different from how things were between you previously?" He looks at me knowingly.

"Yes," I say simply.

"So, your hyper-independent girlfriend..."

"Fiancée," I correct.

"Right, fiancée How could I forget?" He chuckles as he walks around to his desk chair and begins logging into his computer. "So, your fiancée, a woman I've always known to command over request, is getting frustrated with you because you're trying to support her."

"Yeah," I say, my voice lilting up in question.

"Did she tell you she needed this from you?" he asks, his eyes focused on his screen. "Did she say, 'Gunnar, can you load the dishwasher?' or did she simply not do it last night?"

"She said work was stressful and she wasn't feeling great, and I told her to go to bed early. But she said she would do it in the morning before work. But I went ahead and just did it," I tell Emir, who grins in response. "What? What do you know that I don't?"

"You want to support her," Emir states, pulling up one of the reports I get copies of regularly.

"Yes," I confirm.

"Have you ever asked?" This time, he looks at me head-on. "Have you asked her how she needs or wants you to support her?"

Realization dawns with his words.

"Oh," I say softly.

"Yeah." He chuckles and turns back to his computer. "This isn't a mission you're in charge of. She's the one who needs to run point here."

"Shit," I mumble, slumping into one of the leather chairs in front of his desk. "I fucked up."

"Yeah. You fucked up," he says smugly. "The good news is, she loves you for some reason. So, I'm pretty sure you have a shot at fixing things."

"How?" I ask earnestly.

"That's for you to figure out, man." He shrugs, giving me a sympathetic look. "Derek has a sweet tooth as strong as Buddy the Elf. So, baked goods and a blowjob typically fix things for me when it's small. But Selene probably needs something different."

"Yeah. Right," I say, already running through options in my mind. "Okay. I'll figure it out."

"You've got this." Emir gives me a nod and a small smile before turning back to his computer. "Now, tell me who this fucking client is and why the numbers aren't adding up."

"What?"

"Yeah. I noticed it this morning when I reviewed the project reports my team pulled," he says, turning his screen to give me a better view.

"Fuck," I say, running my hand through my hair as I scan the report.

The next few hours are spent reviewing records, and the pieces of the puzzle begin to fit together, giving us a clearer picture of the problem with some errors in the reporting system.

But the entire time, I'm running through options in the back of my mind to make things up to Selene.

By the time we've pieced together enough details to assess the severity of the situation and find the solution. In the back of my mind, I've got a pretty solid plan for how I intend to apologize to Selene.

There's no doubt in my mind that this reporting mess will get cleared up, but I can't shake the knot in my chest over whether Selene will forgive me.

It's not like I was intentionally being an overbearing asshole.

I just was.

Here's hoping Selene can forgive me.

She has to, right?

WHEN I LEAVE THE OFFICE, it's late, but on my way home, I stop at the store to pick up the necessary supplies for my apology, including a cliché bouquet and a card, which I already know she'll laugh at.

When I arrive home, Selene's car is already in the garage. So, I poke my head into the house to see if I can spot her before carrying in my wares.

Thankfully, she's not in the kitchen or living room, which is perfect for me.

I work with purpose to assemble the flowers in a vase and quickly sign the card before turning my focus to the central part of my apology gift.

Swearing wasn't allowed in my mama's house while I was growing up. But, being a typical boy, my language became more foul as I got older, especially during my teenage years.

Thus, the swear jar was established in our household. Anytime I let a swear slip around Mama, she would make me put a dollar in the jar from the money I earned doing chores.

I figure if Mama could cure me of curse words as a kid with a swear jar, then maybe another jar can help manage my jackass behavior.

Grabbing the glass container I bought at the store, I head into my office to find a sticky label and a marker.

After scribbling the words "Jackass Jar" in the best handwriting I can manage, which admittedly isn't great, I go back into the kitchen and find Selene standing in front of the vase of flowers with the signed card in her hand.

"Oh," I breathe out. "I was gonna bring all this to you."

"Apology flowers and a card? Really, Gunnar?" she says, her brow furrowed, but the humor in her voice keeps my chest from seizing up.

"Yeah," I say simply.

She rolls her eyes. "Cliché as it is, I accept."

"There's more," I say quickly, holding the jar out in front of me.

Selene's head tips to the side in confusion, and when I look down, I realize she can't see the label I've applied.

"It's a Jackass Jar," I say quickly.

I turn the jar around so that the label faces her.

Her face blooms with a pleased grin as she takes in my chicken scratch of a label.

"A Jackass Jar. Cute," she chuckles. "So, what's the idea with the jar then?"

"It's like a swear jar, but for when I'm being an ass," I explain earnestly, handing the jar over. "I can't promise to be perfect. I'm gonna get it wrong and mess up, but I can promise to try."

"So, the premise is that when you do fuck up, you're going to put cash in the Jackass Jar?" she asks with a smirk. "What happens to the money once it's in a jar?"

"Whatever you want." I shrug. "Spend it on anything that makes you happy."

"Okay," she says, thinking over my proposition before seeming to come to a determination. "Alright. I decide the amount for jackass behavior, though. I'm sure some things are worth more than others."

I eye her skeptically. "That sounds... reasonable."

"Perfect." She smiles before turning toward Beef Cake's room, where I presume she was previously. "Go ahead and put ten dollars in the jar for the dishwasher debacle."

"What?" I say, astonished.

"You heard me!" she calls over her shoulder as she retreats.

"I did *your* chore, though," I call after her.

She spins around with a grin on her face. "And?"

"I... I shouldn't..." I sputter.

"Flowers die, Gunnar. Cards get thrown away." She shrugs. "Cash is King. Time to pay up, pretty boy. Mama wants to get her first tattoo."

I stand there, stunned, as she turns and walks away, giggling to herself.

"But you hate needles," I mumble as I pull out my wallet and put a twenty into the jar.

Ten for the dishwasher.

Ten for whatever I manage to screw up next.

15

SELENE

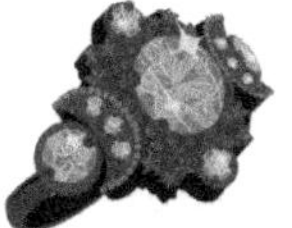

March 14—Scorpio Moon

I returned to my office satisfied with the good deed Oliver and I orchestrated for Elsie, namely, kicking Marshall out of the office for good.

When I'm settled into my chair, I pull up my email and start clearing out what I can to declutter my mind before diving into the final items on my to-do list for the day.

Time flies as I work, and in the back of my mind, I register the sun setting outside.

When the light flicks on, I squint under the harsh light.

"Why are you working in the dark?" The deep rumble sends shivers down my spine.

Blinking away the spots in my vision, I focus on the source of the voice—and there he is, the man who captured my heart and soul.

Gunnar stands in my office doorway in workout wear—no stains though—holding a bag of food.

I glance at the corner of my computer screen, looking for the time.

"Shit. Is it that late already?" I ask, frantically looking back at Gunnar, where he stands.

"Yeah. I thought you'd forgotten about me entirely." He smirks and lifts the bag. "When I checked your location, you were still here. I thought you might be hungry."

"You tracked me?" I ask, my voice pitching with frustration.

Then, my tummy growls, filling the room.

"I guess I was right." He chuckles, ignoring my question, then his expression shifts—more serious, almost reverent. "You're glowing. Just like the Goddess you are."

"Stop," I groan. "Sometimes it's too much."

I chuckle, clearing off some of my desk to avoid Gunnar's intense stare.

Gunnar steps fully into my office and closes the door behind him with a click before he narrows his eyes at me.

"Luna," he says, taking a few steps toward me where I sit at my desk until he's facing me on the other side.

Gunnar walks around the desk until he's face-to-face with me, then slowly drops to his knees.

"Do you know why I call you My Goddess?" he asks, simply but passionately.

"Selene, the moon Goddess. I know my name is one big joke. Selene Aracely Solis de Estrella. Moon Goddess, heaven, sun, and stars. My parents really knew what they were doing when they got married and had me."

"No, Selene. You're my Goddess, my luna, because you're the only thing in the universe that moves me," he breathes out. "Your love embraces me like the heavens, ever expanding like the universe. The ocean's tides would not exist without the moon, and I would not exist without you. You are divine, my love. Divine, and somehow you've chosen me."

It feels as if all the air has been sucked from my lungs. There's nothing left to gasp for because oxygen has ceased to exist.

"I feel like you should kiss me right now," I tell the burly Viking.

"With pleasure."

Gunnar pulls me up from my chair and swaps places with me, so now I'm straddling him, and he pulls me in for a deep kiss.

Already his cock is hardening beneath me, and I can't help but rock into his length.

Our kiss dissolves the reality around us. Nothing exists outside this moment between him and me. Our whole world is centered on each other.

"Fuck. I want you, but I really should get back to work," I say, pulling away from Gunnar.

"Mmh," he hums as his lips trail down my neck with gentle, sweet kisses.

"Gunnar." I press slightly on his shoulders so he has to face me. "Work. I have to work."

"No, you don't." His expression is so earnest that it makes my heart ache. "Quit."

"I can't quit," I exhale.

"Yes, you can. You can quit and go do whatever you want."

He resumes kissing up and down my neck, and the firm press of his lips just beneath my ear at the edge of my jaw nearly makes me cave.

"No, Gunnar," I say, pulling away completely and rising to my feet. "I can't quit and become some kind of tradwife. That's not who I am."

"I know that, Luna," he says as he stands up and looms over me again. "Quit, and you can be whoever you want. Do whatever you want. But do it because it makes you happy. That's all I want— your happiness."

"And you? What about your happiness? Does your job make you happy?"

"No, my Goddess. You do." He smirks and slips his hand up my skirt so his thumb can trace the inside of my thigh. "And if I recall correctly, I owe you something for the jar, don't I? Maybe I can make it up to you now with a reward. And wouldn't that make you happy?"

My breath catches as his hand travels higher and his thumb grazes over my lace underwear right at my slit. His movements are slow as he runs his thumb up and down, making me wet where he strokes.

"I know you want this. Tell me you want this as much as I do," he whispers in my ear.

His hot breath fans over my pulse, which begins to race with each breath he lets out.

"Gunnar," I moan.

"No."

"Sir."

"Better."

"Tell me, little luna. Do you want me to help you then? I can feel how wet you are for me. Should I ease your need, or leave you wanting for later?"

I contemplate the offer, knowing that he will respect my decision above all else, that he treasures me above all else.

"Please, Sir. Can I have some more?"

A rumbling laugh, one he doesn't let out often enough, bursts from his chest.

"Leave it to you to reference Oliver when I'm about to have you ride my hand until you come," he chuckles.

"What can I say? I have impeccable comedic timing." I laugh, which quickly turns into a moan when his fingers push aside my underwear and slip between my folds. "Fuck."

The way he explores my body every time we're together always makes me feel special. With each touch, he reminds me that I'm his.

He's always been this way, always treated me like I'm his most precious thing.

"Tell me something, little luna," he says, pressing up on my clit and sending electricity through my body. "Do you like it when I'm soft? Or do you like it more when I provide you a little pain alongside your pleasure?"

The tips of his fingers move to each side of my clit, and he pinches with just enough pressure to make me jump. His touch turns soothing when I settle back on his hand. I drop my head onto his shoulder when he continues to run his fingers along my most sensitive spots.

"Sir."

"Do you need something, Luna?"

"Please, Sir."

"Tell me how you need me. Tell me exactly how you want me to touch you."

"I want you to fuck me," I groan.

"Not good enough," he says, stopping his movement as he does.

"Please," I plead.

"Tell me, Luna. Be explicit."

"Use your fingers to fuck me. I want you to fill me with your fingers and fuck me with them while I rock my clit on your palm."

"How many fingers?"

"Two, Sir."

"And?"

"And?" I question.

"What else? What should I do with my free hand?"

His free hand slides along the curves of my side, then up to knead my breast. "Should I play with your breast? Tease your nipples?" He continues until the span of his large palm surrounds my neck, pressing gently on my pulse point. "Should I grip your neck until you're lightheaded?" When he lets go, I gasp for breath, but the freedom to breathe doesn't last long before he's shoving his fingers in my mouth. "Or should I make you choke on my fingers as a reminder of how well you choke on my cock?"

I close my mouth around his fingers and suck hard, which makes him grin.

"Mhm. My Goddess likes being gagged, doesn't she?" he says, forcing his fingers a little further down my throat.

I take him greedily down my throat as he slips two fingers into my cunt, and I groan around him.

Baring down on his palm, I rock my mound against the palm of his hand as he crooks his fingers inside of me. The movement has my clit grazing in a perfect rhythm on his hand, and the thrill of the moment begins to climb.

"That's it. Work yourself on my hand and come all over me."

He pulls his hand from my mouth to let me breathe a bit, but my hand goes to wrap around his wrist, and I suck his fingers back into my mouth. I let my tongue run over his fingertips like I would do to the underside of his cock. I tease him with my mouth as he teases me with his fingers.

Pleasure builds in my body slowly as we move together. Every movement brings me closer to my climax, and I'm moaning loud enough to be heard by anyone who bothers to walk by my office door.

I feel like I'm floating, like nothing is real outside this moment of bliss.

My movements grow more frantic, and when I start gasping for breath, Gunnar removes his hand from my mouth, much to my reluctance, but quickly moves around my neck where he grips my pulse points while I struggle for breath.

My eyes close as I struggle for my release. My body tightens as my desperate need for oxygen forces my body to tense.

I need something. Release, climax, a fucking orgasm. I *need.*

When the edge arrives, Gunnar keeps me there. I'm stranded, just one step from falling to my la pequeña muerte.

"Please," I beg, though my lack of breath makes it come out halfhearted and raspy.

"You want to come?" he says, tightening his grip around my neck. "Then come for me. Take what's yours, Luna."

With his express command, gravity ceases to exist. I'm not falling, but floating in a starry, empty abyss. Everything goes black for a moment as I sink into the overwhelming feeling.

Blackness is a blanket that deepens the sensations floating through my body.

I feel disconnected from my body and one with the universe. I'm both myself and not. Everything that was once real ceases to exist, and all that remains is the past version of my old self.

When I come back to myself, Gunnar is holding me tight to his chest, rocking me back and forth, and rubbing his hand up and down my spine.

My body feels too heavy as I reconnect with it, and the world sounds too loud. As sensations return, an overwhelming feeling takes over, and panic begins to claw at my chest.

"Shhh. Luna, breathe with me." I take a deep breath that mirrors that of the man holding me. "You've got this. You're safe. I've got you."

I bury my face in Gunnar's shoulder as my breathing returns to a regular pattern. When I'm finally secure in my body, I pick myself up and lean back to face him.

He wears a smile like one of his gold medals, a smile that's just for me.

"You did so well," he soothes, kissing me on the cheek.

Without effort, he lifts all 280 lbs. of my curvy body to set me back in my office chair.

I can't help the giggle that escapes at the sight of a massive wet spot on his pants.

He looks down and smirks. "More worthwhile than any medal on my shelf."

"Oh, really?"

"Absolutely." He leans down to kiss me on the cheek. "You're the most worthy prize I've ever received."

"Hmmm," I sigh contentedly.

"And right now, I'm taking my prize home."

"I..."

"No arguments. You're done for the day."

"Yes, Sir."

16

GUNNAR

March 18—Moon in Pisces, Mars in Aquarius

Over the past few months, Selene and I have settled into a comfortable morning routine. I get up around 5 a.m. to start breakfast, leaving Selene to her morning rituals. After we eat, we run together through the neighborhood—though on Selene's low-energy days, it's just a walk. By seven, we're ready to head into the office. Even on weekends, our routine stays largely the same, though the timeline is more flexible.

Only on Monday morning, when I come into the bedroom at 6 a.m. expecting to see Selene in front of her mini altar in the corner of our room with her hair in curlers as usual, she's still in bed.

Setting down her mug of tea on the bedside table, I sit beside Selene.

"Luna, are you feeling alright?" I ask her, concern lacing my voice.

All I get in response is a groan, and Selene shifts to turn away from me under the covers of our bed.

"It's Monday," I say softly, my hand resting on her shoulder. "And you're not up. Are you feeling alright?"

I can see the struggle in her body as she turns back toward me.

"Just tired," she groans, pushing herself up in bed with a gargantuan effort.

"You sure?"

"Yeah," she reassures me, shooing me off the edge of the bed so she can get out.

Silence fills the room as Selene walks slowly to the bathroom to start her morning.

I follow her and take my time, just watching as she goes through her routine.

Every movement is languid, and the small noises she makes are not her usual happy chirps as she readies herself for her day. No music or podcast is playing from her phone, and there is no whirlwind of chaos following her in and out of the closet as she picks out an outfit.

She looks exhausted, beyond exhausted.

"I think going all out this weekend at the rodeo was a bad idea." I sigh. "We shouldn't have done three nights in a row plus daytime activities."

She shrugs without a word, and that's what does it.

"You're not going into work today," I say flatly.

Selene spins around to face me, her expression thunderous.

"What? No. I have to go in," she says coldly. "I have work to do."

"You're clearly not feeling well, Luna," I say, taking a few steps toward her, only to have her back away with each step.

I want to touch her, hold her in my arms, and promise her that everything will be okay.

She needs to know I'm here for her in every way.

"Just call in sick and take the day for yourself," I plead.

"No," she states before turning back to the closet to choose yet another outfit option.

Only this time, when she returns, it's with one of her comfort work outfits in hand.

"Selene," I sigh. "If you won't call out, then I'll call out for you."

Her eyes snap to me, with furious flames flickering in her gaze. Still, the tired haze over her eyes dulls its impact.

"And if you do, I'll just go into the office anyway when you leave for work," she says, tipping her hand.

"Then I'll take the day off too." I shrug.

"What? You never do that."

Her eyes are wide and her jaw slack, indicating she really doesn't expect me to do it.

Which only encourages the idea, and I pull out my phone to shoot a message to Emir.

GUNNAR

I'm not coming in today.

His response is immediate.

EMIR

?

GUNNAR

Selene isn't feeling well.

EMIR

Got it. Hope she feels better.

"There, done," I say, looking up from my phone. "Day off secured."

Selene's jaw drops further.

"Now your turn."

"I can't," she starts, her voice small.

"You can. It's not a crime to take care of yourself. You're allowed to take time to rest," I say softly, hoping she'll see how serious I am about this. "You've been dealing with a lot of stress lately, and you deserve a day off. So take it."

I watch as she struggles internally, debating all the pros and cons of the situation.

Her entire body slumps in relief, and I realize I've won this small battle.

"Fine," she says, entirely defeated with a hint of relief in her voice.

Selene immediately drops the clothes in her hands onto the vanity stool and marches back into the bedroom, probably to change into her hermit wardrobe of sweats and a tank top.

I'm sure she eventually shoots off a text to Elsie, too, but the next time I see her, Selene is curled up on the living room couch with Beef Cake and her gaming computer in her lap.

I can't help but smile to myself as I go about my day, finishing the 'honey-do' list Selene asked me to complete the other day.

After finishing a few smaller projects, I go back into the living room to find Selene completely passed out, cuddled up in a blanket.

In the kitchen, I begin making her a comfort meal of rice and marinated sirloin steak, which seems to rouse my luna from her slumber.

"What's for lunch?" Selene says groggily as she comes into the kitchen.

"Beef bulgogi, japchae, some steamed veggies, and rice are in the rice maker," I tell her, hoping my answer will coax a sleepy smile from Selene.

Joy spreads across her face at my answer, and a grateful warmth sinks into my bones.

"Feeling better?" I ask her as she settles onto one of the barstools at the island.

"Yeah, a bit. Thanks," she replies softly.

We settle into a comfortable silence as I finish cooking and plating our lunch.

Selene helps me take the dishes into our dining room, and we sit to eat.

"Don't forget to check your sugar levels," I remind her as we're setting the dishes down on the table.

"Stop," Selene snaps her head up to look at me directly, her gaze sharp and unrelenting. "I already feel like crap physically; I don't need you making me feel awful mentally, too."

"Sorry," I say softly. "I'm sorry. I was just trying..."

"I know," she says with a sigh, her body relaxing as the tension from just a moment ago fades away. "You were just trying to help."

"Yeah."

"I don't need your help, Gunnar. The constant reminders and check-ins? They're more frustrating than anything. They make me feel as though I'm incapable, weak," she says softly, getting up from the table and walking back into the kitchen to the cabinet where her supplies are kept.

I watch her as she follows what has now become a standard routine for her. She takes out the necessary equipment and supplies, pricks her finger to take her reading, and then records everything in her notebook to track her levels.

When she finishes, she puts everything away, but then she stands in front of the cabinet with her hands on the counter.

"Come eat, Luna," I tell her softly, trying to coax rather than demand.

"Yeah," she nods, pushing herself back from the counter. "Yeah. I can do that."

The rest of the meal, and even into the afternoon, passes in silence.

Selene's usual running dialogue with herself is nowhere to be found.

It's like watching the ghost of the woman I love float through the house, and every attempt I make to reach her feels like grasping at air.

She says my support makes her feel weak.
But I don't think it makes her weak at all.
She's the strongest person I know.
If only she saw herself that way, too.

17

SELENE

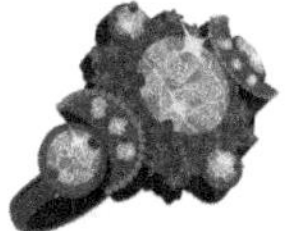

April 5—New Moon Solar Eclipse in Aries

I t doesn't take long before the Jackass Jar has accumulated a few hundred dollars—Gunnar's habit of obnoxiously monitoring my sugar levels being the primary contributor.

The funniest part of having the jar is watching his face whenever he catches himself on the brink of turning into a jackhole. But it has helped a bit overall.

Once the jar was established, I immediately started researching tattoo shops and artists in the area.

After my most recent doctor's appointment, it was decided that a Continuous Glucose Monitor (CGM) would be a good choice for monitoring my blood sugar levels.

The truth is, they're not exactly the most glamorous accessory. Thus began the rabbit hole of figuring out how to feel cute while wearing it.

First came the colorful and patterned bandages to secure the CGM in place. I found some fun ones that helped with the transition to wearing the device, but I still tended to reach for tops and dresses with flowy sleeves, which made the device less noticeable.

Wearing it just didn't feel like me.

The worst awkwardness occurred at the club. Because I love wearing lingerie, it was more noticeable, which invited a lot of stares and questions from people at the club.

So, I searched for a solution in the online forums, groups, chats, and channels I joined at the beginning of this transition in my life.

Hearing about other people's experiences was validating, but most people seemed to settle for 'you get used to it.'

I don't want to get used to it. I don't want this to be something I'm embarrassed about.

If this bitch is going to be a part of my life, then I want to own it.

Growing up in a plus-sized body, I learned early on to hide myself and my body. Making myself small and less noticeable was a measure I took to protect myself from the cruelty of others.

It took a long time to unlearn that shit.

I don't plan on going back to it.

Hence the tattoo idea.

It only took one mention of someone getting a dia-buddy, a tattoo that served as emotional support for getting shots, and I knew that was the path I wanted to take.

If I'm accessorizing in a new way with my CGM for the rest of my life, then I'm sure as hell going to play it up with some ink.

I'm not hiding it anymore.

I'm flaunting it.

Finding an artist whose work I liked was no problem, but I needed more than just an artist whose style I appreciated.

After hearing a few too many stories from people with diabetes about their tattoos literally falling off, I wanted someone who knew their shit. I needed to find someone who understood my body and its unique circumstances.

Enter @ChronicallyInked.

I found Chronically Inked through a friend of a friend, online, of course.

It was a small shop in West Texas, known by those in the industry as one of the best tattoo parlors in the nation.

Looking at their social media and website, I could see why they were so revered and had won so many awards among their artists.

But if you were chronically ill or disabled, you wanted one person.

The owner, Dottie.

After one email and an hour-long video call consultation, which turned into a two-hour gab session, I had an appointment with her for my tattoo.

I took the day off from work to come here, and when I walked into the shop, I knew I had picked the right place.

The space feels bright and airy, with examples from all the artists proudly displayed on the walls, along with other decor that creates a witchy vibe. Plants add greenery to the front waiting area, and there's a bookshelf against the wall opposite the front desk filled with an assortment of books. Soft music plays in the background, enough to add atmosphere to the space without being disruptive or annoying.

The person who greets me at the desk has a smile as bright as their pink hair and colorful tattoos.

"Hey! Welcome to Chronically Inked!" they chirp. "I'm Zeph. I use she/they pronouns. Are you here for an appointment?"

I'm awestruck momentarily and stand there in shock before finally finding my words.

"Yeah. Sorry. I'm Selene. She/her," I start, shaking myself out of my stupor. "I have a 1 p.m. appointment with Dottie."

"Oh, my Gods! Yes!" Zeph says with a confident grin. "Dottie's been working on your design this week, and it's *incredible*. You're going to love it."

"Yeah, the concept sketches they did were amazing. I can't wait." I smile back at them. "I'm a little nervous, though."

Zeph glances up and down my body, clad in a tight-fitting workout top and comfortable shorts that show most of my blank skin.

"First tattoo?" I nod. "Don't worry. Dottie is the best. They'll take good care of you."

The confidence in their tone is reassuring, and with their demeanor and the calming atmosphere of the studio, I can't help but believe them.

"Okay. Boring stuff first," they say, unplugging a tablet from the charger and tapping on it before handing it over. "If you could fill this out and sign it, that would be great. If you have any questions, let me know. I'll go let Dottie know you're here!"

I take the tablet from them and head for one of the comfortable-looking velvet couches to follow instructions and finish up the necessary forms.

Zeph returns quietly and checks in about halfway through me finishing the forms. But just as I sign the final one, a smooth, dulcet voice echoes through the space.

"Selene?" I turn to see Dottie, who's much taller than I expected from our call, approaching me. "Do you hug? I'm a big hugger."

Her arms are already wide, and the simple gesture causes my muscles to relax as I stand to embrace them.

"Yes! Hugs are great," I say as they wrap themselves around me.

This may genuinely be the best hug I've ever experienced. The way they embrace me, with pressure but not exerting sheer strength, somehow eases the last of my nerves.

"You give amazing hugs," I say in awe as I pull back from them.

"I've been told that a few times." Dottie winks. "A few repeat clients joke they'd pay big bucks just for the hugs."

"Solid business plan," I joke with them.

"Oh, for sure." They laugh before becoming a bit more serious. "Ready?"

"As I'll ever be," I say.

Dottie turns around and heads back in the direction from which they came. They guide me through a hallway that branches off into various rooms, each filled with unique styles of art.

When we reach the end of the corridor, Dottie guides me into the biggest of the rooms I saw.

"Okay. Door open or closed?" they ask.

"Closed, please," I request, and they nod in acknowledgment.

"So, we're doing dia-buddy tattoos today," Dottie says, strolling over to the desk in the corner. "I've been working on some concepts based on your approved sketch. So, let's go over those, and you let me know if you want any changes. Then we'll do placement until we get it perfect. Then the actual tattoo. Sound good?"

"Yeah. That sounds great," I confirm as I set my stuff down on the ground by the chair next to their desk.

"Perfect," they say as they start pulling out sheets of paper, face down.

When they have them all out, they turn to me with a serious expression.

"Okay. Before we get swept away by pretty things and forget, let's review the health-related things," Dottie says seriously. "You're diabetic, so that means you have a higher risk for infection and such. I want to ensure you're fully on board before we start."

I nod, knowing we already covered all of this in our consultation, but grateful we're reviewing it again. "Yes. I appreciate going over it again."

The way Dottie reviews all the details of the tattoo process, from preparation to healing, is eerily similar to how the doctor who did my tubal ligation last year explained that process.

It makes sense, since part of the reason they're so highly recommended in the disability community is their background as a nurse.

It's clear that the training stuck with them.

By the time we're done, I have sheets of paper with all the same information we just covered, including a list of specific things to watch out for and care instructions for me since I'm diabetic.

"Okay. Now that the info dump is done." They pause, and excitement rushes through me again. "Wanna see your options?"

"Yes!" I say eagerly, leaning forward to get closer to their drafting desk.

Dottie flips through three designs that are similar in style but have slightly different elements on each.

The idea for the tattoo is to place it on the back of my arms, which are two of the areas where I'm most likely to wear my CGM regularly.

Each features the elements of a night sky I requested—a moon and surrounding stars—plus a kitty curled up on the moon on one side of my body.

Immediately, I know which design I want, and Dottie starts prepping the design to lay the stencil down. Thankfully, after figuring out how high the design needs to be, we only have to shift the placement of one stencil so that I can safely place my monitor on my arm without interfering with the design.

Dottie has me lie down on her table and begin the final prep steps, but the anticipation of the tattoo and needle has me tense up.

"You're welcome to listen to something, sleep, or do whatever makes you most comfortable," Dottie says with a gentle hand on my shoulder, but I can't relax despite her calm demeanor. "Do you want to chat? Sometimes talking helps distract the mind."

"Yeah," I say, my head resting on a pillow so I'm facing opposite where they sit, ready to begin tattooing.

"Okay. So, what's going on in your life right now?" they ask as the needle begins to buzz in the machine.

"Nothing? And a lot?" I chuckle, trying to keep my body still. "My life is pretty much work, wedding planning, and wishing my fiancé wasn't so nosy about all my health stuff."

"Oof." They breathe out as the needle penetrates my skin. "I've seen a lot of people over the years who are going through big life changes, but a wedding and a new diagnosis all at once? That's a lot to juggle."

"Yeah."

"You're not alone, though," they reassure me. "It just takes time to adjust to a new normal."

New normal.

If that isn't the truth.

"It feels like starting over, you know. It's part of the reason it took me so long to do anything about it," I tell Dottie. "I knew for several months before I actually started following my doctor's recommendations. I know it was a bad idea, but it was just too big and overwhelming. You know?"

"I can imagine," they say as they continue to work. "How are your family and friends handling things?"

"Mixed bag," I sigh. "Most people are fine with it. It doesn't affect them, you know? But Gunnar took it really hard when he found out."

Dottie murmurs a noise of support, but I let the conversation settle into silence. A knot tightened in my chest the entire time until I couldn't help but speak up.

"He just took it really hard. The not knowing," I say, breaking through the steady buzz of the tattoo machine. "To him, it was a betrayal of trust or something, me not telling him immediately about my diagnosis. But to me, I just wasn't..."

"Wasn't ready," they fill in when I trail off.

"Yeah."

"It's a big change," Dottie says calmly.

"Yeah. There's a part of me that just wants to go back to how things were before." Dottie hums in acknowledgment. "I feel like I've lost a part of myself. I thought I knew who I was and what I was capable of, only to discover that everything I knew had to change."

Dottie remains silent for a minute, graciously giving me space to continue if I want. But I don't want to keep going; I'm tired.

Of all of it.

"There's a grief process involved in this kind of stuff," they explain. "I've seen a lot of people in front of me—both as patients in the hospital and as patrons here—and anytime there's big news, especially medical diagnoses, there's a certain look people get."

I feel Dottie's hands leave my arm for a moment, and I hear her breathe deeply for a few breaths before resuming her work and our conversation.

"The look. It's like they're unsure, or more like lost. Like they don't know how to carry on. Their whole world stops and resets without even a second to really understand what's happening."

Their words hit me square in the chest.

The buzz of the tattoo gun starts up again, and they continue their work.

"Yeah. Exactly. How do you keep going when you can't even see the path?" I murmur as the now-familiar feeling of a needle carving a wound into my skin returns. "And Gunnar... He keeps forcing me forward. I haven't had a second to process because everything happens quickly and there's so much pressure to do everything correctly."

"Well, y'all are engaged. So, at least you know he's not going anywhere," Dottie suggests.

"Sometimes I wish he would, though," I chuckle. "It's part of the reason I didn't tell him I was coming out here. He's on a work trip and doesn't get back until Sunday."

"So, you drove six hours across the state and didn't tell anyone?" Dottie asks, shock evident in her voice.

"Oh, I told my best friends. The girls definitely know," I reassure them.

"Thank Goddess," they breathe out as they continue working.

Conversation switches from the current chaos that is my relationship with Gunnar to talking about different things: work, wedding stuff, video games, tarot, and other witchy shit.

Time warps as Dottie works, and suddenly we've switched to my other arm, this one with far less detail, and before I know it, we're done.

"Okay. Let's take a look before we wrap it up," Dottie says, standing and helping me up from the table where I was lying.

They hand me a mirror and position me so I can see the finished work in the mirror, and I gasp in shock.

It's gorgeous.

Simple black lines make up a night sky, complete with a moon and stars. On my right side, there's a kitty curled up in the crescent moon.

"It's perfect!" I tell Dottie with a squeal.

"Good. Because it's permanent." They laugh. "Let's get some pictures. Then... would you want to do dinner? There's nothing fancy out here like you'd find in the city, but we have some good bars serving excellent greasy food—and a Tex-Mex restaurant that's to die for."

"Fuck yes! I'd love to," I reply eagerly, smiling back at them.

A quick photoshoot later, and we're off to a place called Boot 'N Scoot, where I've been promised the best wings I'll ever have.

The crew from the tattoo shop is having a great time, and they even try to teach me a few line dances when their favorite songs come on. I catch on to those pretty quickly, but two-steppin' will never be one of my talents.

I'm at the bar, getting another round of drinks, water for me, when Zeph comes up next to me, holding my phone in their hand.

"Hey. Your phone is going nuts with texts and phone calls," they say with a sympathetic look on their face. "Looks like someone named Gunnar really wants to get ahold of you."

Taking my phone from them, I scroll through all the text, call, and voicemail notifications.

"Fuck," I murmur.

The bartender lays the drinks down in front of us, and I look over at Zeph.

"I'll take these back to the group. You take care of that," they say, nodding to my phone.

"Yeah. Right," I sigh. "I'll be outside."

I nod to the security woman at the door and step back from the entrance for a bit more quiet, but stay close enough to be in her line of sight.

As I'm bracing myself to hit call on Gunnar's contact, my screen lights up with a call from him.

I accept the call and bring my phone to my ear.

"Hey," I say.

"Shit, Selene. You've had me worried sick," he says frantically. "Where the fuck are you?"

"What do you mean? I'm at home." I try to keep my tone light and casual.

"Well, that's a fucking lie because I've been calling you *from home* for the past two hours," he snaps. "And when I couldn't get ahold of you, I called Elsie to see if you were still at the office, which you're not. Then I had Emir track your phone to the middle of nowhere, West Texas? What the hell is going on?"

"First off, that's extremely invasive and a major breach of

boundaries," I sass back at him. "Tracking my phone? Really, Gunnar?"

"You weren't picking up. I can't file a missing person report for 48 hours," he says frantically. "What was I supposed to do?"

"You wait," I say, gritting my teeth. "You fucking wait for me to look at my phone and text or call you back, like a fucking normal person. You don't go all bounty hunter and track me down, Gunnar."

I take a deep breath before realization dawns.

"And what the hell are you doing home? You said you wouldn't be back until Sunday," I defend.

"I came back early. Figured I'd surprise my fiancée and take her out this weekend," he grinds out. "Only, she's not fucking here."

"Hold your horns, Viking," I scoff. "I made plans. That's all. I don't need to tell you everything."

"Well, maybe you should. And I think you should start sharing your location with me," he grumbles.

"Not fucking happening. You won't, or can't, for work reasons, and I'm allowed to set that boundary too," I argue before sighing. "Gunnar, what are we even fighting about?"

"You *left*," he growls. "You left, and I've been worried out of my mind. And you won't even tell me what you're doing in the middle of nowhere."

"I got a tattoo. I told you about that a while ago," I argue. "This is about my body. My life. My choice. This doesn't impact you at all."

"Like hell it doesn't," he says, real anger now evident in his voice. "You can't just go galavanting off and not tell anyone where you've gone, Selene."

"Actually, I can," I snap. "I'm hanging up. I'll see you when I get home tomorrow."

"Sele..."

But I don't let him finish saying my name before I cut the call. Fucking men.

18

GUNNAR

July 4—New Moon in Cancer, Mercury in Leo

By the time the fireworks show is set to start at 9 p.m., the sun has long since dipped below the horizon, and we've already spent hours outside drinking and eating with friends.

None of us gives a particular fuck about the holiday itself, but Ivy worked her ass off to pull off a night of celebration sure to impress all the resort guests.

The fireworks are set up on the other side of the Colorado River, and we're all sitting on blankets and lawn chairs in the area she set aside for our group.

Selene has been playing hostess to our small group of friends as usual. Things even feel normal between us since the tracking incident. She even gave me permission to use her location in the event of an emergency, which requires blood, fire, or death according to her definition.

The night started with a handful of us who could make it this weekend, but it quickly grew to include several new couples and singles who had the good fortune to sit near us. Our circle quickly expanded, and once acquaintances noticed our presence, a steady flow of people came over to say hello.

Standing at the back of our group, I'm chatting with Alvie and a new friend, Archer Warr, a world-renowned astronomer. The man is brilliant as fuck and, as the stars start to come out against the dark backdrop of an unpolluted Texas sky, he proudly begins to tell us about the backdrop of our evening of fireworks, which we have the honor of joining. The funniest part was seeing Selene's confusion as she worked through the differences between an astrologer and an astronomer, which gave me quite the chuckle.

At nine-fifteen on the dot, music filters from the speakers hidden among the surrounding trees, signaling the show's start. They've already run their tests to ensure everything goes off without a hitch, earning plenty of oohs and aahs on their own. But the swell of music around us has everyone settling into their seats, drinks and food in hand, to enjoy the show.

Selene makes her way through the crowd of blankets and chairs toward me when the first fireworks explode. The sudden noise startles her enough to cause her to stumble.

"Whoa there, Luna," I tell her, catching her by her elbows, my nearly empty bottle of beer now discarded on the ground. "Don't go hurting my fiancée."

Selene gives me a mocking smile, silently telling me she's fine.

"Where's our blanket again?" she asks.

"I moved it a little further back," I tell her. "We were right in the middle of everything."

A smirk creeps up on Selene's face. "Which is exactly where I like to be, Viking."

"I know you do," I tell her, smiling down at her. "But I want you all to myself tonight."

The way her eyelashes flutter makes my heart stop, and I am unable to focus on anything but her stunning beauty.

Selene may sometimes see me as too much, but I will never get enough of her.

"Hey, assholes. You're blocking our view," someone snaps with a chuckle from behind us, drawing my attention away from the one thing worth noticing.

I take her cup from her and set it on the ground near the cooler. Then I take her hand and lead her out of the throng of people, passing by a smirking Alvie as we go.

When we reach the edge of the group, I keep walking while Selene starts glancing behind us.

"Gunnar, where are we going?" she asks me, but I keep walking.

The music from the speakers fades a little as we keep walking through the trees until we come upon an opening.

I hear Selene's gasp as she takes in the magical space Ivy helped me create today. In the center of the grove of trees is a large blanket, held down at the corners by a basket of food and a cooler of wine. Electric candles are placed all around, giving the alcove a romantic glow.

"Gunnar," Selene says breathlessly as the fireworks go off in the background.

I turn to her and walk backward until we're in the center of the blanket.

"I found this place a while ago on one of our other visits during a run," I tell her, kneeling before her.

"Gunnar. You've already proposed. There's no need to do it again," she laughs.

"I can't help myself, Luna," I smile at her. "I'd ask you to marry me every day if I didn't think you'd end up throwing your shoe collection at me each time."

"That's a lot of shoes," she chuckles.

The soft sounds of music and fireworks drift around us as we gaze at each other, taking in the most important person in our lives.

"I'm asking again, though, because this is where I want to do it," I tell her, looking at the nature around us. "I want to get married here."

Selene glances around, taking in the space and seeing the vision for herself.

"Okay?" she says with a lilt in her voice, her gaze wandering around as she thinks and talks to herself. "We can make that work. An outdoor wedding in March shouldn't be too bad. Yeah. We can definitely do that."

Looking back down at me, she smiles brighter than the stars, and fireworks frame her.

"Perfect," I say with a growl.

I tug her down into my arms, which earns me a squeal of delight, and hold her to my chest to keep her from falling.

She's whole body laughing as I lower her to the ground and adjust her so she's comfortably lying on her back. Then, with my entire body coiled tight with need, I crawl up her body. Each inch of progress I make moving up her perfect curves allows me a moment to kiss and caress each part of her.

Every touch of my lips and fingers against the fabric of her dress elicits shivers of anticipation from my girl until she's truly shaking with need.

"Fuck," I groan into her breasts when I reach them and lean down to rest my head between them.

With a featherlike touch, I play with her nipple, and it perks up at my attention. Leaning over, I pull it into my mouth and tug it between my teeth.

"Goddess, you're perfect," I whisper when I pull away.

Selene pushes herself up a little to look me in the eye.

"I know," she says with a grin. "Now show me how much you believe it and fuck me like I deserve."

Returning her grin, I quickly lean up to look down at her. She's dressed in a light blue floral button-up dress, which has me growling in approval.

Selene goes to unbutton her dress, but my patience and my quickly hardening cock can't take the slow, methodical way she's going about it.

Like the Viking she calls me, I reach for her buttons and pull until they pop free, leaving only her breasts hidden by the lingerie beneath.

"No panties?" I ask with an eyebrow quirked.

"Well, I was hoping you'd fuck me tonight. But I imagined myself riding you among our friends with my dress still on." She laughs, leaning up to take my face between her hands and kiss me.

With one easy swipe of her tongue across my lips, I open for her. The warmth of her tongue delving into my mouth makes me shiver with need for her.

Reaching my arm around her back, I pull her close and let my free hand go to her breast. One of her hands immediately goes to push mine down away from the swells of her chest to her core, where she wants me.

With her dress wide open, my fingers easily find her slit as we continue to kiss. Running a single tip through her center tells me she's already wet and needy for my cock.

She's always ready for me, always desires me. It's the greatest honor a man could ever ask for.

Letting myself explore her center, I feel my way through her curls and into the center of her core. I tease her by circling her opening but never entering. Then I play with her clit, which has her clutching at my shirt and moaning into my mouth.

"Goddess," I groan. "Please. I need to be inside you. I want to worship your tight cunt with my cock."

Releasing me, Selene leans back to look at me. Surely she sees how wrecked I am, how hopelessly devoted I am to her.

"You remember my rule, right?" she says slowly, her voice hitching when I brush against her clit once again. "My pussy. My pleasure."

"Yes, Goddess," I breathe out, my voice deep and needy. "Nothing but your pleasure."

She stares at me for a minute, looking for something, then seems satisfied with whatever she's found in my expression.

She gives me a single nod before reaching for my belt and unbuckling it. Then the button and zipper to my pants are opened, and the only thing containing my cock, keeping it from her blissfully warm cunt, is my briefs.

Reaching over, she palms me through the soft cotton, and I feel myself twitch at her touch.

"Someone was thinking of me when they made you, you know," Selene says, looking at me with fire in her gaze. "They knew one day you'd find someone who would need you to be your best self to please them. The Gods knew that when they crafted you." She gives me a wink. "And your cock."

A groan slips from my lips as she crashes hers to mine.

Selene reaches into my briefs, her small hand wrapping around my cock with a strength I'm always impressed with. The feeling of her warm hand moving up and down my length has me shivering with anticipation, the memory of the feeling of her cunt wrapped around me already pushing me close to the edge of coming.

Lying her back down carefully when our kiss breaks apart, I hurry to take off my clothes fully.

Spreading her legs, Selene invites me to her. She brings her knees to wrap and lock with my own before pulling me down for a kiss by the collar of my shirt.

Being so close, my cock finds the slit of her pussy waiting for me, warm and welcoming.

I rock into her, every glide of my length brushing against Selene's opening and her clit, eliciting moans from her as we kiss.

The music around us changes to something slower and more melodic, and the energy between us shifts.

"I need you, Gunnar," Selene groans, bucking her hips up into me. "Now. I need you now."

Leaning back, I line my tip up with her pussy and brush myself up and down her opening. I let myself graze her clit on the way down and circle her center lightly.

Soon though, the teasing is too much for me.

I cannot deny my Goddess any longer.

Pressing the head of my cock into her, I lock my gaze with her hazel eyes. Every inch she takes of me is another victory in my eyes, an honor for being allowed to partake in the pleasure she wrings from my body.

I sink into her fully and lean down to kiss her lightly on the forehead.

"No," she growls, a hand coming to wrap around my throat. "Fuck me like you mean it, Viking. Fuck me like the machine I know you are."

"Yes, Goddess," I tell her, my voice strained as I hold back my pleasure.

Positioning myself above her, I cage her in with my arms and pull my hips back so I can thrust back into her. When I push back in, Selene sucks in a gasp and arches her back. Her cunt squeezes around me as I try to pull back, silently begging me to stay in place.

But I know what's been asked of me.

I know how to please her.

So, I persevere.

My hips find a steady rhythm with the music that surrounds us. The swell of the orchestra matches the pace of my hips. Each crescendo of the music coincides with the swell of her pending orgasm—every drive I make into her pushing her closer to that edge of bliss.

Sweat builds on my face, and I pick myself up to wipe it away so it doesn't drip on my girl, but the movement changes the angle of my cock, and Selene screams in pleasure just as the music crashes at its peak.

"Fuck. Gunnar!" she pants. "Right. There!"

I keep myself hovering above her on one hand, my free arm going behind my back to keep it out of the way, and I thrust into her at this new angle.

"Yes," she chants. "Yes. Yes. Yes!"

My finale is so close, but I push it back, willing it to hold off just long enough to let her find her release before I do.

But the surge of pleasure through my body has me picking up the pace without thought.

Selene reaches up to grasp my neck, pulling me down close enough to feel her breath on my lips but too far to take it with my own.

"Make me come, Viking," she growls ferociously. "Now."

I drop my hand back to the ground and start fucking her in earnest now. Every movement is firmer and harder than before, but I keep the pace just as she's shown me, which feels best.

Then, I feel it.

Her pussy flutters around me once, then twice, before clamping down hard—almost to the point of pain—as she tries to push me out and keep me in her at the same time.

She cries out in time with the fireworks that explode overhead just as her own body ignites with pleasure.

"Mierda!" *Fuck!* Selene gasps, pulling me into her so I don't slip out.

When her nails dig into my back and ass, there's no stopping my release. I come with a groan, filling her up enough that it's leaking out of her and down onto her torn dress beneath us. My body convulses as I spend the last of my energy rocking my cum back into her.

We're both breathing heavily as we come down from each of our orgasms. Finally, my cock softens enough to slip out of her, and I know our moment is over.

"How was that for a fireworks show?" I ask, rolling us to our sides so I don't crush her with the weight of my own body.

She laughs, a beautiful sound that makes my heart swell with pure love for her.

"It was perfect," she replies, leaning over to kiss me on the nose.

Pulling her close to my chest, I lean over and pull one corner of the blanket to wrap around us.

Despite the heat of a Texas summer, Selene loves her blankets. She burrows into them while tucking her head into my chest.

Lying under the stars with the woman who is the center of my universe, like this, feels right.

"So now that we've fucked here..." I start cautiously. "Are you still okay with getting married here?"

She looks up at me with glittering hazel eyes and a smile.

"Fuck yes," she chuckles. "I'll walk down the aisle to you here any day. Just know I'll be thinking of this night the whole time."

My lips press against her forehead, and her eyes flutter closed.

"Good," I say softly. "I will be too."

19

GUNNAR

July 22—Capricorn Full Moon

Things with Selene have been good since the Fourth of July weekend and our evening under the fireworks. The tension that occasionally pops up is no longer between us, but rather because of something work or wedding related, which is an incredible relief.

Selene and I have been busy at work, and thankfully, Ivy has been handling most of the wedding planning.

Today, though, is the day every groom looks forward to: the wedding menu tasting.

I've actually been looking forward to it all week, but when Emir walks into my office with a frown on his face, I know my plans for the day are screwed.

"Who fucked up?" I ask, a frustrated growl already in my voice.

"It doesn't matter who fucked up, Gunnar. Just that we have to deal with it," Emir says patiently.

"Tell me who, Emir," I repeat.

"Like I said, it doesn't matter," he replies calmly.

Emir has always been the more even-tempered of the two of us in the workplace. It does help that part of my job involves beating the shit out of our employees regularly in training, though.

It's for their betterment.

I swear.

"Okay. So how are we *dealing with this*?" I ask, leaning back in my chair and crossing my arms over my chest.

Emir winces a little, but he does his best to hide it.

"I need you to go to Chicago," he starts, his expression relaxing into a more neutral one. "Meet with some of your contacts there."

I raise an eyebrow at him.

"And you need me to go today, don't you?" I infer.

He nods silently.

"Can it wait?" I ask, with a little more pleading in my voice than I would like.

"No." He pauses, taking a deep breath. "There're kids involved. This needs to be resolved quickly and quietly."

"Fuck," I say, already rising from my chair and reaching for the go bag I keep in the corner of my office.

"Ash is going with you." Emir backs up and lets me storm out of my office. "They're waiting for you at the airfield. The plane is already fueled and cleared for takeoff."

"I'll grab my equipment from the armory," I shoot over my shoulder.

"Already here, Sir." My assistant—someone I resisted hiring for the longest time but who has been supremely helpful since starting—stands with the case for my gear in his hand.

"Thanks," I say, shifting my bag to my shoulder and taking the case from them.

I flip the case up onto the shelf of their desk and open it to confirm everything I need is there, which it is.

I give my assistant an approving smile and close the case before turning back to Emir.

"Guessing a car is already downstairs," I say, my voice less a question and more a confirmation.

"Of course," Emir says, handing me a tablet. "I'll call you with the details and fill you in on what you need to know, but this has the basics."

"Got it." I take the device and turn toward the lobby.

Stopping at the elevators, I turn to Emir, who's followed me.

"Fuck," I murmur.

"What?" Emir asks.

"The tasting. Selene's going to be so pissed." I sigh. "I'll call her from the car."

"She'll understand," he says.

Only Emir doesn't know how fragile my relationship with Selene has been recently, not entirely.

I genuinely don't know how she's going to react to this.

"I hope so," I tell him.

The ride to the airfield passes slowly.

I tried calling Selene three times, but she sent me to voicemail each time.

By the time I've reached the plane and greeted Ash, I am frantically checking my phone to see if Selene has texted.

Finally, when the pilot announces we're taxiing to the runway, I cave and send her my text.

GUNNAR

I'm not going to make the tasting today.

Headed out of town last minute.

I'll be dark for a while. Not sure how long. Sorry.

I promise to make this up to you.

Love you, Luna.

With great hesitation, I power off my phone for the duration of the flight and this trip.

I'm so fucked.

20

SELENE

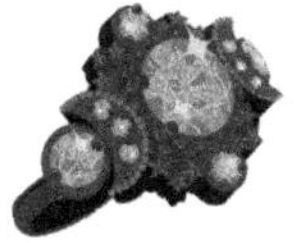

OVERTHEMOON

SOS. CALL ME

MINDFUCKMASTER

I'm in class. What's up?

OVERTHEMOON

GUNNAR LEFT ME

MINDFUCKMASTER

WHAT?????

OVERTHEMOON

Okay. He didn't *leave me*, leave me. He went out of town last minute.

MINDFUCKMASTER

GIRL YOU CAN'T SAY SHIT LIKE THAT

DAMN NEAR GAVE ME A HEART ATTACK!!!

OVERTHEMOON

Sorry. lol

MINDFUCKMASTER

So, he went out of town?

OVERTHEMOON

Yeah. He left town and only sent me a text to let me know.

screenshot of texts from Gunnar

And we're supposed to have our tasting today. And a bunch of other appointments for the wedding this weekend.

MINDFUCKMASTER

Oh, Lena.

OVERTHEMOON

He's supposed to be here. 😭

I need him here and he **LEFT**

MINDFUCKMASTER

I'm sure it was important if he had to leave last minute.

OVERTHEMOON

Better fucking be.

I just… I needed him here with me.

This wedding stuff is all so overwhelming. And he keeps telling me that it's all up to me because he wants me to have the wedding of my dreams.

But I don't want it to be all up to me. I want him *with me*. You know?

MINDFUCKMASTER

Of course you do. He's your partner. He needs to show up for you.

OVERTHEMOON

Yes! Exactly!

MINDFUCKMASTER

Though, I have trouble imagining a world where Gunnar isn't like 100% all in with you.

OVERTHEMOON

Well, yeah. He's all in when it comes to certain things.

Like he's hyper aware of all my health stuff. Annoyingly so…

MINDFUCKMASTER

But?

OVERTHEMOON

But like, wedding stuff? Isn't that something we should be doing *together*?

MINDFUCKMASTER

I would think so… but I've never planned a wedding either.

OVERTHEMOON

It's fucking a lot. And he just abandons me for work?

MINDFUCKMASTER

Question…

OVERTHEMOON

Shoot

MINDFUCKMASTER

Why do you think Gunnar is staying out of wedding planning?

OVERTHEMOON

I don't understand the question.

MINDFUCKMASTER

He left town and is missing all these appointments.

OVERTHEMOON

Yeah

MINDFUCKMASTER

He said he had to go last minute. Do you believe
him?

OVERTHEMOON

Well… Yeah.

MINDFUCKMASTER

So… is he missing the appointments or is he
avoiding them?

Right now, your emotional mind is feeling this like
a full force betrayal. Like you said, it feels like he's
abandoned you, left you alone.

OVERTHEMOON

Yeah. That's definitely how it feels.

MINDFUCKMASTER

That's totally understandable. He's your partner
and you expect him to show up for you. You
expect him to keep his word.

OVERTHEMOON

Of course I do.

MINDFUCKMASTER

Okay, so lean into your logical mind for a minute
and look at your history with Gunnar. Has he ever
given you reason to believe that he's unreliable?
That he's not someone to keep his word? Or that
he would lie to you?

OVERTHEMOON

Gunnar's the most dependable person I've
ever met.

And he's never lied to me before. He's never had
a reason to.

MINDFUCKMASTER

So, would it stand to reason that he's telling you
the truth? That he's just going out of town, right?

OVERTHEMOON

Yeah, probably.

It just hurts.

MINDFUCKMASTER

Of course it does. Your pain is valid, even if he
didn't intend to hurt you.

OVERTHEMOON

Thank you

I don't like that you're right though.

MINDFUCKMASTER

Gunnar's still in the dog house, isn't he? 😆

OVERTHEMOON

Fuck yes! I'll put a bowl out for him and
everything.

MINDFUCKMASTER

LENA! You can't make me cackle like that in
class. Everyone probably thinks I'm crazy now.

OVERTHEMOON

It's part of why I love you though!

MINDFUCKMASTER

Love you too, Lena.

I'll call you after class.

OVERTHEMOON

lol

21

GUNNAR

July 24—Capricorn Full Moon

Turning my phone back on when I got on the plane to come home made my heart race faster than when I first learned to diffuse a bomb.

The barrage of texts and calls waiting for me is as overwhelming as I expected. Each notification makes me cringe internally and curl into myself even more.

By the time we land, I've just finished going through the last of Selene's texts, not even bothering with the voicemails since I already know what they'll say.

Luckily, airplane mode spares my fellow passengers on the flight. I have to wait to call Selene until I'm safely inside the company SUV that's been left for me to pick up.

The phone rings until it's automatically sent to voicemail. But instead of embracing the momentary relief I feel at not having to face my fiancée's ire immediately, I end the call and try again.

It takes several more tries, enough to get me halfway home from the airport, before she finally answers.

"Hello." Selene's voice is cold.

"Hey, Luna," I say, bracing myself for Selene's rightful anger. "I just got back."

"Oh, good. Glad to know you didn't actually die," she says. "Too bad you're dead to me."

Then she hangs up on me.

I expected Selene to be angry, and she's entirely justified in her anger.

I literally dropped off the map for two days without any real notice.

Of course, she's outraged.

But hanging up on me?

I quickly hit her contact again and wait for the call to connect.

"Dead people don't use cell phones."

She hangs up again, and yet again, I call her back.

"I'm not dead, Selene," I say before she can hang up on me again.

"Well, sometimes dead is better."

She hangs up again, and I don't try calling her again, knowing it's futile.

The simmer of frustration turns into a raging boil that I do my best to contain as I finish driving home.

By the time I pull into the driveway, I'm barely hanging onto my last thread of sanity.

I'm already out of the car before the engine is even off and storming into the house.

"Selene!" I call out when I'm through the front door and slam it behind me.

All I hear in response is silence, sending me hunting through the house to find her.

I'm exhausted, and all I want is to wash up and cuddle on the couch with my fiancée, but instead, she has me so worked up that I need a session in the gym on a punching bag more than a hot shower.

I find her in Beef Cake's room, curled up in a chair with the cat napping on the backrest, and just seeing her calms me a little.

Only when she looks up at me, there's a look of shock, and her eyes keep flicking behind me.

"What? What are you looking at?" I ask, following her gaze.

"I must be hallucinating," she whispers, her eyes wide and the smallest of smiles on her lips. "I see dead people."

Then her expression turns murderous, and she stands.

"Only, no. I don't, because I would very much like to kill you myself right now," she says, her voice laced with the most venomous poison.

"Selene," I plead.

"No," she growls out, her frustration from earlier on the phone returning to her voice. "How *dare* you? How dare you drop off the map like that? I know you have work trips, and I know I'm not always allowed to know the details of those trips. I know you're away for those missions. I can live with that."

There's no defense that I can mount, so I just let her vent her anger, and with each lash she whips out, my frustration dissipates.

"But this?" she shrieks. "I got your text and immediately called Emir. He said you were dealing with some kind of company business? Since when do you need to go off the grid for two days to deal with a business matter? In all your trips since we've been together, you've never pulled a stunt like this."

"It wasn't..." I try.

"Ugh. Don't start. Nothing you can say in your defense would make this better," she seethes.

"Selene, you're not being fair."

She scoffs. "Do you know how *embarrassing* it was to show up to the tasting and wait around for you not to show up? Incredibly, by the way. The wait staff kept looking at me like I'd lost my mind being there alone since Ivy told us that she wouldn't be there."

"I'm sorry," I say, pushing down my frustration. "But I tried to tell you what was going on."

"It's fine," she huffs. "Nothing to do about it now."

"For the record. We were helping resolve a conflict that involved some missing kids," I say, my words devoid of emotion, which is the only way I can manage these things without breaking down. "I got called in to help because of my tracking and profiling experience. I was there to help *kids*."

Selene's jaw drops, but I don't give her a chance to respond, feeling just as dead inside as she claims I am to her.

Instead, I march out of the room.

"Dead people don't stomp!" Selene calls after me, but I keep going until I'm in the pool house where Marshall used to live.

In the kitchen, I open the fridge and, thankfully, find a few cases of beer inside.

I rummage through the drawers until I find a bottle opener, then crack one open and down it like I'm back in college.

Immediately, I open another and settle onto the couch. Instead of turning on the television to distract myself, I lean back and stare at the blank screen.

The funny thing about staring at one spot for so long is that you start to hallucinate at a certain point. But instead of some fantasy coming to life, it's like I'm witnessing my life as if it's a horror movie or tragic drama.

There's no good ending to this story.

Not with the way things are going right now.

22

SELENE

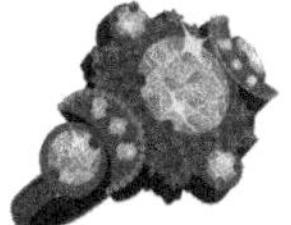

August 19—Aquarius Full Moon

It only took a few days of staying in the pool house for Gunnar to worm his way back into my bed.

Doesn't mean I've fucked him since then, though.

I'm trying to forgive him. I don't want to stay mad, but it's hard to reconcile how Gunnar wants to be involved in every part of my life while not offering the same transparency in return.

I understand that I don't need or want to know every detail about his job, but I should be allowed certain access and knowledge about it.

The tension in our household has made for an uncomfortable atmosphere for the last three and a half weeks.

Worse than the awkwardness is the lack of orgasms.

Going through an ovulation cycle while you're on a sex strike? Not advisable.

Especially not after a tubal ligation, which messes with my hormones anyway.

I've been horny for days with only my vibrator to get me through the waves of lust I experience several times a day.

My sex drive has always been high, and when I was single, taking care of myself seemed enough. But I've clearly become spoiled by having near-constant access to dick.

My cunt is *needy*.

Every morning when Gunnar comes back from his morning run, his skin glowing and glistening with sweat, it takes every bit of strength I have to keep myself from jumping him and riding his dick like the hoe I am.

At this point, I've resorted to straight-up avoiding Gunnar like the plague.

Within a week of our argument, I found a new routine. Waking up early and going into the office, and then staying late, has become a daily occurrence. I go out with friends whenever possible to avoid being in close proximity to him for meals. At night, I catch myself falling asleep in Beef Cake's room in my comfortable reading chair rather than going to bed. Yet, I somehow always wake up in my bed anyway.

I want him desperately. I always have.

But it's the principle of the matter.

Lysistrata and the women who ended a whole fucking war were definitely stronger than me.

I feel guilty, but it's necessary.

The orgasm thing has been a major problem, though. And masturbating in front of your cat is a little awkward.

Which is why I found myself changing my routine today.

I woke up early and got ready for cycle class, but instead of heading straight to work afterward, I texted Elsie saying I'd be working from home and turned my ass around to head home.

I know for a fact that Gunnar has a big work presentation today for a potential new client because he was rehearsing his part of the presentation for me last night.

Still, when I get home, I check the entire house to make sure he's not hiding anywhere.

A sigh of relief escapes me when I finish checking the last room in our home and head to our bedroom.

I take my time with my morning routine. When I step out of my everything shower, I feel more relaxed than I have in weeks.

I towel myself off, go through my beauty routine, and even take the time to let my hair fall into its natural waves instead of blow-drying it straight or leaving it to air dry.

I feel like a completely new woman by the time I really get to start my day, more like myself than I have in weeks.

When I walk into the bedroom, still wrapped in my towel, I walk over to my altar space by the window and sit down to go through my morning meditation and spiritual rituals.

Instinctively, I reach for a deck of tarot cards, picking out one I don't usually use. It's a romantic deck; the cards' imagery is illustrated in an Art Nouveau style and embossed with gold.

I shuffle the cards seven times before cutting the deck and drawing three cards from the top, one by one.

The Empress.

The Star.

The Queen of Wands.

Each card has unique elements that hint at its meaning. None of the cards came out in reverse, which gives the reading a positive energy.

The Empress embodies sensuality, beauty, and self-worth. She represents the divine feminine in her fullest form—lush, gentle, receptive, and magnetic. She looks directly at me, wearing a crown of stars. It's as if she's gazing at me expectantly, waiting for me to embrace myself as she drapes herself over her throne like a woman who knows her worth and has experienced ecstasy.

Next, I look at the Star card, which shows a naked woman under starlight. She's kneeling and pouring water from a vessel into a reflection pond. This imagery tells me I should be pouring into myself right now, prioritizing myself and especially my emotional well-being. I imagine her slipping into the cool water, letting it envelop her. Her nakedness is both a symbol of vulnerability and sensuality.

Finally, the Queen of Wands sits confidently on her seat of power with a scepter. Everything about her exudes confidence and self-assurance. Her presence is magnetic. She embraces her sexuality and radiates inner fire. She encourages me to embrace my desires and see my pleasure as sacred. She looks like... me. She even has a cat at her feet who reminds me a little of Beef Cake.

I lay the cards neatly on my altar and sit with the reading for a moment, trying to decipher its meaning.

Or rather, bring myself to accept its meaning.

Shaking myself out of my thoughts, I go to the dresser to pick out my undergarments for the day. However, when I open the drawer, I'm not drawn to the plain bra and underwear I usually wear.

Instead, my eyes land on a matching set of lingerie that Gunnar got me as one of his many apology gifts. I haven't tried them on yet out of principle, but the brilliant teal color calls to me.

I pick them up, running my fingers over the lace, which is placed strategically on a sheer base fabric to hide certain anatomy and show off others.

The responsible adult voice in my head tells me I should get dressed in my practical undergarments and go to my office to get work done.

But I can't bring myself to put the teal lingerie down, my eyes flicking over to the cards still displayed on my altar.

"Fuck it," I say, closing the drawer and turning to dress in the teal garment.

Every cell in my body hums with the heat of sensuality. There's an intense desire to connect my spirit with my body, to explore my body and pleasure as if navigating vast oceans.

My mind made up, I dress in the teal garments and head to my bedside table. Opening the cabinet, I reach for one of the boxes there and pull out my favorite wand and a dildo, which is longer and a bit thinner than most of the ones I have.

It doesn't usually do it for me when Gunnar and I are fucking regularly, but after a few weeks without a good dicking down, I think it will be perfect.

I take them into the bathroom and wash them with the toy soap I have in my medicine cabinet before drying them off with a fresh towel. Then, I bring them back into the bedroom and set them on the waterproof blanket I grabbed from the linen closet.

The universe wants me to embrace my sensuality.

Fine by me.

A girl could use a great orgasm.

I lay out the blanket and climb onto it.

Starting with the vibrator on the lowest setting, I push my panties to the side and run the bulb of the toy up and down my center, making sure to avoid my clit directly while I warm my body up.

The flames of desire don't take long to spark to life under my skin.

I shift and adjust on the pillows to allow me better access to myself.

With one hand focused on using the wand to ramp up the energy in my body, I let myself push down one cup of my bra and pinch my nipple. The small bud hardens under my touch as I circle it, occasionally brushing against it directly.

The buzzing in my body radiates out from my pussy until there's a steady ringing in my ears, which blocks out the rest of the world.

I let myself get lost in the sensations that flow through my body.

My body craves an orgasm, seeking its pleasure *now*. But my mind wants to hold on to this feeling of temptation for as long as possible.

I edge myself with the toy and my touch. I allow myself just enough variation to avoid falling over the edge, but push my body to the edge of bliss with brief moments of consistent sensation that tempt me to abandon my commitment to a prolonged exploration of my body.

Time no longer exists, and I'm merely following the path my body has laid out for me.

Only when my eyes flutter open briefly does the movement in the doorway startle me out of my headspace.

"Fuck," I cry, sitting up in bed, closing my legs, and staring at the man in the doorway to our bedroom. "Gunnar, what the fuck are you doing here?"

"I came home to check on you," he says, his words a little breathless. "You came back after your class, but you didn't leave to go to work. I got worried."

"Well, don't do that then," I huff, collapsing back on the bed with an arm over my eyes. "And tracking me again? When there's no blood fire or death? Fucking hell."

I murmur the words to myself, but he manages to hear me.

"Don't stop," he says with lust in his voice. "Keep going."

I glare at him for a minute before deciding the orgasm will be worth it, and start the vibrator again.

Closing my eyes, I try to focus back on the sensations flowing through my body.

But my pussy is a demanding bitch, needing to be filled. So, I reach for the dildo next to me.

I guide it to my opening before pressing it in.

Though a sharp intake of breath from Gunnar distracts me from enjoying how the length of the dildo presses into me.

Closing my eyes, I try to ignore him and begin thrusting the dildo in and out of my channel, but I get nowhere.

My frustration mounts the longer I go, and whatever heated pleasure sizzled under my skin quickly dies out.

"Shit," I sigh, going limp on the bed. "It's like my body knows your dick is here, and now my pussy won't cooperate. Now I'm gonna have to deal with blue ovaries all day."

"Let me help then," Gunnar says, taking a few steps toward me.

"It's fine," I say, gathering my toys and heading for the bathroom to clean them off.

Gunnar's Viking build quickly blocks my path, and I look up into his crystal blue eyes.

"Let me touch you," he says softly. "I want to."

"I said it's fine, Gunnar," I mumble, pushing past him.

Only his hand comes to my shoulder, and the heat I thought had fled my body flames back to life under the warmth of his touch.

"You're still mad at me. I get it. You have every right to be." He slowly turns me to face him. "But Gods. I fucking miss you, Selene."

The way guilt floods his face makes me soften in front of him.

"Don't walk away. Stop hiding from me." His free hand rises to touch my cheek.

"I'm not..."

"You are." He cuts me off. "I should know. I know because my world is much darker without your brilliant light in it."

"I can't just..."

"Can't what?" he asks earnestly.

"I don't know how to get past this," I tell him honestly. "My body wants you." A smile begins to form on his lips. "But my head? It's conflicted. And my heart is hurting."

"I did that. That's on me," he admits. "Let me fix this."

"You can't fix feelings, Gunnar. They just are. Until they're not." I shrug. "It hurts. It just hurts. I'm too in my head when I'm around you."

"Then I'll get you out of your head," he says simply.

His confidence makes me huff and smirk.

Of course, he thinks that's all I need.

I look at him, studying his expression.

And therein lies the problem.

The sincerity of his gaze breaks down the walls I've built around myself recently.

"Let me do this for you. Let me make you feel *good*," he pleads gently. "Please."

His tone is what breaks me.

What can I say? I'm weak.

Fucking hormones.

"Yes," I tell him softly, still unsure of myself.

"Yes?" he repeats, his hands moving from my jaw and arm to rest around my waist. "I don't want a reluctant 'yes' from you, Selene." He pulls me in tight. "I want the confident 'fuck yes' of my Goddess, the woman I worship."

I suck in a sharp breath, and electricity zips through me.

The heat of his fingertips sinks through my skin and down to my bones, fueling my desire.

It's not just lust I feel.

Not just that base need to float on a cloud of bliss, but also a need for him.

"Fuck yes," I say, my usual confidence back in my voice. "I want you to worship me."

Before I can blink, Gunnar moves to lift me, so I'm forced to wrap myself around him to keep from falling backward.

He turns and walks toward the bed and lays me down gently.

Hovering over me, his gaze connects with my own, and his devotion makes me melt.

The way he looks at me tells me he wants to kiss me, but something is holding him back.

Rocking my hips up into him, I silently plead for him to kiss me, touch me.

"If you want something, then tell me. Command me like the Goddess you are," he says, a tease in his voice.

"Kiss me, Viking," I breathe out.

Any hesitation he had disappears, and his lips are now on mine.

The kiss is gentle but insistent. There's an eagerness in the way his lips caress mine, which sends a thrill through me.

His tongue traces against my lips, silently asking me to open for him, and he lowers himself so his body presses further into my own.

I let him in; his tongue tangles with my own, but there's no battle between us. We move together, seeking each other out with each caress.

Tilting my lips away from him, I lift my chin to allow him to continue his ministrations down my neck and to the spot where my neck meets my shoulder. He bites down firmly, and my whole body arches at the sensation that shoots through me.

He doesn't stop there, though; his kisses and caresses continue down my body. He moves from my neck to my shoulder and then my breasts, giving them plenty of attention after tugging down the cups of the bra I'm wearing.

The way he worships my stomach—with such adoration and gentleness—makes me melt. He nips at one spot where my stretch marks are most prominent, and I lift my hips at the sudden sensation with a gasp.

I push him down to where I want him the most, and he dives in like a man who's been given his favorite dessert.

He licks up my center, making my back arch up off the bed as he focuses his attention on my sensitive bud. My body moves with each wave of sensation that shoots through my body, straight from my clit. His entire world right now centers on my pussy and my pleasure.

"More," I moan, needing something beyond the pleasure he's already pulling from my body. "I need more."

He grins up at me, and after shifting his weight off one of his arms, he spears me with two of his fingers.

The intrusion has me crying out, my system shocked by the sudden fullness, but the way he strokes my inner walls has me quickly relaxing into his touch.

After years of studying my body, Gunnar knows how to work me to the edge quickly, but I don't want to fall apart like this. I don't want to find bliss without him.

I grab him by the roots of his hair and tug him up my body, while he continues stroking that sensitive spot on my upper wall.

"Is there something you want, Goddess?" he asks, his eyebrows raised as though he already knows my answer.

His fingers press up hard into my most sensitive spot, and my vision blurs out in a combination of pain and pleasure.

"I need you to fuck me. I need your cock inside me when I come," I pant as I come back to myself. "Your fingers aren't enough. I want to be full."

"You want my cock, little Goddess?" he asks. "Then come and take it for yourself."

I push at his shoulders to give myself space to rise and immediately reach for the bulge in his pants.

He's already hard for me, throbbing under my touch as blood rushes to fill his cock.

"You want me. You want my pussy," I state, knowing he does just by how he looks at me.

Reaching for his belt, I unbuckle him and go for the button and zipper on his pants.

When his pants are undone, his cock is hidden only by his boxer briefs.

"Off," I command, and Gunnar responds eagerly, pushing his underwear and pants to the ground.

He's warm in my hand, and I stroke him gently as he removes his shoes and rids himself of his clothing.

Without asking him to, he pulls off his shirt with one hand, revealing his toned body to me in all its glory.

He may call me his Goddess, but this man looks like a god.

Grabbing him by the hips, I pull him to me, and he crawls on top of me on the bed, allowing his hips to settle in the space I've left for him between my legs.

"Fuck me, Gunnar," I murmur, pushing up to kiss him lightly. "Fuck me like the Viking you are, hard and fast."

He rocks his hips, letting his cock settle between my folds and gathering up my wetness to coat his length. The way he grazes my clit with each pulse has me rocking up into him, searching for more pressure.

"Fuck me, Gunnar," I growl, which only makes him smirk.

I dig my nails into his ass.

"Such a demanding woman," he chuckles.

"I know what I want. And right now I want your cock," I moan.

Reaching down, I take hold of him and guide him to my opening.

"Fuck me," I plead breathlessly.

"As you wish," Gunnar says, kissing me lightly on the forehead.

All of my senses hone in on the feeling of him as he enters me; the world around us no longer exists as our bodies join together.

He starts slowly, thrusting with even movements that allow me to open up to him more.

With every pump of his hips, I grow wetter, allowing his cock to glide in and out of me effortlessly.

A whine erupts from my lips, and he takes it as his cue to pick up his pace. Each push into me increases in both strength and speed.

I let my head fall back and my eyes flutter closed as I focus on the sensations emanating from where our bodies join together.

A buzz pulls me from my meditative state, and when I open my eyes, I see that Gunnar has turned on the vibrator I had discarded on the bed beside us.

He leans back, opening up the space between us, and places the toy directly on my clit. The setting he has it on is a steady vibration, which lights my body on fire.

Bliss is inevitable with the way my body responds to the combination of being fucked full of Gunnar's cock and the buzz of the wand.

"Come with me, Gunnar," I pant, nearing the edge of pleasure.

Gunnar cages me in with his body, and my hand snaps to the handle of the wand to keep it in place.

All those hours honing his body come in handy in moments like this. He holds himself above me at the perfect angle so that each time he thrusts into me, his hips push the bulb of the wand into my clit harshly, making me cry out.

I'm a writhing mess on the bed, tears of frustration streaming from my closed eyes.

I can feel it; my collapse hovers before me, but I can't get there.

Without a word of complaint, Gunnar seems to know what I need.

He picks up his pace and shifts his body to free one of his hands, which comes to wrap around my throat.

The way he presses down on the sides of my throat has me gasping for breath, and I become lightheaded.

I become wholly focused on the pleasure invading my body; there's nothing to keep me from it. No sound or sight can permeate the bubble I'm in, and I have no breath to interrupt the increase of pressure in my body.

"Now," Gunnar growls.

The singular word sends me over the cliff of pleasure, which has taunted me.

My body goes into free-fall. There's no end in sight to the pleasure overwhelming me—only me and the buzz of bliss hovering behind my eyes.

There's a flood of warmth between my thighs, which brings me back to earth. Gunnar's groan of release grounding me in the moment with him.

"Fuck," he groans, rocking his hips into me as he fills me with his cum. "Fucking hell, Selene."

My hands release the fabric of the bedding I'd been desperately grasping onto, gliding around his rib cage and to his back. I pull him down to me, and he rolls us to our sides so we can grasp each other like we're the only thing keeping us on this planet.

Each of us is breathing heavily as we come back to ourselves.

Gunnar's cock goes soft, and he draws himself out of me slowly, letting his cum leak out with how much he released into me.

The sticky warmth of his seed has me smiling, knowing this is something only we share.

We lay together for a while in silence, but my thoughts are running one hundred miles a minute. The calm from earlier is gone, and instead it's replaced by a tightness in my chest.

"What's wrong?" Gunnar asks, pulling back from me to study my face. "You look distressed."

"I..." I stutter. "I don't..."

My breathing grows rapidly, panic closing my throat for a new reason now.

"I can't even get myself off without wanting to involve you somehow," I whisper, the realization of the reason for my anxiety dawning.

I roll away from him and give him my back.

"What do you mean?" Gunnar asks carefully.

"I don't like feeling dependent on you like this," I murmur over my shoulder. "I can't... I don't know how to do this."

Pushing myself up from the bed, I head for the bathroom.

"What do you mean you don't know how to do this, Selene?" Gunnar asks rapidly, following me into the bathroom. "Us? You don't know how to be together, is that what it is?"

I slowly start the shower and get it to the right temperature.

"I don't know how to depend on you," I say softly, glancing over my shoulder to gauge his reaction. "I just... I need to figure out my shit."

Gunnar's face falls at my confession, but he doesn't let that stop him from climbing into the massive shower next to me. He reaches for my shampoo and begins to lather it between his hands before massaging it into my scalp.

We're silent for a while, the only sound the water falling from the shower-head as he washes me reverently. I'm grateful for the connection his touch creates between us.

He speaks softly when I come out from beneath the water after rinsing my hair. "You need time to figure things out."

I shrug, unable to find the explanation I know he's hoping for.

"Okay," he says. "I can give you that. I can give you time."

"And space, Gunnar," I manage to say, placing my hand on his chest. "I need room to breathe, to think."

"Okay. Okay," he murmurs to himself, filling his palm with the perfect amount of conditioner. "Time and space. I can do that."

He looks up at me with determination.

"I can't stop myself from taking care of you," he starts. "But I can give you what you're asking for."

I have to.

That's what his gaze tells me.

He'd rather suffer and struggle with his instincts than tell me I can't have what I need.

At this moment, I realize that this man would truly do anything for me.

Including letting me walk away.

And that thought scares me more than anything.

23

SELENE

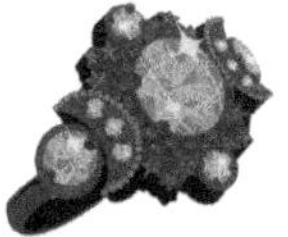

September 14—Virgo Sun, Sagittarius Moon

It feels wrong to celebrate Elsie's birthday at the club and enjoy ourselves with alcohol flowing freely when the birthday girl herself can't drink.

Granted, she's 37 weeks pregnant. She's seemed off all night, yet she's smiling and having a good time. And it's not like she isn't glowing in that way only gorgeous pregnant women do.

The girls and I have been hanging out with her in the party area we had Ivy reserve for all of us for the evening. Considering how tipsy many of us are, all the most delicious tea has already been spilled now that the drinks have been freely flowing.

The highlight of the evening is all the Jell-O shots Zuri made for everyone, including alcohol-free ones for the birthday girl.

Nothing beats a good 1 a.m. Jell-O shot.

The night is going smoothly, and everyone is having a good time, until everything comes to a screeching halt.

"Selene!" Gunnar's voice booms over the sound of the speakers. "Selene Aracely Solis de Estrella!"

His warm hand gently presses my shoulder to spin me around

to face him. I nearly drop the two small plastic cups containing the shots I was about to take.

"What?" I ask, looking at him incredulously. "What on earth could be so important that you need to shout across the club and storm all the way over here?"

"What's in your hand?" he demands.

"Jell-O shots. Duh." I smile broadly, a tease in my voice. "Want one?"

The contents of the cup jiggle as I extend my hand out to him with my offering.

"No. I don't want a shot, Selene," he says sternly while pushing my hand away. "What I want to know is, why do *you*?"

"Because they're yummy. Duh," I reply.

"Selene," he warns. "We've talked about this."

"Yes. And I disagree." I shrug, turning back to my friends and speaking over my shoulder. "You think it's your responsibility to monitor everything that goes into my body. I think I should be able to fuck around and find out if I please."

Gunnar's hand comes back to my shoulder to spin me around, more forcefully this time.

"Selene," Gunnar says sternly. "I won't watch you do this to yourself."

"Do what, Gunnar? Spend time with my friends? Enjoy myself and get a little tipsy at the club?" I roll my eyes. "There's nothing to say I can't have fun here. Having a few Jell-O shots isn't going to kill me."

A bright light flames in Gunnar's eyes at my petulance, and suddenly I'm being swung onto his shoulder and hauled away.

I'm sure my whole ass is on display to everyone who's watching him carry me out of the club, and with each step he takes, my frustration mounts.

"Put me down, Gunnar," I command, banging on his back as he carries me through the lobby of the club and out into the courtyard entrance. "Gunnar Herleif Rees! Put me down, right this instant!"

Gunnar's abrupt halt has my head swimming, but I straighten myself out soon enough.

"Gunnar, you can't just haul me off like a stolen bride. We're not at that part of the wedding yet," I joke.

His hand is wrapped tenderly around my elbow, and his look is one of pure concern now.

"I won't watch you do this to yourself," Gunnar says, pure tenderness in his voice. "I can't watch you hurt yourself like this."

"So what? Watching me get beat on a cross every other weekend by Alvie or Bex is fine, but taking a Jell-O shot isn't?" I scoff, rolling my eyes at his hypocrisy as adrenaline pumps through my veins. "Where's the fucking line, Gunnar?"

When the door to the club swings open, my gaze falls on Naomi and Ivy standing there.

"Everything alright?" Ivy calls out.

"Yes," Gunnar calls back, but I'm already pulling out of his grasp and walking toward my friends now that he's distracted.

"Everything is most definitely not alright, Gunnar," I yell back at him as I walk towards Naomi, who has her hand outstretched. "You're being a controlling, overprotective asshole."

There are only a few steps leading up to the landing where the girls now stand outside the club doors.

"Selene? Girl, you okay?" Ivy's voice is laced with worry.

"I'm okay," I tell her. "Just scraping off my barnacle for the night."

Gunnar's touch makes me jump when he catches up and touches my shoulder.

"Don't touch me," I growl, spinning on him. "I need you to let this go. Just... Goddess. Leave me alone for like one fucking hour."

"Selene." His voice is dark, and his gaze is narrowed on me. "I won't leave you alone. Especially not when you're committed to destroying yourself like this."

"It's my right! It's my fucking body, Gunnar!" I shove my finger into his chest, and he catches me by the wrist, but I struggle free and start backing away. "I swear. You need to stop. Now."

"Stop what, exactly? Caring? Making sure the love of my life will be around for the next few decades?" he asks, his voice dark and insistent, which grates on my nerves.

I spin around, stride towards the doors, and pass my friends back into the club lobby.

The Playground features a grand lobby with terrazzo flooring and high ceilings adorned with chandeliers, surrounded by cages. There's seductive art on the walls and a dark, intimate atmosphere that greets everyone in the club.

But right now, the distance between me and the entrance back to the club cannot come soon enough.

I've nearly reached the freedom of the club, my fingers clasped around the door handle, when Gunnar calls out once more.

"Selene! Listen to me." His voice booms through the space, all command in his words.

The sound of his raised voice is like gasoline on my flame of frustration.

My fingers tightly grip the door handle, and I take a deep breath before turning around.

Everything turns dark, and it's like my soul leaves my body.

"No. You listen to me," I say lowly.

The overwhelming feeling that comes over me is the opposite of his vibrant anger.

Everything sits low in my belly, a furnace which fuels me steadily rather than a hot flash in a pan.

"Listen to me. Very. Clearly." My voice is quiet but carries across the space, evident in the looks on my friends' faces standing between Gunnar and me. "You are not my guardian. Not my savior. I don't need saving."

"Yes, you do." Gunnar's hands clench into fists. "From yourself."

Something snaps inside of me.

"No. You're not listening, not *hearing* me." I take a few steps to close the gap between us.

Despite how he looms over me and I have to tilt my head back to meet his eyes, I feel a thousand feet tall right now. He sees it in me, and his body instinctively takes a step back without a second thought.

"I don't need this—your hovering, your planning, your days of controlling me are over, Gunnar." I speak slowly and clearly. "I may have chosen you at one point, but I don't need you."

As I face off with him, a bubble surrounds us. No sound can permeate it, and it's the only thing containing the dark energy rippling off me right now.

"I don't. Need. You." My voice is darker than the starless Texas night sky outside. "Now leave me. The fuck. Alone."

I let him absorb my words, unidentifiable emotions flashing behind his eyes.

When I'm sure he's finally understood my message, I turn around and break the barrier that contained us.

Naomi and Ivy look at me with pure shock on their faces, but as I approach them, their expressions turn protective.

A few steps past them, I feel their presence close behind me as they form a barrier between Gunnar and me.

I turn around to see them doing just that, allowing me to talk to him with a shield between us.

"You know the funny thing?" I say with a smug smirk. "All of this is over a Jell-O shot. Which, if you'd just let me take it? It would have helped regulate my system because I *am* paying attention to my body. I *am* taking care of myself. Just fine, in fact. Without you."

His expression folds in on itself as I turn away and walk toward the club doors.

My girls fall in behind me, their heels clacking in rhythm with my own.

A warm feeling of satisfaction blooms in my chest at the solidarity I feel just from their mere presence behind me.

These women would throw down with me without a word of explanation.

I'm proud of the friendships I've made at The Playground.

They're my people.

My community.

Now is one of those moments when I remember why.

No matter what, I know these girls will show up for me.

Partners may come and go, but your friends and life partners, are forever.

THE SECOND FLOOR of The Playground Club is designed specifically for play. It features a central balcony overlooking the dance floor below. The balcony has bars that give it a cage-like feel, and recently installed plexiglass muffles the music just enough so you can hear the moans and cries coming from the play spaces.

On either side are two play spaces that mirror each other, with a central public play space and private rooms surrounding the area. One side features a St. Andrew's cross and a voyeur bed, while the other has a spanking bench that can be removed for rigging from the room's hard point above.

Ivy and Naomi have followed me up the stairs to the suspension space where Alvie and his wife, Bex, are setting up for a scene. However, Ivy quickly wanders off to talk to some of the onlookers, as is part of her role at the club.

"Naomi! There you are!" Bex cries as she spots us weaving through the crowd gathered to see our resident riggers perform.

I imagine Naomi gives Bex some signal from behind because one moment the beautiful brunette is smiling, and the next her expression goes flat.

"What's wrong?" she asks, glancing between us.

Stopping before her, I turn back to look at Naomi.

"Gunnar and I…" I stop.

I don't actually know what just happened with Gunnar.

Did we break up? I'm not sure.

How do I explain the dark and heavy feeling in my chest?

Bex takes my silence as a cue to change the subject.

"Alvie," Bex calls over to her partner. "Come here."

Alvie, a tall, tan cowboy with a talent for rope, crosses to us.

"We had talked earlier about suspending Naomi tonight," Bex says, Alvie listening in. "But it looks like you might need to get out of your head. Any chance you'd like to go up tonight?"

Bex glances over her shoulder at Alvie, who nods, understanding the situation without a word.

My shoulders drop, and I am thankful for the understanding my friends so freely give me.

I turn to Naomi. "You okay with that, Nay?"

"Oh, hell yeah," she says with a smirk and a chuckle. "I've been dying to see you up in ropes ever since you told me about that one time you were fucking with Alvie and doing inversions while he was working on your suspension."

"Heard you've gotten pretty good at fucking with him, too," I laugh, lightness returning to my chest as I joke with my friends.

"Alright if I supervise?" Alvie asks. "Bex has been working on rigging with Naomi, and she's getting really good. Would you be comfortable with her putting rope on you?"

I look over at Bex, who's sheepishly smiling.

"You're a rigger now?" I ask, pride swelling in my chest.

"Yeah. And she's getting really fucking good," Naomi says, coming around to stand beside her girlfriend while she beams with a similar look of pride.

"I'm so down for that," I tell the trio, looking between them as they stare back at me with the same excitement I feel.

"Perfect!" Naomi claps before glancing over to her partners with a huge smile. "Can I help? I don't get many opportunities to be helpful when I'm in the ropes."

"Oh, but you're such a good girl when you're in ropes," Bex purrs, her finger coming beneath Naomi's chin as she leans in for a brief kiss. "You're *very* helpful, bunny."

Naomi blushes, but the way she leans into Bex tells me everything I need to know about how much she loves this woman.

"Is Gunnar going to be watching? I presume he's going to provide aftercare?" Alvie asks genuinely.

"No," I snap icily before softening. "I'm not sure where Gunnar is, but he won't be participating."

Alvie looks between the two girls. Bex gives him a sympathetic shrug, but Naomi shakes her head, silently telling Alvie to shut the fuck up.

"Okay," he says, drawing out the word. "No, Gunnar. Got it."

He looks back at me, his dominant side returning to the forefront of his mind as he thinks through the plans.

"Why don't you, Bex, and Naomi talk through the scene. I'll set up all the rigging equipment and prep the ropes for y'all." He turns to his girls. "Bex, you're in charge of the tie. Naomi, I want you to focus on assisting and making an aftercare plan for your girl."

"Yes, Sir," the girls reply, ever the responsive submissives to their Dom.

He gives them a nod and turns back to me.

"I'm going to tell you the same thing I tell everyone I put in the air," he says, holding out his hand for me to take. "If anything feels off, tell us immediately, even if it feels silly. Got it?"

"Yes, Sir," I repeat to him like his girls did.

"And you know my deal. Rope is supposed to be fun, but sometimes it can make feelings surface," he tells me, a soft understanding in his eyes, even though he doesn't know what's happening. "Ride the wave. Let us know what you need. Talk to us and we'll help you through it all."

My earlier bravado falters as his softness and sweetness hit me full force.

The throuple is looking at me with such love and adoration, making my heart swell with gratitude.

"Yes. Of course." I nod to all of them. "A rope bottom will always be their own best advocate. I promise to tell you what I need."

"And we'll check in with you too," Bex says sweetly. "I know you go nonverbal sometimes. So, we'll negotiate hand signals and such, too." She turns to Naomi. "That will be part of your job too; look out for those."

"Yes, love," Naomi says with a smile, clearly loving the way her girlfriend takes command of her.

There's a moment of silence between us, during which our connection seems to fall into place, and I can tell the scene has already begun.

Alvie gives us a nod and squeezes my hand before setting up all the rigging equipment, while we girls dive into walking through the scene and the aftercare plan.

Not long after, Bex has me at the center of the mat, underneath the hard points, holding up a long, four-inch-diameter bamboo rod.

"What do you need help with?" Naomi asks the woman, who holds a length of jute rope in her hand.

"Nothing right now, bunny," Bex replies softly. "Just enjoy the show and watch for what you normally communicate to Alvie and me when you're suspended. Plus, the things Selene told us as well."

Naomi gives her a nod and goes to kneel in the corner of the pad, which defines the zone people should stay out of while Bex is tying me. Alvie stands behind her, and my heart swells with love for her at the sight of them together, her kneeling at his feet with his hand running through her perfectly curled blonde hair.

There's something special about the connection between a Dom and their sub, a connection that I'm suddenly jealous of.

It's been a long time since I've felt that way about Gunnar, a long time since we've had a connection that goes beyond the physical.

Ever since he found out, it's like the only thing he can see is my chronic illness. What makes me feel weak and vulnerable is exactly what I need his help to build me back up from. I don't need him hovering or caretaking all the time. I need his support, his encouragement.

Gunnar treats me like the center of his universe, but it isn't gravity that keeps us together.

It's choice.

Every day I choose to love him with my whole heart, but it's difficult to see the man I love sometimes when all he seems to see is my illness.

I miss how he used to look at me—like I was his match, challenge, and equal. I ache for the thrill of being seen for my strength instead of my fragility. I want the heat in his eyes when we locked onto each other in a crowded room, the unspoken promise that we were in this together. More than anything, I want us back in that place where love was the fire that kept us both burning, not just the shelter he thinks I need.

Bex asks me for my consent for her to put a rope on me, and I give her verbal confirmation.

First, she guides me into position. I relax into her touch as she moves my arms behind my back and supports me there carefully while she begins her tie.

The first length of rope running across my skin is soothing and sends a shiver down my spine. The slightly rough texture grounds me as Bex places it around my wrists in a single-column tie.

The whole time, her hand, which holds the running ends, never makes contact with me; instead, I can only feel its presence through the pressure it applies to the rope as it surrounds me. Her free hand stabilizes me as I'm wrapped, sometimes tightly and other times with a feather-light pressure. Each wrap around my body involves her hugging me tightly as she works, the pressure relaxing me further.

My mind wanders as the process continues, allowing me to focus on only the sensation. I'm keenly aware of every part of my body, its function in the tie, and the beauty of how the rope frames my curves.

In the periphery of my mind, I notice when Bex begins the process of running her lines to the hard point. But I'm more focused on how the rope hugs me firmly like a comforting embrace after a long day.

And what a day it has been.

I'm half aware of each of my legs being maneuvered and tied in a futomomo and brought up by their lines until I'm fully suspended, but the moment I'm fully in the air is when everything slips away.

The feeling is pure freedom.

Despite being encased in the jute rope, I feel freer than I have in months.

There are no demands from others at this moment, and no one

is telling me what to do or how to feel. There's nothing but my body existing as it should.

A haze takes over as I sink into my liberation from reality.

Time passes, but there's no telling how long it is.

When the position starts to put strain on my joints, I shift my hips and use the momentum to invert myself, allowing the pressure to shift within my body.

Again, I can slip into the nothingness that's settled in my mind.

A gentle hand touches my face, drawing my focus back to the world around me, and I'm met with my best friend's welcoming smile.

"You've been up for a while," she says, just loud enough to be heard over the music that starts to filter into the background of my focus. "Do you want to stay? Or come down."

Biting my lip, I think about it for a minute.

On the one hand, I feel so good. The stubborn, invincible part of me believes I can stay here forever if I want to. But the slight ache in my body tells me I need to come down soon.

"Slowly?" I tell her.

"Yeah. We can do that." She looks over her shoulder at Bex. "I think it would be best to let her leg down first so she can kneel on the ground."

"Of course." Bex takes a few steps toward me, placing her hand on the center of my back. "I'll help you invert again and then bring you down."

I give her a nod, my head feeling heavy alongside the rest of my body.

Rope runs around me as Bex lowers me slowly and smoothly to the ground. Both of my legs are free from the confines of their ties, but I can still feel the patterns of rope marks left on my skin.

When I finally kneel on the ground, Naomi helps me shift to one side so I rest on my hip while Bex undoes the Takate Kote on my upper body.

Each brush of the rope against my skin sends chills down my body. The combination of smooth, consistent motion and the roughness of the fibers on my skin is the perfect combination.

I feel a new sensation as the pressure on my body is released. It's heavy but comfortable, leading to a sleepiness that I want to sink into. Bex helps me return my arms to my sides. She moves her palms up and down my arms, before helping me stretch out the now free muscles and helping return blood flow to various parts of my body.

Alvie's soft voice comes through my haze. "Bex and I will help you to the couch, okay?"

I nod, letting him know I understand.

When I'm settled on the couch, wrapped in a blanket with a bottle of water and a snack, Naomi sits beside me.

"How are you feeling?" she asks.

"Floaty," I answer with a small smile. "Free."

"Ah. Yes. The best kind of feeling," she replies, smiling back at me. "I know it well."

Wrapping her arms around me, she leans in to kiss me on the forehead and begins playing with my hair.

We watch as people approach Bex to tell her what a beautiful scene we did and ask her and Alvie questions about their craft. I can't help but giggle internally at how Naomi tenses whenever someone reaches out to touch one of her partners. It's pretty amusing.

A familiar deep voice nearly has me jumping out of my skin, though, when it calls out my name.

My head whips over, and my eyes widen at seeing my tall Viking looking a mess. His hair is disheveled as though he's been running his hands through it and tugging on it anxiously. His eyes are wide with concern, but for what I know not. Every muscle in his body is coiled tightly, ready to spring or snap.

Naomi is standing in front of me before he can get within reach.

"I don't think this is a good idea, Gunnar," Naomi says slowly, glancing around at the eyes that are already shifting in our direction. "I think you should leave her with us for a bit."

"I just want to take care of her," he says, his voice gravely and rough. "I'm the one who takes care of her."

"She didn't ask you to this time, though," Naomi says softly, lightly touching his chest. "We've got her, Gunnar."

"She's..." He takes a shaky breath. "I just want to..."

Another, much larger hand comes down on his shoulder, tugging him back a step.

Alvie turns Gunnar to face him more directly, his frame slightly slimmer but still matching Gunnar's.

"She's okay, man," Alvie tells his friend. "We've got her."

"Just..." Gunnar takes a step back, trying to turn in my direction so he can look at me. "Let me know when you want to go home?"

I glance between him and Naomi, then at Alvie, who waits patiently.

"I don't want to." My voice is small, much to my frustration. "I don't want to go home right now."

"Selene," he says, his voice soft but firm. "I don't think..."

"I don't really care what you think right now," I snap as my fire returns.

I can feel how others in the room are paying attention to us, but I ignore the watchful eyes.

I stand and look over Gunnar's shoulder, ignoring him in favor of speaking with Alvie.

"Alvie, would it be alright if I stay with y'all for a while?" I ask, then turn to Naomi and speak softly to her, silently hoping she understands what I really mean. "I want to go home with you, Nay. I want to go to the ranch."

She gives me a sad smile. "Then that's what we'll do."

Bex moves next to her husband, and I see something unspoken pass between them and Naomi, who's still protecting me from my fiancé.

My question was directed to Alvie, but after the glances between the three of them, Bex is the one to speak for their household. "Of course. We were going to head back tomorrow morning. Do you want to stay with us for the night?"

Naomi looks back at me with a bright smile and takes my hand from under the blanket I'm still wrapped in. "You can stay in the extra bed in our room. I'll snuggle between Bex and Alvie for the night."

"Selene. We don't have to do this," Gunnar interjects, making my body tense.

Turning around, Naomi faces off with Gunnar for a final time.

"Selene has expressed what she needs." Her expression is like stone. "It's not you right now."

Gunnar's eyes go wide with the same shock I imagine a person experiences when they're hit with a bullet to the chest.

I don't think Gunnar and I have genuinely had a fight of this magnitude before. The way he's looking at me, with a look of such betrayal, tells me this might, in fact, be our first real war.

Naomi squeezes my hand, drawing my attention away from Gunnar's distraught expression.

"I just..." I trail off, trying to find the words to express myself. "I need time to myself. Okay?"

Despite the hurt clearly written across his expression, Gunnar nods and turns around to speak with Alvie.

I can't hear their exchange, but it's like all the fight leaves me at that moment, and I'm suddenly drained. The freedom I felt earlier is but a faint memory in my body.

Sitting back down in my spot on the couch, I let the exhaustion take over. My head leans against the arm of the couch, and I curl into myself under the blanket with my eyes closed.

When Gunnar is done speaking with Alvie and Bex, I hear him turn to address my guard dog.

"Naomi, can I speak with her for a minute?" he asks, his tone clear and deliberately calm to mask his inner feelings.

Naomi must decide it's okay, because a moment later, there's a light touch on my knee, making me open my eyes.

"I'm going to let you have your time, but this isn't an ending, Selene." Determination returns to him as he speaks. "You're my person, my everything. When... when you're ready to talk, let me know. Okay?"

My throat closes with emotion, and I'm unable to speak, so I simply nod in response.

Watching him walk away breaks my heart, but I also feel a mix of relief, which is what I choose to focus on.

This is what I want, what I need.

I just need a moment to breathe.

An hour to collect and check in with myself.

A few days away from being under the microscope of his constant attention.

I love Gunnar with all my heart.

But you can't thrive if you can't breathe.

He says I'm his sun, the center of his universe.

Only a sun blocked, overshadowed, is simply an eclipse.

You can't see her at all.

It's as though she's not there.

24

SELENE

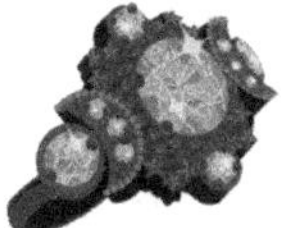

September 16—Mars square Neptune, Moon in Capricorn

My friends were more than willing to let me hide at the ranch, even if they didn't entirely understand what was happening between Gunnar and me.

Nevertheless, the next morning, Alvie let me pack my bags and throw them in the back of his truck with the rest of Naomi and Bex's stuff. We girls drove back in Bex's car while Alvie provided bag transport, and we chatted the whole way back to the ranch as though nothing was wrong in the world.

Arriving at the ranch, though, the mood in the car shifted.

"Do you want to stay with us in the house, Lena? You can stay in the extra guest room," Naomi asks, turning over her shoulder from the passenger seat to face me directly. "Or would you prefer to stay in one of the cabins?"

"Either is fine with us, sweetie," Bex says.

I already know what I need, though.

Just time.

Time alone.

"A cabin would be great," I reply, the answer slipping off my tongue easily. "I think I just need some time alone with my thoughts."

"That sounds like a good plan." Bex nods, still keeping her eyes forward as we pass the main house and weave our way down the rural back roads of the property.

"But maybe not too much alone time?" Naomi says. "If you're gonna be out here, I demand bestie time."

Laughter bursts from my chest. "Of course, Nay."

"Oh! Maybe we can do morning yoga together," Naomi cheers. "Bex and I have started doing it pretty regularly, and it's way more fun than I thought it would be."

I raise my eyebrows at my best friend, who's not known for being the most athletic person.

"I know, I was shocked too," she chuckles. "But it will be fun. Promise."

"Nay..." Bex says, her tone implying there's more to the story.

"We do it at 6 a.m., though." She cringes at the reminder. "But we do breakfast after, and it's a great way to start the day!"

I chuckle at her insistence. "Babe, you forget I'm a Pilates girl —7 a.m. classes four times a week. Just come, grab me, and I'll join. I'll need to borrow workout clothes, though."

Naomi beams. "Of course!"

Just then, we pull up to the cabin, and my shoulders drop in relief.

"I'll text you the code for the keypad," Bex says, pulling out her phone as Naomi exits the car.

Climbing out of the car, I round the vehicle to meet her on the cabin's porch.

My best friend looks at me with sympathy. I resent it, but the love behind it calms the feeling, so it doesn't hurt at all.

"I'm so sorry," Nay says softly, taking my hands in her own.

"What for?" I ask

"I was so caught up in my shit for so long with Bex and Alvie...

It was rough there for months, and you supported me through it. Then things were good, and I ... I didn't see how unhappy you were."

"I'm fine," I lie.

She studies me for a minute. Her eyes roam every bit of my face, looking for every cue I can't help but hide from her.

"No," she says, her inner therapist calling me out on my bullshit. "You're not happy, Lena. And I'm a shitty friend for not realizing sooner."

Silence settles between us, and I look over at Bex, who's still sitting patiently in the car, to avoid continuing the line of questioning I know Naomi wants to pursue.

"Thanks for letting me stay," I tell her as I turn back to face her.

"Of course. You're always welcome here. It's a good place to think." She pauses. "And heal."

"Yeah. Thank you," I reply, knowing that's exactly what I need.

"Can I?" she trails off. "I'm gonna go into therapist mode for a minute."

I chuckle, knowing she couldn't help herself if she tried.

"You're always welcome, of course. But something needs to change," she tells me. "Whatever happened at the club? It's not good for you. You seem... unsure?"

"I think you're right, Nay," I reply, tears starting to well in my eyes.

"Oh, Lena," Naomi says as she wraps her arms around me.

"It hurts. It all hurts." I breathe deeply, trying to get myself under control.

"I know. I know, Lena," Naomi says. "You're grieving. Life has changed a lot for you since your diagnosis."

"I haven't lost anything. No one died."

"You did, though. You lost yourself. The person you thought you were? That person no longer exists." She sighs, hugging me tighter. "You don't need to justify your grief. Heartbreak is a process, not a moment in time."

My breathing evens out. "When did you get so wise?"

"I've learned a few key lessons this year," she chuckles, pulling back to look at me. "Are you and Gunnar okay?"

"I hope so," I tell her honestly.

"You will be. He loves you." She smiles hopefully.

"Sometimes love isn't enough, Nay," I tell her softly. "What if..."

She cuts me off. "You can't fixate on the 'what if' scenarios, Lena. You'll drive yourself crazy."

"Yeah, ain't that the truth." I laugh, my voice becoming watery again. "So, what now? What's next?"

"I don't know, but if you figure it out before I do, don't keep me in the dark. I want answers, too." She laughs.

"Same."

"Deal?" she asks.

"Deal," I promise her. "I love you, Nay."

"I love you, Lena."

September 17—Full Moon in Pisces

Waking up to the rising sun after a night alone after such an emotional fight is sobering.

Watching the world come to life as the rhythm of nature plays its song is breathtaking, but the knowledge that this isn't forever casts a shadow over whatever joy I felt on the porch this morning.

By the time breakfast with Naomi and her partners rolls around, I'm entirely drowning in my depressing thoughts. Thankfully, the trio mostly leaves me to indulge in my internal spiral.

Relationships take work, but I don't believe they should be hard.

The first requires time and effort to be successful, whereas the second is a tax forced upon you simply for connecting with another person.

Relationships shouldn't feel like tax season.

After breakfast, I let Naomi know I'm going to go on a walk to the river that runs through the property. I'll probably go for a swim while I'm down there since the temperature is still in the eighties despite it being mid-September.

Naomi lets me borrow a bathing suit and towel, which I gratefully accept, though she becomes annoyingly pushy about slathering me with sunscreen. She even sends me off with a cooler of food and a large full water bottle.

Ultimately, the journey to the river doesn't take long from the main house, and before long, I'm lounging on a towel on the dock Alvie built into the riverbank, soaking up the sunshine.

The peace and quiet of my surroundings settle into my bones, the sun melting away the tension that has had my body coiled tightly for the past months. The sounds of nature fill the air around me, and I let myself get lost in the peace of the moment.

When the sun is nearly burning me alive and I've flipped and flopped my way to an even tan, I decide to take a dip in the river.

The cool water of the Guadalupe River envelops me as I make my way down the ladder and into the water. Once fully in, I take a deep breath and submerge my head beneath the surface.

Sound is muffled down here. It's like being in a sleeping pod where nothing can disturb you. It's just you and the water.

When my lungs start burning, I come up for air. My hands smooth back my hair from my face, and I tilt my chin up to take in the rays of the sun still shining bright as ever.

With the water enveloping me, I let it carry away the tension and fear that have plagued me since my diagnosis. I let tears of relief slide down my face and into the water as I grieve my old self and the life I once lived.

With my emotions purged, I let myself enjoy the moment, floating in the water until my fingers are prunes before I haul myself out and gather my things to eat in the shade of the cypress trees along the riverside.

By the time I finish the lunch Naomi packed for me and the entire bottle of water, I'm dry enough to slip my shoes back on and make my way back to the main house.

When I enter, greeted by the cool AC, I see Naomi sitting on the couch with her craft supplies.

"Hey, Nay," I say, setting the cooler back in the kitchen and unpacking what's left inside into the fridge.

"How was your swim?" she asks, not looking up from her embroidery project. "Feeling better?"

"Very much. A lot more relaxed," I tell her, walking around the kitchen island and into the living room to join her on the couch.

"Good. That's good," she says, nodding before stopping her task and looking up at me as I sit down. "Your phone's been going crazy this morning, though."

She looks guilty, and I already know she's looked at the previews my phone gives.

"Who's been texting?" I ask.

"Gunnar?" she says, her voice lilting up at the end of his name.

I can't help the sigh that escapes, though.

For as perfect as this day started and as peaceful a morning as I've had so far, there was no way it could last forever.

Reality was bound to come crashing back in at some point.

Getting up from the comfy couch, I walk to the kitchen island where my phone is plugged in.

I'm met with a flood of notifications when I tap the screen.

I scroll through the calls and texts on my locked screen, taking in the overwhelming number before summoning the courage to open my phone and confront the notifications directly.

Most of them are from Gunnar, asking questions about how I

am, updates on Beef Cake and more about wedding planning. All of them are bids for attention, Gunnar trying to connect with me in whatever way I want him to.

I take my phone back to the couch, and Naomi silently hands me a blanket to wrap myself in while I scroll through everything.

There are also two texts from Ivy.

> **IVY**
>
> I'm so sorry. I didn't realize that email was going to turn Gunnar into Groomzilla. I've been fielding calls from him all morning.
>
> I owe every bride I've ever worked with an apology.

Compared to Gunnar's texts, Ivy's actually manages to elicit a smile out of me, and I shoot off a quick response to her before tackling Gunnar's string of messages.

I try to keep things short and concise to minimize the number of responses I get.

> **SELENE**
>
> I'm good. Went for a swim this morning in the river, which is why I've been away from my phone.
>
> Beef Cake looks very handsome today. Thank you for the photos.

I sigh, knowing this last message is going to get a reaction. Every fiber of my being wants to avoid sending it, but it's necessary at this point—for my health and my sanity.

> **SELENE**
>
> Also, I want to pause wedding planning. I think it's too much right now, and I need a break.

Immediately, my phone starts to ring, and Gunnar's contact pops up on my screen.

I glance up at Naomi, whose attention is now focused on my phone.

Looking her in the eyes, I can tell she sees my sheer panic. Putting down her project on the coffee table, she crawls over to me on the couch while my phone continues to ring.

I'm frozen in place. I can't move, can't breathe.

What have I done?

What am I doing?

"Do you want me to answer for you?" Naomi asks earnestly.

I can only bring myself to nod.

Naomi takes my phone from my hand and answers for me, putting it on speaker so I can hear both sides of the conversation.

"Selene?" Gunnar's voice comes through the phone's speaker.

"It's Naomi, but Selene is here with me," Naomi says.

"Can I talk to her alone?" Gunnar asks.

Naomi looks over at me; all I can do is shake my head.

"Not right now. Sorry, Gunnar." Naomi pauses. "I know you love her. *She* knows you love her. I think she's just overwhelmed right now and needs a break."

Naomi glances at me, sadness in her eyes—a look that clearly shows she understands how I feel.

"I just want to talk to her. She can't just send a message like that and not talk to me," Gunnar says. "She can't call off the wedding and not talk to me about it."

Naomi looks at me with wide eyes and a slack jaw.

"I'm not calling off the wedding," I interject defensively. "I just need a break from all the questions and decisions, okay?"

"There you are," Gunnar says with relief in his voice. "Luna, I just need you to talk to me."

"No," I say firmly. "I've said everything I need to say. *You're not listening to me.* That's the whole problem here."

"I am listening. Or I'm trying to," he says.

"Well then, *hear me* when I tell you I need a break from

wedding planning, not you or our relationship. *Wedding planning.* I need the escalator to stop. I need off this rollercoaster." I take a deep breath, looking at Naomi for support and grabbing her hand from underneath my blanket. "If you need anything, have your people talk to my people. Okay?"

Silence crackles through the air as I wait for Gunnar to respond, but he says nothing.

"I need time for myself—to breathe, to simply exist as me," I say softly. "Please give me that."

Naomi squeezes my hand, and my shoulders relax as we wait for Gunnar's voice to filter through the speaker once more.

"Okay. I can do that," Gunnar acquiesces, talking to himself more than to me. "It's like a spiritual retreat. She's going on one of her spiritual retreats. I'll let her go off for a while, and then she'll be back."

He takes a deep breath, and I can tell he's steeling himself and shutting away the vulnerabilities he's facing right now.

"Okay, but you can't go radio silent on me," Gunnar finally says, with more strength in his voice than before.

"Agreed," Naomi interjects, with a concerned and understanding look.

"Okay. I can agree to that," I say.

Gunnar sighs, and I can practically see how he sags with relief through the phone.

"I love you, Luna," he says softly.

"Love you, Viking," I reply.

"Awe. Love y'all too!" Naomi says with a sassy smile, drawing a chuckle from Gunnar and me.

"Okay. Well, bye ladies," Gunnar says after a few moments of silence.

"Bye," I tell him before hitting end on the call.

Naomi waits as I settle back onto the couch, letting me sit with whatever I'm feeling.

Only I don't know what I'm feeling, and I don't really think there's a script here to follow. There is no code to tell me what needs to happen next, or an error code to tell me what to fix.

Soon, the unidentifiable feelings in my chest overflow, and suddenly there are tears streaking down my face.

"Oh, Lena," Naomi says, shifting me so I can fall into her lap and cry while she runs her fingers through my hair. "It will be okay. It will all be okay."

"You can't promise that," I sniffle. "It's like part of your therapist code or whatever."

"Well, it's a good thing I'm your friend and not your therapist, then, isn't it?" She chuckles. "I'm fully in support of any delusional dreams you want to have right now. I'm choosing the option where this all works itself out. Sound good?"

"Sounds perfect," I hiccup.

"Wanna watch a movie and eat our weight in ice cream?" Naomi asks hopefully. "There are gallons of Blue Bell in the deep freezer in the garage—even that nasty bride's cake flavor you love."

"Why on earth would you have it if you don't like it?" I giggle, pushing myself up to look at my best friend.

"Because I asked Alvie to go to town last night to stock up and asked him to get some for my bestie. That's why." She smiles, giving my hand on her thigh a squeeze. "Anything for you, Lena."

Tears threaten me again, but I hold them back and choke down the sobs that want to escape from my throat.

"Okay. Ice cream and movie time," Naomi says, all seriously. "Let's go."

GUNNAR

September 19—Sun Trine Pluto

It's been two?

Three?

It's been a few days since Selene texted me to tell me she wanted to pause wedding planning.

Since that one message, I haven't moved from my spot on the couch.

My whole system is in shock.

How did everything go so terribly wrong so quickly?

My phone chimes, and I glance at it to find a text from my friend, Emir.

EMIR

Open up. We're outside.

When I don't respond after a few minutes, banging filters through the house from the front door.

GUNNAR

Try the door handle. It's unlocked.

Moments later, the door swings wide, letting in voices from outside.

Fuck. I don't want to be around anyone right now.

When Emir walks into the room and spots me on the couch, he tries to look furious, but his concern comes through clearly as day. Marshall, on the other hand, who is only steps behind, just looks shocked as he takes in the room and me.

I must look like a total mess. I haven't showered in... a while, nor have I bothered to clean up the bottles of beer and takeout boxes littered around the living room.

"You haven't been to the office in four days, man... You haven't taken a day off work like... ever," Emir starts, taking in the room in all its chaos. "When I said to take a few days off, I wasn't really picturing you on the couch in your boxers and socks looking like you haven't showered in several days."

"Well, I *haven't* showered in several days. So, fuck you, man," I growl under my breath.

"Dude," Marshall snaps, his tone very contrary to his usual happy-go-lucky demeanor. "The fuck is wrong with you? We're here to help."

"Well, unless you know a way to keep Selene from giving back the ring and breaking up with me completely, you're not very fucking helpful," I snap, immediate guilt flooding me as I look at my friends.

Quiet fills the room as they absorb my words. There's a silent expectation, an insistence, for me to fill them in on everything, but it just feels exhausting.

"I just wanted a beer and a few days away. I didn't think I'd have to explain my life to you all." I sigh, running my hand down my face.

"A beer? Dude. This is at least six packs that you've downed," Emir says, looking around the room at the carnage I've managed to inflict upon my home. "I'm finding trash bags."

Looking around the room, I realize how bad things have gotten over the past few days. The space around me reflects my mental state: cluttered, overwhelmed, and sad.

As Emir wanders off to the kitchen to find what he's searching for, Marshall comes over cautiously and sits in the chair to my right.

"You're really not looking good, man," he says with understanding in his voice. "Talk to us."

"I... I don't know how." My voice is smaller than I would like, lacking all hope.

"Start with telling us why, maybe?" Marshall prompts, his eyes conveying a gentle comfort I need right now. "What happened with Selene?"

"I fucked up with Selene, but I'm not really sure what I did," I tell him, letting my head hang. "She paused wedding planning, which kind of sent me spiraling."

Marshall's eyes are wide when I look back at him, his mouth agape in shock.

"Why didn't you tell me?" he asks, hurt in his voice. "Emir called this morning saying you needed an intervention, but he didn't say why."

"He didn't know either." I sigh. "I just said I was taking a few days. He didn't know. I didn't tell anyone."

"Well, that's fucking shitty of you," Marshall says, the frustration in his voice evident.

His outrage almost shocks me out of my paralysis.

"I didn't think anyone would care," I tell him. "So, it seemed pointless to mention it to anyone."

Marshall shakes his head vigorously. "We're your friends. Whether we get it or not, we'll always show up for you. So, now that we're here, talk."

"I..." My words are cut off by Emir re-entering the room.

"Your pantry is shockingly immaculately organized for

someone who can't pick up a fucking empty bottle," he says, tossing trash bags in our direction. "Marshall and I will clean. You're taking a fucking shower, Pig-Pen. *Then* we can talk about your shit."

Coming around to where I sit on the couch, he shoves me until I'm on my feet, and he's able to usher me to the stairs in the direction of my bedroom and shower.

"And change your sheets," Emir yells up the stairway as I get to my room. "If they smell anything like you, you'll thank me later!"

Taking my time, I start by changing the sheets on Selene and my king-size bed, knowing it will make me feel better at the end of the day.

Looking around the room, I pick up some of the mess I've let accumulate over the past few days before stripping down and hopping in the shower.

Twenty minutes later, scrubbed within an inch of my life, I step out of the shower.

When I wipe down the mirror, I'm confronted with the reflection of my misery.

I may be clean, but the sorrow that has taken up residence in my chest is just as present as it has been since that single text from Selene after our phone call.

SELENE

The wedding is just too much right now. I need a
break from everything.

She didn't say it, but the implied "a break from you" was there nonetheless.

It's what started the spiral, but my brain has been replaying every moment of the past nine months. Every conversation and touch with her is examined under the same microscope I'd use to review security footage.

But nothing I can think of helps me understand her any better.

She's a mystery to me.

When all I want is to *know* her.

Dressed in a fresh pair of sweats and a t-shirt, I make my way downstairs to find my depression cave has been swept away by my friends.

Emir and Marshall sit on the couch, each with a cold beer.

Another bang comes from the front door, and Emir wanders over to answer it.

When Alvie steps into the room, I finally manage a small smile.

"This isn't nearly as bad as I thought it'd be," he says to Emir at his side as he glances around the room. "And he looks fine."

"Should have seen it all when we got here," Emir gripes. "He looked about as messy as the room did and smelled worse."

Alvie lets out a hearty laugh, filling the room with an energy that hasn't been present for several days. He settles in with the rest of us on the couches, but we hear the front door swing wide open before we can dive into conversation.

"Food's here!" Emir's husband, Derek, can be heard from the foyer, his voice bouncing through the room as he strides in carrying multiple bags of takeout.

I glance over at Marshall, who's gone into total shock despite meeting the man several times now, and reach out to close his mouth.

"That's Derek Bonner," he whispers to me in awe, just as he does every time he sees the massive linebacker. "Derek-fucking-Bonner."

I nod, chuckling at Marshall's continuous star-struck state whenever he sees the man. It's 100% a total man-crush at this point.

Derek comes in, utterly unfazed by Marshall's stupor.

Once we're all settled in with food and have caught up on

everyone else's lives and the shit talking is done, attention turns back to me.

"Your turn," Emir says, using his Board of Directors voice. "Either you tell us what's been going on, or we use your interrogation techniques against you."

I cringe, knowing how good Emir has become at those.

"Alright," I acquiesce, then dive into the past nine months of my life, which I've been keeping to myself.

It's late, and the sun has long since set by the time we're done with our lively discussion about my love life.

When there's a lull in the conversation, Alvie fills the silence. "Alright, guys. I think it's time I head home."

Protests arise from the group, but Alvie has a look in his eyes that I know well. One that's full of love and longing for his people.

"Nah, guys. Let the man get home to his partners," I cut in with a smirk. "Let him abandon me in my time of need for some girls."

Alvie's brow furrows at first, then he bursts into laughter.

"Yeah. Those girls have me whipped better than I could ever dole out in a scene," he jokes, the lighthearted guy I know, coming back in a mere instant.

Alvie rises, and the rest of us follow. Hugs are exchanged, but I'm the last for him to say goodbye to.

"Selene asked me to bring Beef Cake back with me," he says gently, but my heart stops regardless.

"Right. That makes sense. Selene probably misses him," I tell him after taking a few calming breaths, then I turn to find the blasted fur-ball. "He's probably in his room."

"He has a *room*?" Alvie asks, shocked by the idea.

"Yup," I shrug. "He's really the man of this household. Selene tells me all the time that he outranks me."

"You're kidding me," he says from behind me as we walk through the house toward Beef Cake's room. "I swear, our women are unhinged. Naomi insists we let Milkshake sleep in the bed with us now. It's a fucking cattle dog. She should sleep in the barn, but when I said that, Bex gave me this disappointed look, and Naomi looked like she was going to cry."

"I'm guessing the dog sleeps in the bed now," I say, knowing Alvie and how much he loves his girls.

"The dog sleeps in the bed now," he gripes, but when I turn back to look at him, there's a smile on his face.

Sure enough, when we reach Beef Cake's room, he's asleep in his bed by the window.

We close the door behind us and, after instructing Alvie to go to the closet and grab the cat carrier, I move slowly toward the beast.

"Don't make this difficult, boy," I tell the cat quietly as I approach him.

I'm able to scoop him up, but the second he's in my arms, he yowls and claws.

"Fuck! Such a dick!" I shout in pain when he scratches me especially hard.

Alvie and I wrestle him into his carrier, but the massive cat continues to vocalize loudly how incredibly offended he is by our behavior.

I pack a second bag with his dry and wet food, treats, and toys before leading Alvie and the cat to the front door.

Alvie slips out with Beef Cake, still screaming at us in annoyance, and I follow them down to his truck.

He secures the cat's carrier in the passenger seat with the seatbelt before turning to take the bag of supplies from me.

"Thanks for making the trip," I tell him when he closes the door on the vocal cat. "And sorry you're gonna have him to deal with the whole drive home."

"All good, man," Alvie says with a genuine smile. "Worth it to see you and the guys."

"Yeah." I look back at the house where the other three men

remain. "I'm grateful for y'all. I really am. I needed this more than I knew."

"Anytime," Alvie says, opening his arms for another hug, which I gratefully accept.

Wrapped in each other's arms, we stood outside like that for a while, long beyond what might be normal for two guys to hug.

When I pull back, Alvie is looking at me with understanding.

"You'll be okay," he says. "It will work itself out. Just give her a little time. Everyone fucks up, and Selene is a good woman."

"Too good for me," I admit. "She deserves better."

"No." His eyes narrow at me. "She deserves you. And you're worthy of her. I promise."

We give each other another brief hug before he lets go and rounds his truck to drive away with a wave.

Looking up at the sky and the moon, which shines brightly, I take solace in the knowledge that Selene is under the same sky as I.

She might not be here physically. But as long as the moon is in this universe, she's still with me.

26

SELENE

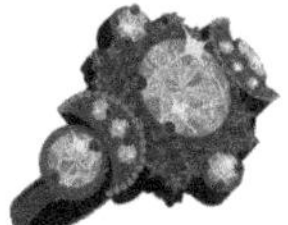

September 24—Moon in Virgo, Mercury trine Uranus

The call came in *early* in the morning, early enough that sleep mode was still enabled on my phone. But only a short list of people can break through during my precious hours of sleep.

So, when Elsie's number popped up on my phone around 4 a.m., I answered immediately. Well, as immediately as my groggy self could. We knew she was due soon, but she had her C-section scheduled for next week. A last-minute trip to the hospital at that hour was not part of the plan.

But in that one call from Elsie's phone to tell us that she was in labor, Marshall let us know they were already at the hospital. It was enough for me to rouse from bed and rally the troops to pack up and head into the city.

One phone call to Naomi and the Silva-Hall household was up and packing their bags so they could stay in the city for a few days to support our friends.

Within an hour, we were on the road, driving the two and a

half hours to the medical center in their SUV. For nearly the entire drive, I was texting *someone* to catch them up to speed.

First, I announced it to the group chat, minus Elsie, who was a little busy at the moment, which earned a lot of exclamation points in the thread. Then, I started reaching out to the others in our friend group.

Though fearless as I may seem to others, Gunnar was still the last person I called.

"Pick up, Gunnar," I whine as I call his phone for the third time. "Get your ass out of bed."

I understand not wanting to have a television in your bedroom, but not having your phone seems like a step too far. Which means I fully plan on holding this over his head for a while as a perfect example of why he should have it more easily accessible.

"Hello?" Gunnar's deep, groggy voice comes through the speaker. "Selene? Are you okay? What's wrong?"

"Yes. No. Ugh." I take a deep breath before everything comes tumbling out. "I'm fine. Nothing's wrong. Elsie is in the hospital and is in active labor. Alvie is driving me and the girls to the medical center now. We should arrive in..." I check the center console for the estimated maps. "Fifteen minutes. Get your ass over there now. There should already be a few people there to meet you. Try calling Emir first. Okay?"

"All I heard was Elsie and hospital before you switched to Spanish, Luna." I can hear the satisfied smirk through the phone, which only riles me more.

"Get your ass to the hospital ASAP. I'll text you the info. And call Emir. He should be there already to meet you," I tell him more slowly.

"Of course. I'll leave now." I can hear him pulling open drawers, likely to grab clothes to change into, and then they shut again before he speaks. "Do you need me to bring anything for you?"

"No," I tell him. "I've got everything in my bag."

"Your bag?" he asks, hope in his voice that I wish wasn't there. "You're coming home?"

I sigh. "Just for this. Don't make it into some big thing. Okay?"

"Okay," he says, more stoic this time. "I'll see you at the hospital."

"Sounds good."

"Love you, Luna." He says just before hanging up.

Sighing, my heart heavy, I let my head rest against the window until the eyes burning into me from all directions brings my attention back to my fellow passengers.

"No comment," I tell Bex, who looks like she's starved for information.

"You're gonna have to catch them up eventually," Naomi tells me.

"Yeah. Just... not right now?" I ask, hoping no one in the car will push the issue at this early hour.

"You've been hiding out for almost a week at my ranch, Selene. And I haven't asked a single damn question." Alvie says, his voice lacking the judgment I presumed would be there. "But I love that fiancé of yours like he's my brother and, while my girls may have my balls for this..." He glances over at Bex quickly before his eyes return to the road. "If you break that man's heart, you'll find yourself out on the highway faster than a cat lappin' chain lightnin'."

I look over at Naomi, who just shrugs with a small smile.

"I don't want to, Alvie." I sigh, which only earns me a quick glare over his shoulder. "I mean, yes, sir. I'll do my damndest not to break his heart."

"Good," he says, nodding like I've given him exactly the answer he was looking for.

"You're right, honey," Bex says with a grin. "We will have your balls for it, though."

ELSIE AND MARSHALL never told us *not* to show up at the hospital. They said nothing about whether our presence was requested... or not.

My motto is 'ask forgiveness, not permission' when it comes to these types of things. So what if it wasn't an explicit invitation? I was going to show up for my friends in whatever way they needed me.

This is how Naomi, Bex, Alvie, and I, along with a handful of Elsie and Marshall's closest friends, all arrived in the hospital's waiting room in the early hours of the morning to welcome their new baby into the world.

Ivy called out of work completely, which was fine with her boss, Juliana, who told Ivy to pass along well wishes and sent the most enormous bouquet of assorted yellow flowers I've ever seen.

With her next product launch coming up, Zuri had to step out for a few meetings, but she always returned with coffee and food for everyone throughout the day.

Emir and Derek were there for the first few hours before they both had to go to work and practice, respectively. Their attendance nearly caused the father to have a heart attack when he realized one of his sports idols was at the hospital for *his* baby's birth.

When Gunnar arrived, the small group I had been talking with fell silent. By this point, everyone knew *something* was going on between the two of us, even if they didn't know what it was.

Already pissed at him for how late he was, I was so close to wheeling around and laying into him when I noticed everyone staring.

But as I turn, I notice the multiple large bags he has in his hands, and the scolding on the tip of my tongue disappears.

The man had brought presents. Presents that he had clearly been holding onto for a while, which I didn't know about.

"What is all this?" I ask him as he makes his way toward me.

"This?" he replies, lifting the bags a little. "Just some things I thought the group might need."

"Gunnar," I warn.

"Don't freak out," he says, his tone already telling me that I'm absolutely going to freak out.

"Marshall filled me in on his plans for after the baby is born and the surprise he got for Elsie," Gunnar says slowly. "I figure we can contribute to the surprise while we're here."

He hands me one of the bags, and I open it like a clown is about to jump out before peering inside.

"Boxes?" I ask, staring at him blankly.

"Photos. For their new house," Gunnar explains. "Evidently Marshall bought a house and has been collecting a ton of furniture and things, then storing them in the pool-house. I caught him moving boxes out earlier this week, and he told me what he's been doing while she's at work every day."

"Hold on. He bought a *house* for her?" I stop him. "When did this happen? Does she know?"

"No, absolutely not. But it must have been recent—I'm not sure when he closed," Gunnar says with a shrug. "His mom has been helping him decorate, and I've been helping put together these photo albums for them. Figured it'd be a good activity for us while we wait."

My heart swells at the sight of this incredibly thoughtful man.

All the thinking I've been doing over the past week has only made me even more confused now.

I take the bag silently and walk into the waiting area, the rest of our group already there, with Gunnar trailing behind me.

When I don't say anything further, Gunnar starts explaining his plan, much like an activities director at a retirement home on craft night.

For hours, people come and go from the waiting room down the hall from Elsie's delivery room. Every single person stops to help with Gunnar's project for at least a few minutes before they announce their departure. Texts constantly come in through the group chat, and updates are sent out immediately after every time Marshall comes to talk with us.

The energy in the waiting room was beautiful. Everyone in attendance was filled with pure joy and excitement.

The tension between Gunnar and me?

It wasn't nearly as pleasant as the feelings among the rest of the group.

Around hour ten, Marshall came out looking both exhausted and distraught.

"Selene?" His voice floats over the crowd, and a hush falls over us. "Elsie's asking for you."

"Me?" I squeak, standing from the couch where I was sitting with Naomi.

"Yeah." I can see there's more to the story, hovering just behind his eyes. "The nurses said you're free to come back to visit."

"Oh. Okay. Yeah." I scramble to gather my bag before following Marshall down the hall to Elsie's room.

"Hey, princess," Marshall says soothingly as he enters the room.

"Oh, fuck off," Elsie snaps back at him, her fury and pain clear on her face.

"Okay," he says, drawing out the last vowel. "I'm gonna go."

Glancing between them as he makes his escape, I send out a silent question to my friend from where she sits in the hospital bed.

"He's getting on my nerves," Elsie says, followed by a chuckle, when I'm done closing the door behind me. "But what's new with that?"

"You sure you want me here?" I ask her hesitantly as I approach her bed.

"Yeah, girl. I need you here," she says with a small smile. "You're my people."

Tears spring to my eyes at the genuineness of her remark.

Many in our industry know Elsie as the ice queen, but hearing her call me *her people* is truly heartwarming. With her, that kind of admission doesn't come easily—especially after everything she's gone through with her dad.

"Elsie," I wobble out.

"Don't you dare start crying, or I'm going to cry," she says, her expression deadly serious.

"Yes, ma'am." I give her a little mocking salute. "What's up, boss?"

"I'm not your boss right now. Just your friend." She pauses, her face scrunched in pain.

Reaching out, I grab her hand and mirror her breathing.

"Sorry. These contractions are a bitch," she says, collapsing back on her bed. "I need to talk to you about something important."

"Okay," I reply tentatively.

"You and Gunnar are going through something, but you're both so important to me and Marshall. I don't think we would have made it this far without all your meddling."

"It's not meddling!" I defend jovially. "It's just a series of encouraging nudges."

Elsie rolls her eyes at me before continuing. "Whatever you're going through, I know you'll make it out the other side together." She takes a deep breath. "You know about my family, or lack thereof. But I don't think you realize how much you saved me when you brought me into this group, this family. *My* family."

"Elsie." Tears bubble to the surface. "You're gonna make me cry."

A watery laugh escapes her lips.

"Stop that right now." She chuckles before taking a deep

breath. "Selene, you are truly one of the most wonderful people, and I'm so honored to have met you. You taught me what it means to love someone, to be open to *being loved*. And I want that for my child, too."

The tears are coming in earnest now as she continues.

"I know we haven't talked about this, and it's a big undertaking. But I would love it if you'd agree to being my child's godmother. I want you in their life. I want them to see what I see in you. A woman who gives her heart freely to others and loves them with every ounce of her being. I want this child to be surrounded by love. For me, that means you."

Elsie's grin overshadows her tears and her pain for a minute as she looks at me.

So many emotions rush in all at once. Surprise and confusion come first, followed by a bright warmth that overwhelms me.

"Elsie, I..." I choke out, and a furrow forms in Elsie's brow.

"I know you don't want to have kids, but I was hoping..." she starts, but I cut her off.

"Oh, my Goddess. Yes! Sorry." I laugh through my sobs. "I would love that. I would love that very much."

"Oh. Good." She settles back into her bed. "Thank Goddess. I thought you were saying no, and I don't know if I could've handled that."

A cocoon forms, protecting this moment from the world around us. Tears run down our faces as we silently look at each other for a minute. All the love in the world that I have for this woman pours out as we cry together, adoration in every tear, laugh, and sob.

"I..." The words are in my heart, but I don't quite know how to vocalize them. "I would love nothing more than to be a godparent to your baby. I want to be in their life and yours for as long as I'm allowed."

"You'll always be welcome with us," Elsie replies, wiping a few salty tears. "Now, let's just hope that Gunnar says yes when Marshall asks him."

"He'll say yes," I say without hesitation. "I know he will."

Elsie smiles. "Yeah. He's good like that."

"He is." Tears spring up again.

"You want to tell me what's happening with you two?" she asks, her hand tightening on mine and her teeth gritting together as another contraction rolls through her body.

"This doesn't really seem like the right time to get into my messy love life," I chuckle, holding her hand through the pain.

"Trust me, this is the perfect time for a distraction," she finally replies a few moments later when the contraction is finished.

I nod, knowing I would give this woman the bra off my back.

"He loves me. So much." Elsie smiles at me with an understanding in her gaze that comforts me. "He loves me so much it's suffocating sometimes."

A laugh bursts from her lips. "I know that feeling."

I can't help but smile back at her, knowing her story and the journey went on with her partner, Marshall.

Then, I tell her everything. All of it. It all spills out in a flurry of words.

When I'm done, we have a moment of silence before Elsie speaks again.

"Don't ever keep us on the outside like this again. You take care of us all the time and show us how much you love us every day," she says, squeezing my hand tightly. The complete command with which she lives her life returns to her voice when she says, "When you do keep us in the dark, you deny us the opportunity to show you how much we love you. To show you that you're not alone. You're never alone, Selene. Never."

"I know," I say, with a little shame in my tone.

"I don't think you do yet." She shakes her head, but she still has a slight smile. "But we'll just have to start reminding you more often."

Another contraction hits much sooner than the last one.

"Fuck. I fucking hate pregnancy!" she shouts, the pain more significant than before. "Motherfucker!"

"I think I need to go get Marshall," I say, my eyes widening.

"Yes. Please," she pants. "That asshole is going to suffer for this."

I chuckle to myself. "And he'll love every second of it."

"Yeah, he will," she says through deep breaths. "He's a total masochist."

"You gonna be okay?" I ask, letting go of her hand.

She waves me away without a word, and I run through the halls back to the waiting area.

When I reach the large room, Marshall and Gunnar are standing to the side. Both of them have red rims around their eyes, as though they are crying just as much as Elsie and I were.

"Marshall! I think you should go back now," I call across the room. "And maybe call the doctor on your way."

Marshall bounces on the balls of his feet before giving Gunnar a quick bro hug and bounding back in the direction I came from.

Walking over to Gunnar, I eye him carefully.

"Did he ask you?" I ask quietly, mindful of the group of people that surrounds us.

"Yeah," he sighs, but a smile forms on his beautiful face. "You?"

"Yeah," I say, tears threatening me once again at the memory of Elsie and my moment.

Reaching for me, Gunnar brings me into his embrace, and I soak in his warmth as he holds me.

"I love you," he whispers into my hair.

"I know," I reply, holding back tears. "I know."

27

GUNNAR

September 25—Moon enters Libra, Mercury sextile Neptune

The nurses forced us all out around 9 p.m., but Selene was up and ready to go at 7 a.m. the next morning, so we could head back to the hospital when visiting hours were open again.

Around hour thirty of Elsie's labor, we learned that she had delivered a beautiful baby girl.

Marshall came striding into the waiting area, like the proud papa he is, and made the announcement to our cohort, which had gathered once again to support our friends.

"Bridgit Gabriela Law, born at 10:47 a.m., weighing in at seven pounds nine ounces and measuring 19 inches tall," he announced to the group with his signature broad smile. "She's perfect."

Emotion filled all of us. There were cheers and tears of joy from some of us and a mix of both for others. Many of our group passed along congratulations to Marshall and Elsie before taking off, promising to come back and visit another time to meet the baby. Still, Elsie had instructed Marshall to ask Selene and me to stay.

And Selene was not going to deny her friend anything.

It took a while for the doctors and nurses to clear Elsie for visitors, but we waited as patiently as possible to meet the new family member.

Marshall's mom was the first to see little Bridgit, followed by a few of his sisters who managed to make it into town for the occasion.

Finally, after what felt like forever, Marshall came back to the waiting room with another huge smile and an invitation for my fiancée and me to come back.

Immediately upon entering the room, both Elsie and Selene were crying.

I stood back near the doorway with Marshall to give them a moment together.

A look was exchanged between the new father and me, telling me this was a moment we would all remember forever.

It's one thing for a new member to be brought into our inner circle. Selene is constantly making new friends, many of whom have become quite close to us.

But this baby. Little Bridgit is an addition to our clan that inspires true wonder.

After the girls cry their fill, Elsie motions for me to join them.

"You ready to meet Uncle Gunnar, Bridgit?" Elsie whispers to her daughter.

My whole world tilts on its axis when I look down at the little girl.

I *know* that I'll protect her just as I would my own family because she is my family now. I've been given the honor of being part of her life, and I take that very seriously.

"She's gorgeous," I tell Elsie softly.

"Isn't she?" Marshall's voice comes from the other side of the hospital bed where he now stands, hand on his little girl's head. "She's perfect."

"She really is," Selene says with a small smile. "You realize I'm going to start shopping for her immediately, right?"

I suppress a chuckle, but my face must tell Elsie everything, anyway.

"I would expect nothing less, Selene," Elsie says with a glowing smile.

"Good," Selene says, satisfactorily. "First things first, this girl needs more glitter in her life. And a pair of sparkly boots to match her auntie's when she's big enough."

The three of us laugh openly at how seriously Selene makes her declaration, knowing she's dead serious about it all and probably making a list a mile long of all the things she will spoil this little girl with.

Selene leaves the bedside to get her bag, likely to grab a notebook to start writing down her list in her little world, and I step closer to my goddaughter.

The little bundle pops a hand out of her swaddle and reaches toward me, and I can't help but reach out my massive hand to meet hers.

Her tiny little hand with even smaller fingers isn't able to wrap around a single one of my fingers when she grasps onto me, and the feeling of her hand on my skin sends radiant warmth through my whole being.

"She's precious," I breathe out, looking up at her parents. "Thank you for the honor of allowing me into her life."

"Of course, man," Marshall says.

"We couldn't think of any two people we would trust more with her than you and Selene," Elsie says softly, looking down at her precious daughter.

A moment of silence passes with the three of us positioned like this, me looking down at my goddaughter in awe.

Then, Elsie looks at me with the same stern confidence she's known for. "Selene told me what's been going on."

"Oh."

"Fix it," she commands.

"I don't know how. If I did, I would have by now," I tell her honestly.

"A life with Selene means giving her the space to be independent from you, Gunnar," she says patiently. "But she's always going to need you. She's always going to come back. She's always going to love you. You don't have to worry about that."

"Then what is?" I ask.

"Worry about yourself. Your independence." Elsie smiles. "Selene loves all of us exactly as we are. She loves us because of our uniqueness, not despite it."

"I know that," I reply, probably a little too defensively.

"No. I don't think you do. Maybe it's becoming a mother that's making me wiser. So, I'm only going to tell you this once." Elsie sighs. "Selene is your whole world. Hell, your entire universe. She's the sun and the stars and all that. But a universe contains multitudes. You have to be equal to her to deserve her, Gunnar. Match her; don't stifle her. You can't contain an ever-expanding universe, so don't try."

I look up at Marshall, who has a knowing smirk.

"She's right, you know." His gaze moves down to Elsie, and he has the same wonder on his face that I have when I look at Selene. "Our girls aren't meant to be contained. They're meant for more than us; we're just lucky enough to be a part of their world."

I'm dumbfounded at Marshall's astute observation, his wisdom that surely has been lurking behind his Playboy facade this whole time.

Just then, Selene comes bounding back over, list in hand.

"Okay. So..."

I don't hear a word of what she says. I'm only able to focus on the radiance that she exudes.

I don't know how much time passes with the four of us there, but soon enough, a nurse who needs to do her job interrupts us, and Selene and I are ushered out of the room.

I'm still in a daze as we make it to my truck to start our way back to the house that hasn't felt like home since Selene went to stay out at the ranch.

"Gunnar? You okay?" Selene asks as I start the vehicle. "You've been awfully quiet. More than usual."

"Yeah. I'm good, Luna," I tell her honestly. "Just... it's a lot."

"Yeah," she says with a smile. "Bridgit is so cute. I can't wait until she gets a little bigger and I can squish her little cheeks and play with her."

I nod, the only thing I'm able to do at the moment.

Selene chatters the whole way home about one thing or another, and I nod along, following her wandering thoughts as best I can.

Parking the truck in the garage, I sit there as the engine turns off.

Quiet descends upon the cab when Selene realizes I haven't moved to get out and turns to face me fully.

"Gunnar? Everything okay?" she asks.

I look over at my fiancée, noticing how her brown curls have escaped her messy bun to frame her round face. The bright, twinkling eyes and wrinkled forehead staring at me with a worried expression, I want to wipe from her face forever.

"I want to be deserving of your love," I start, taking a deep breath as I prepare to lay my heart on the table. "I want you to choose me. Every day. I want to explore and conquer the universe with you."

"Okay," she says, drawing out the word.

"But I understand it better now. I understand *you* better now," I tell her earnestly.

"How's that?" Her brow furrows even deeper.

"I just..." I take in another steadying breath. "Just because you're off exploring on your own doesn't mean you aren't safe or that you won't come back. You've always been good on your own and always will be."

I reach out to her, cupping her face in the palm of my hand, satisfied when she leans into my touch.

"I've always felt pulled toward you," I tell her. "I'd follow you to the ends of the earth and beyond. But I'm realizing now that you have the same pull to me. While you pull me out into the universe, I'm your anchor to home."

"Gunnar," she says softly.

"You don't... I don't..." I sigh. "I want to marry you. To follow you on this journey of life. When you're ready, just let me know and I'll be right there in a heartbeat."

Selene's hand comes up to cup mine, and I lean in to kiss her on the forehead.

"I know you want to pause wedding planning. I respect that. It's a lot," I say, drawing away from the warmth of her tanned skin. "When you're ready to walk down the aisle with me, I'll be there, waiting for you."

28

SELENE

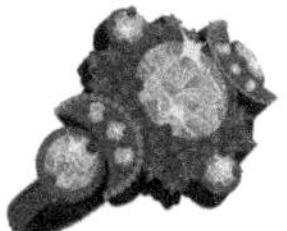

Gunnar's words are still echoing in my head, tangling with Elsie's earlier advice, as I sit in the car staring at the garage wall. It's impossible to ignore the truth in what they both said—or the ache it stirs in me.

I've been so focused on protecting my independence that I've built walls even he can't climb, forgetting that love isn't supposed to be a cage for either of us. But beneath all that, I know why I love him... It's the way he sees me—not the Goddess, not the challenge, not the fragile thing my illness sometimes makes me feel like— but *me*, and somehow still chooses me every single time.

In the beginning, Gunnar's infatuation with me was sweet, but over time, the realization of just how genuine that devotion was became awe-inspiring.

Gunnar has an incredible ability to show up for me exactly how I need him to. He comes with his heart open and mind eager to help and solve. I've always admired this about him, especially because he never seems to ask for anything in return.

Though that seems to be part of the issue, doesn't it?

How do you show up for someone completely without losing yourself to their needs and desires?

How do you maintain your independence while giving a person everything they need?

I may not have known Gunnar was it for me when I met him, like he did with me, but I've known for a long time that he's it for me.

If I were wishing upon a star, he's everything I could have asked for in a partner.

My mind starts circling his words.

I'll be waiting for you.

Though he may call me his Goddess, Gunnar has the patience of a saint.

He would wait forever if I asked him to.

If I said I wasn't ready, he would wait without question.

But I *am* ready, aren't I?

The way my thoughts are beginning to swirl has my breath picking up pace and my worries mounting.

The air around me seems sparse, and I'm having difficulty getting full breaths.

Frantically, I grab the door handle and yank the door open to let in some fresh air. Grabbing my purse, I get out of Gunnar's SUV and stumble over to my own car.

Settling into the driver's seat, I grip the steering wheel like my life depends on it and try to slow my breathing.

Once I've calmed myself enough, I put the car in reverse and back out of our driveway.

"I'm not running," I promise myself. "I just need to think."

When I get out of the garage, I circle through our half-moon drive and get onto the street. From there, everything happens on autopilot, and the next thing I know, I'm going 75 mph on the loop at noon.

My focus is only on the car beneath me and the road in front of me. Music floats around me as I drive, and I lose myself in the rhythm of the road.

I don't know how long I've been driving, but I don't recognize the streets listed on the exit signs like I do in my neighborhood.

A startling sound rings through the car's cab, and my notification system alerts me to an incoming call from Naomi.

I pick up on the second ring.

"Hey, Nay," I say absentmindedly.

"Lena? Where are you?" Naomi's voice is urgent. "We stopped by the house to drop off Beef Cake and the rest of your things, and Gunnar said you had gone out, but he didn't say where."

I force myself to breathe out before I respond. "Yeah. Just took myself for a drive. Needed to clear my head."

"Okay," she says tentatively, and I hear a door close behind her. "You wanna tell me what's going on? I'm alone now."

"I just…" I sigh, keeping my eyes on the road while trying to gather my thoughts. "Nay. How do you know when you're in love?"

"Oh no. We're full-on spiraling, aren't we?" Nay says with a forced lightheartedness in her tone.

"Fully," I confirm.

"Do you want delusional support or do you need to be talked back down to earth?" Naomi says helpfully.

"Can't I have both?" I pout, my lip pushed out, and all.

"I guess you can," Naomi chuckles. "Delusion first or last?"

"I don't know," I tell her honestly. "I'm overwhelmed. And Gunnar is so good…"

Naomi lets my words hang in the air. I know she's trying to wait me out, but my brain is too scrambled to put words together.

"And Gunnar being good is a problem?" she asks.

"Well… yeah," I tell her. "He's so perfect. And I'm so not."

"Nobody is perfect, Lena," Naomi reasons.

"Nay. Delusional spiral. I asked for delusional," I snap, a shaky laugh spilling out of my throat.

"Ah. Excuse me." She takes a dramatic breath. "Yes, Selene.

Gunnar is a perfect being, and you are just a speck of dirt on his shoe. Better?"

Her sarcastic insult manages to pull a giggle out of my throat.

"I don't know how to be with him anymore, Nay." I let the words fall out quickly, just to get them out of my head. "He's so good and does all this nice stuff for me. I don't know how to do it."

"Oh, woe is you. Life is so hard with a fiancé who loves you too much," she chuckles.

"No. Really." I take a deep breath in. "He does all these things for me without asking, and it's suffocating. I know he wants to be helpful, and he thinks that's what he's doing, but it's exhausting. I can't keep up."

"Then just let him," Naomi says flatly.

"What?"

"Let him. It's as simple as that," she continues. "If this is how he wants to show up for you in your relationship, then let him. That's his choice to make. You're only responsible for your own choices."

"I know that, but..."

"But what? He knows his capacity—or he should." I can practically hear her shrug through the phone. "I don't think this is a question of whether he's capable, but whether you'll let him prove just how willing and able he is."

"I don't understand," I say softly.

Naomi pauses, and I can hear the therapist gears in her head grinding against each other.

"You asked how you're supposed to know when you're in love, right?" she asks without giving me a moment to confirm. "Everyone sees love differently. There's no single way to define love or one universal experience of being loved."

Naomi pauses for a minute, and I wait for her to continue, curious to see where she's taking this.

"Lena, do you love me?" she finally asks.

"What? Of course I do!" I scoff. "Why would you even need to ask that?"

"Exactly. But you're not overthinking it, are you?" She takes a breath. "How do you know I love you? What is it that reminds you that you are loved?"

"I..." My voice catches in my throat before I admit. "I don't know."

"Think about it while you get your ass home," she says softly.

"Okay," I tell her, "I love you, Nay."

"Love you too, Lena," she replies.

Naomi's words run on a loop through my mind as I make my way home.

I pull into the garage, and when I walk through the door into the kitchen, I find Gunnar leaning over the counter, waiting for me.

His gaze whips to me, and he looks distraught.

"Selene," he starts.

"Wait." I stop him. He seems to settle a bit, though he's clearly still bracing himself for whatever I say next. "I'm really overwhelmed right now. I talked with Nay, and she gave me some really good things to think about."

He nods, giving me space to process.

"I'm exhausted in every way imaginable," I say, tears threatening me at the edge of my vision. "I need time. I'm not going anywhere. I need to get back to baseline."

"Of course," he says.

"Thank you," I sigh. "I'm gonna go curl up with Beef Cake if that's okay."

He nods, and I take a few steps towards the hallway before Gunnar's voice stops me in my tracks.

"Can I?" His words are cautious. "Dinner is in the oven, and I was going to make some tea here soon. Can I bring you something when it's ready?"

I can't help but smile at my big Viking and his thoughtfulness.

"Yeah. That would be great." I smile and walk over to him.

When I'm standing before him, I take his hand in mine and give it a squeeze. When I go up on my toes, he leans down so I can kiss him on the cheek.

I know he needs this.

Everything he does shows me how much he loves me, even when I'm being a bitch.

29

SELENE

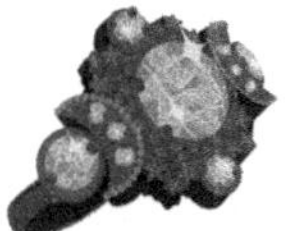

September 26—Moon still in Libra, Mercury still sextile Neptune

Gunnar and I moved through the rest of our day like ships passing in the night. Not a word was said between us since my speech.

What is there to say, really?

I spend hours going through what Naomi said over and over again as I settle myself back into the house a little more, unpacking my belongings from being out at the ranch and doing all the laundry I have from my trip.

I don't know when I decided to stay, but no part of me wants to return to the ranch. I belong here.

Every word he said to me earlier makes that even clearer now.

Though he's clearly seeking a specific answer, I don't know how to respond.

Not to mention my conversation with Naomi.

How do you know you are loved?

What kind of therapy bullshit is that?

It's to the point where it keeps me up most of the night, tossing and turning in bed until I can't take it anymore.

Around 5 a.m. I give up on sleep and go into the kitchen to start the coffee and begin making breakfast.

When I open the fridge, I see stacks of containers with ready-made meals from my diabetic friendly nutrition plan, each labeled with the dish's name and preparation instructions.

"Goddamnit," I whisper, choking on the words as they come out of my mouth.

Slamming the door to the fridge open, I turn violently on my heel and storm upstairs to our bedroom, where Gunnar is still fast asleep in our bed.

"Wake up, asshole," I say, my voice filling the room as I enter.

Gunnar stirs, but he doesn't wake up, prompting me to storm to his side of the bed.

I've always known what a big deal it is for Gunnar to feel safe enough to sleep so deeply with me around, what an honor it is. But right now I really need him to snap to attention.

"Gunnar," I growl, shaking his shoulder. "Wake the fuck up now."

He groans and tries to turn away, but I force his shoulder down so he can't move, which is quite the feat on my end, considering his size.

"Gunnar Herleif Rees, wake the fuck up now or I swear to Goddess..." I growl out.

"What?" Gunnar says groggily, batting at my hands where they push on his shoulder. "What is it, Selene?"

"You had someone meal prep for me," I snap. "Even while I was gone."

"For us," he replies, rubbing sleep from his eyes as he sits up in bed.

"You had someone come into our home and fill the fridge with food that's already made," I huff, watching as he swings his long legs over the edge to face me.

"Yes, that is in fact what meal prep means," he says, attempting to joke in his sleepy state.

"I can't believe you would... I'm so..." My hands fist at my side. "How *dare* you do something so... thoughtful!"

"What?" His gaze snaps to mine. "Selene? Your words are saying one thing, and your tone is saying something completely different."

I huff, trying to gather myself. "I'm so mad at you. And so thankful. And I just..."

Trying not to cry, I shake my head, and the emotion disappears.

"I don't know what changed. I don't know when it changed," I sigh, my temper cooling. "Maybe it was what you said to me yesterday? I don't know. But..."

"But what, Luna?" he asks, sleep now gone from his face and voice.

"I want to get married," I say, my voice sure and confident.

"Well, I would hope so. You do have my ring on your finger after all," he chuckles, which earns him a swat on the shoulder.

"No. Well, yes," I sigh, frustrated beyond measure that mind-reading isn't real.

Looking down at my ring, the most perfect ring that could ever exist, I know this is the right path for us.

"I want to get married soon." I steady myself. "Like this weekend or next, if we can make it happen."

"What? Why?" The surprise on his face is genuine, and I'm a little offended at how shocked he is at the idea.

Scowling, I tell him, "I don't want to wait. You're my person—my forever person."

There's a pause before he speaks again. A pause that lasts far too long.

"And you're mine," he says softly.

"I can see it, though. I know what I want."

Visions of the perfect day, the beautiful ceremony, and reception flash through my mind. But mostly, the people.

"And what is it that you want, little Goddess?" Gunnar asks, his hand reaching for my own to tug me close. "I'll move the sun and stars for you. You know that."

"I do." I smile at him, mesmerized by the small flickers of green hidden in his blue gaze.

"Mhmm. I love hearing those words on your lips." He grins.

"I know you do." I squeeze his hand. "And I want to say them. I do."

His sleepy expression is gone now, replaced by a mesmerizing smile.

"One more time, my Goddess," he smirks.

"No. Not until it's the real thing," I tell him, pulling away and turning on my heel.

He pulls me back, and I can't escape his grasp on me.

"Let me hear it, Luna. Tell me one more time," he purrs in my ear as he nestles me closer into his body.

He's all strength and softness, hard muscle covered in a layer of comfort. I look over my shoulder at his face and take in the slope of his crooked nose and the glint of light in his eyes.

"Tell you what, my Viking?" I tease.

"You know exactly what I want to hear, little luna." His stubble scratches along the soft roundness of my cheek, making me shiver at the rough feeling.

"Kiss me?" I tease.

"Happily. But those aren't the magic words, little luna," he growls in my ear.

"Fuck me?" I press my luck.

"Wrong again. Think really hard, Luna," he says, his deep timber driving a shiver through my whole being.

"Marry me, Gunnar."

Suddenly, I'm airborne, and Gunnar has me in his arms. He carries me back to the bed before tossing me down roughly, just how I like it.

"I love it when you talk marriage to me," Gunnar growls, prowling up my body until he covers me with his own. He leans down into my ear and purrs. "Makes me think of our wedding night and how good I'm going to fuck you then."

"And what about now?" I tease. "Are you really going to wait until the wedding night to take advantage of all of this?"

Thrusting my hips up, I grind my pelvis into his quickly forming erection.

I love how his body reacts to my own, how a shiver of pleasure and delight ripples through him enough for it to vibrate into my being.

"No, I'm not waiting any longer. I'm going to worship my Goddess as she deserves. Right. Fucking. Now," he growls, punctuating each of his last words by grinding his erection into me.

"Then I really think you should fuck me, like a good devotee should," I say.

Gunnar leans back, perusing my body as if seeing a side of me he's never noticed before.

"Fuck. I'm a lucky man," he says softly, running his hands gently over my hips and up to my stomach, drawing up my nightgown as he goes.

Leaning down, he kisses his way across the stretch marks on my skin and down to the sensitive spot hidden in the curve of my inner hip, the curve of my hips just below my waist. That soft crevasse that leads into the junction of my leg and pelvis. Every touch of his lips sends a spark of electricity through every nerve in my body.

As he worships my curves, his hands continue to push up my

silken gown until my breasts are exposed to the cold air, making my nipples pucker to tight little peaks.

My shiver at the sudden change in temperature draws Gunnar's attention away from where he was giving attention to my inner thighs and back up to my face.

"Do you need something, my Goddess?" he asks, a blonde eyebrow quirked in question.

"My breast," I pant out. "I want your lips on my breast and your fingers in my pussy."

My hips squirm in anticipation as he makes his way up to face me. Every brush of his chest hair on my skin sparks along the path he takes up my body.

"Sounds like my woman is making demands again, isn't she?" Gunnar smirks, his fingers brushing the curls at my center while he looks me straight in the eye.

"Yes," I breathe out, my eyes falling closed as I wait for the sensation of his thick fingers plunging into my core.

"But I'd so much rather hear you beg," he rumbles.

My eyes snap open, a spark of frustration flaming to life in my chest. "A Goddess doesn't beg."

"What does she do then?" Gunnar asks, provoking a dangerous part of me.

My hand snaps up to wrap around his throat, giving it a light squeeze.

"A Goddess takes what she wants, what she deserves," I say with a devious smile.

"Then take it," he tempts back.

I push on his shoulder, and he easily falls on his back in bed despite his size.

As I push myself up, I admire Gunnar's already hardened cock standing at attention. His length is throbbing, twitching with need.

My mouth waters at the sight, and I reach over to take him in hand before leaning down and wrapping my lips around his quickly purpling tip.

A deep groan slips out from between his lips, driving my need for him higher. But my desire to have him squirm beneath my touch is stronger. I take him into my mouth, sucking him down to the back of my throat, gagging on his cock until I can't breathe.

Up and down I bob on his length until his hips are bucking up into me, forcing his cock even deeper down my throat.

I push myself up, putting all my strength into keeping his hips pinned to the bed. He squirms from side to side, but he's given in to my desire to keep him immobile.

He's well and truly throbbing with need for me now, and my pussy is screaming at me to fill myself with his thickness.

Steadying myself with where my hands are placed on his hips, I bring myself to kneel above him, looking down at his perfect body.

Silently, I straddle his hips. My pussy sits just above his aching cock, and I slowly lower myself down until my opening makes contact with his length.

"You think you deserve this pussy, Viking?" I ask, rocking myself across his length and allowing my clit to gather all the pleasure it can take from the sensation. "You think you've earned this cunt?"

"Yes. Please, Goddess. I've been good, haven't I?" he grits out from between his tightly clamped teeth.

"And you thought it would be so satisfying to hear me beg, didn't you?" I laugh. "But it's so much prettier when the words slip off your lips."

"Fuck," Gunnar groans when the tip of his cock catches on my opening, but I lift myself up and away from him before he can slip in.

I'll take his cock when *I'm* ready for it.

And no sooner than that.

"Tell me, Viking. What is it that makes you deserving of worshipping my body? Of pleasing me?" I ask, a grin on my lips as I study his sharp jaw and high cheekbones.

When he settles down, I lower myself again over his length, and his hips buck up into me again at the touch.

"Nothing," he pants. "Nothing makes me worthy."

"But?"

"But I want to be. I swear. I want to be good enough for you." His eyes open, and the tenderness with which he looks at me is heartwarming.

This man truly loves me.

He'd do anything for me.

"And I, you," I tell him reverently, rising on my knees and grasping his cock in my hand.

I guide him to my opening, readying myself to sink onto his thick length and take him into my needy cunt.

"I'm going to give you what you so desperately want," I tell him, pressing his tip into my opening. "But only because *I* want to."

He nods frantically. "Yes, Goddess."

"This is about me. Not you," I remind him.

When I sink further down on his cock, his hands whip out to grasp at my hips tightly, and he groans deeply.

I'm so worked up that I can already feel my channel fluttering around him when I'm fully seated on his cock, ready for the first orgasm I'll give myself.

Following the cues my body gives me, I start rocking against him. His cock shifts inside me, rubbing against the sensitive spot inside me while my clit grinds into his pelvis.

Quickly, I work myself up to my first orgasm, and before I can even think to hold it off, the wave of pleasure crashes over me.

My whole body shivers atop Gunnar, and his hands grip my hips tighter with each squeeze my cunt gives to his cock.

"Fuck," I pant out. "I needed that."

Leaning back a little, I let the sensation waft through my body and enjoy the aftershock of the orgasm.

Soon enough, the sensation subsides, and the need comes back with a vengeance.

I shift my weight and push myself up enough to keep him barely inside me. Hovering there above him, I pulse on his tip. I let myself push an inch down and then pull back up again, over and over, until Gunnar's breath becomes a series of desperate, short pants for air.

"Fuck, Selene," he groans out.

"Not Selene," I snap, sinking fully onto his cock. "I'm your wife."

Pulling up and pushing myself back down, I force my pussy to take every inch of him that I can handle. Each bounce on his cock pushes me further down until I'm able to take his full length inside me.

I increase my pace, my hair falling around my face as I move, but I reach up to push it back, exposing my breasts openly to Gunnar, who very quickly reaches up to grasp them and play with my nipples.

I push myself through one orgasm straight into the next until I'm overstimulated and exhausted.

There's likely only one left in me as I pull up on him for the last time, my hips so close to giving out on me. But I'm chasing the sensation, the pleasure of connecting with him like this.

"Take it," Gunnar grunts out. "Take everything I can offer."

That's it. His words send me over the edge, and I careen straight into the final orgasm my body can handle.

When I collapse onto him, Gunnar begins thrusting up into me. It's not just to chase his orgasm, though I can tell that he's close, but instead to bring me down slowly from my own as he comes and fills me.

Everything is dreamy and beautiful. I'm in the arms of the man I love, the man I'm going to *marry*. It almost feels too good to be true.

Once the dreamy haze of my last orgasm has passed, reality crashes in, and my mind is suddenly full steam ahead with plans and logistics for the wedding—the excitement of the prospect propelling me forward.

I know exactly what needs to happen now, and the list is forming in my mind. My body is like an automaton that can't stop until interrupted.

"We could get married at Alvie's place, the Silver Rope Ranch," I tell him, flipping over on the bed so my torso rests on his chest. "A sunset wedding over in the grove of trees where Bex, Naomi, and I do yoga. I want to be surrounded by our closest friends, too."

Gunnar looks at me, my excitement mirrored in his gaze.

"What about your family?" he asks cautiously.

"They... I don't know." I pause, trying to think of a solution to involve my family without figuring out the logistics of getting mi familia here from Puerto Rico. "We can figure something out to make them happy. But I don't want to wait anymore."

"Okay. So, a ranch wedding," Gunnar states patiently, waiting for me to continue rambling until I get it all out of my system.

"Yes. An outdoor wedding," I confirm, though my mind goes blank, and a long pause follows.

"In the Texas heat?" Gunnar fills in the silence, but my brow furrows at his words.

"It's October! It will be fine. Right?" I'm tempted to pick up my phone and look up the forecast, but I resist the urge. "Surely it will cool down by the evening, too."

"Supposedly." He rolls his eyes, earning him a playful smack on the arm. "Okay. Okay. That sounds doable. Assuming Alvie's good with us invading his property."

"Of course he will be," I scoff. "He loves us! I'm sure they'd be happy to have us get married on the ranch."

"If you say so, wife." Gunnar smiles at me, pure joy in his expression. "I'll make it happen. You won't even have to lift a finger."

"Okay. Wedding ceremony in the grove. Then a party in the barn," I continue with my plan.

"With those Edison bulb string lights you love," Gunnar supplies, knowing me so well.

"Yes! And we do a signature cocktail for the evening."

"And have Fort's cater with barbecue." He pauses, and his expression grows more serious. "What about flowers, cake, rings? All of those details. Do you want to plan all of those? Or do you want me to handle things?"

I bite my lip as I consider taking on all that planning, and how freeing it was not to worry about that for the past couple of months. "No. I don't. I trust you to handle it. You know me inside and out. It's why I love you. More than I know how to express sometimes."

"I know, Luna. I love you, too."

I give him a light kiss on the lips, which quickly deepens and allows me to get lost in his touch.

"So?" I ask.

"So what?" he chuckles, his voice still deep and rumbly this early in the morning.

"I take it this means you're on board?"

Gunnar's grin breaks out into a full-blown smile.

"Of course I'm on board." he says, then suggests. "You should probably text the group chat if we're going to make everything happen in time."

"Oh! Yes!"

To: The Safe Word Is Brunch

SELENE

I'M GETTING MARRIED!

NAOMI

Yes, we've known that for quite a while. 😂

SELENE

No. Like... soon. We want to have the wedding next weekend.

Which, @Bex... any chance we can invade the ranch for the wedding?

BEX

Next weekend? • •

SELENE

Yes!

BEX

Of course. Send me the details when you have them.

IVY

DID YOU MAYBE WANT TO RUN THIS PAST ME BEFORE MAKING A DECISION?

SELENE

It was kind of a last-minute decision?

IVY

Clearly... Fine. I'll call you when I get into the office.

SELENE

So like... thirty minutes?

IVY

Make it an hour. I have a few things I need to do first.

ZURI

CONGRATS!

@Naomi, text me, and we can have a bachelorette
party this weekend. I have new toys to give out!

NAOMI

On it!

BEX

Alvie said he can clear the big barn for the
reception.

SELENE

Perfect! That's what I was hoping. Also... How
well do you know Fort?

BEX

I'll call him about catering lol

SELENE

Thank you!

ELSIE

We won't be able to make it, but I'd love to call in
if we can.

SELENE

Boss... this isn't a board meeting. It's a wedding.

ELSIE

And I have a newborn. I literally haven't even left
the hospital yet.

SELENE

I was kidding! Yes, we will figure out a way for you
to attend.

ELSIE

Thanks. Send me details when they're ready.

REKA

I'll be there! Symon will be in town next weekend.
So he'll come too.

For the next hour, the group chat blows up. Enough time for Gunnar and I to shower and get ready for the day, plus make us breakfast that he brings to me in bed.

He starts spooning me food as my fingers fly across my keyboard, responding to texts and emails from everyone.

"Take a break, Luna," Gunnar finally says after I refuse another bite of food. "It's okay to rest. I'll take care of it."

Looking over at my handsome Viking, I know he's right. He *will* take care of everything, of me.

"I love you," I tell him softly, putting my phone on the side table and crawling to straddle his lap. "I love you so much and can't wait to walk down the aisle to become your wife."

"I'll be waiting for you," he says, gripping my hips tightly like he's afraid that if he lets go, I'll drift away. "I'll always be home for you, if you want me to be."

"You're such a sap," I tell him, bringing my face a breath away from his own.

"But I'm your sap," he replies, bringing himself even closer until our lips lightly touch.

"Yes. Yes, you are." I smile, giving him a soft kiss.

"And I will cherish you for life," he says, drawing back with a serious face. "Until death do us part, Mrs. Rees."

"I know," I tell him, leaning back for another kiss. "In life and in death, I will always love you, Mr. Rees."

START BACK at the beginning with *Used* and see how one plus one equals three when the ice queen meets her golden retriever in Book 1 of The Playground Club series.

Get your copy!

If you want to keep reading, the series continues in Book 2 with *Bound*, a spicy FFM romance with *two* plus size ladies who have the hots for each other and a cowboy who's *very* good with rope!

Get your copy!

To stay up to date on news, sales, and releases from Shannon Elliot, join her newsletter here:

Join the newsletter!

SELENE

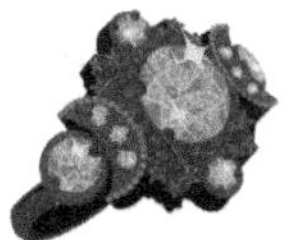

October 5—Sun, Moon, and Mercury in Libra

It turns out, ten days is all that's needed for my chosen family to throw together a wedding. One text to a group chat with everyone I love from The Playground spurred everything into action.

Ivy runs a tight ship, but she truly went full-on taskmaster tyrannizer to get it all organized. Every list in the binder we had been working on for months got tucked away to gather dust, and a whole new plan was outlined within hours of my texting the group. Calls and texts at all hours of the day and night would ask Gunnar and me about one thing or another, to the point where I had to send Griffin's meta, who is a doctor, Sage Morgan, over to check on her. This resulted in several IV fluid bags being pumped into Ivy's system to replace the amount of caffeine she'd been consuming and a supervised nap to make sure she slept. I don't think she's happy with me about that one at all.

Three days was all it took for Naomi and Zuri to put together the perfect bachelorette party for me and all the girls at the resort, including Elsie, who video called us so we could all coo over her baby girl, Bridgit, for a few minutes while her mama was still recovering. Having the luncheon at the resort was a smart move, though, because we were all far too tipsy by the end of it to go anywhere but our rooms upstairs for a good nap before the guys were to join us in the evening at the club for a joint celebration.

Bex and Alvie dropped everything to prepare the ranch for us, too. All the regular duties of running a ranch were left to their foreman so that they could focus on wedding preparations. They even called in reinforcements from their small-town community to help ready the grove for the ceremony and the barn for the wedding reception.

Cakes were tasted, and the menu was set. Dresses and boots were bought. Tuxes were dry-cleaned and pressed. It all happened in a blur, but it came together quickly and beautifully.

Now I'm sitting alone on a settee in a little cabin, dressed in lingerie and staring up at a dress we found on a clearance rack that I would have never imagined getting married in. Yet it feels *right*.

Everything about today feels good, like it was meant to be this way.

There are no nerves or jitters, just a calm sense of knowing that my life is in alignment with the universe at this moment.

Everything is as it ought to be.

A knock at the cabin door draws me back to the moment, and I call out to tell the person to enter.

Clad in a pastel pink gown covered in delicate rosettes that hugs her body beautifully, Naomi appears from behind the door and brings a broad smile to my face.

"Hey, Lena," she says softly with a grin that matches my own. "You ready?"

"Yeah. I am," I say, feeling every bit of the confidence I hear in my voice. "Will you help me get into the dress?"

"Of course."

I can tell she's holding back tears, probably just as much as I am.

But my mascara is fifty-fucking-dollars, and while it is waterproof, I refuse to ruin all the hard work Ivy did to make everything about my appearance perfect today—the woman is truly multitalented.

Naomi and I take our time getting me ready, allowing me to savor the last quiet moment I'll have today.

When I'm finally dressed from head to toe in my bridal regalia, we stand before the full-length mirror and take in the vision of the two of us together.

"You ready for this?" Naomi asks after a minute of silence.

"Yeah," I smile back at her in the mirror. "I am."

Alvie is waiting outside in his truck and helps us into the vehicle's cab as gracefully as possible in our wedding attire.

We pull up to the event tent where I'll be hiding out until it's time to make my grand entrance, and when Alvie helps me out of the truck, there's a sheen in his eyes.

"You make a beautiful bride, Selene," he says softly. "Gunnar is a lucky man."

I smile back at Alvie, my own eyes starting to fill with tears.

"Y'all are all dead set on having me cry today, aren't you?" I say with a wobbly voice.

"Pretty much." He smirks and leans in, pressing a kiss to my forehead. "Enjoy today. You only get so many of these kinds of moments in life."

"Would you do it again?" I ask him.

"For my women? In a heartbeat," he says without hesitation.

"Well then, tag." I poke him in the chest. "You're it."

I turn and head into the tent, where I find Naomi waiting with Ivy and Bex. They are performing our ceremony, as Alvie will be standing next to Gunnar.

"Stunning," Ivy breathes out, coming over to fuss at something as she speaks.

"Truly," Bex confirms. "You look incredible, Selene."

"Thank you," I reply with a smile.

After she finishes fussing, Ivy runs off to check on the video call for Elsie, Marshall, and baby Bridgit to join in and watch the ceremony so that things can get underway.

One by one, the women leave until I'm alone in the tent, waiting for my cue to walk down the aisle. Because no matter how loud the world gets, he's the one who always finds me. He sees me—past the walls, past the scars—and loves me for every piece, even the ones I've tried to hide. Walking toward him now isn't just about vows or rings. It's about choosing the only person who has ever been my home.

Finally, Ivy pokes her head in to have me come out, and it's like the whole world slows to a stop when I reach the beginning of the aisle.

Gunnar is on the other side of the rows of chairs, beaming at me with tears in his eyes.

He looks so handsome in a charcoal gray suit with a dark pink tie, a few shades darker than what we put Naomi and Alvie in. His smile is blinding, but it's the love in his eyes that makes me forget to breathe—love for me.

Everything focuses on him and me as I go down the short aisle, probably far too quickly for what a proper procession would require.

But I just want to be with him, and when I reach him with his outstretched hand, I take it tightly in my own.

Most of the ceremony passes in a blur as Gunnar and I stare at each other. Bex even has to tap me at one point to get me to repeat the words she needs me to say.

Then comes the part I've been most excited about: the hand-fasting.

Bex explains the meaning of the ritual to the small group we have gathered.

She has Gunnar and me cross our arms and take each other's hands before reciting our vows as she wraps a cord around our joined hands.

"Selene," Gunnar starts. "You are my everything: my sun and stars, the center of my universe. I'm the luckiest man in the world to get to call myself your partner, and I'm honored that you'd consider me to be your husband. I can't imagine any part of my life without you in it. A life with you is one that's truly worth living. I cannot wait to see where this journey takes us and the adventures that await."

Tears fall freely as he speaks, and he pauses momentarily to take out his pocket square and hand it to me to blot my tears.

"When I first saw you, I thought, 'That's the woman I'm going to marry. I should learn her name.' And it's the best decision I've ever made. I will forever be grateful to the universe for placing you in my world, allowing me to gravitate to and be in your presence. You're everything I could have wished for and more, Selene. I will treasure you for the rest of my days and worship you as you deserve. I love you, little Goddess."

When he finishes, he looks at me expectantly, and I realize it's my turn, but I'm too overwhelmed by emotion to really get out more than a few words.

"Gunnar," I choke out, trying to gain my composure. "I love you endlessly. You are a better partner than I could have ever dreamed of, and I'm lucky to have found you. You've always said you knew I was it for you since you laid eyes on me. That you needed to learn my name because I was the woman you were going to marry one day. There's something so special about that kind of love. I'm the one who is honored to be on the receiving end of your kindness and devotion. I want to be the woman who gives you that, too. I want to be the person who makes you feel like a god among mortals."

"You do," he interrupts earnestly.

"I'm glad." I smile at him genuinely. "You're my Viking, a protector and warrior who will fight for me no matter what. You call me your Goddess and worship me as such, but I promise to show you the same adoration. I promise to love and cherish you, for all the days of my life."

When I'm done, Gunnar and I are both actively crying, and then Bex pronounces us husband and wife as she unwraps the cord from our hands.

Once we're free, Gunnar's lips are on mine before Bex can even get out the words to kiss the bride.

I melt into the kiss.

Our tears mix as our tongues caress against one another. The passion with which he kisses me has me feeling boneless. If it weren't for him holding me up, I'd surely be on the ground in a puddle.

We pour every bit of our souls and love into the kiss, and when we pull apart, there's a new light in Gunnar's eyes.

"I love you, Luna." He says against my lips.

"I love you, too, Viking," I murmur back.

WANT MORE OF THE PLAYGROUND CLUB?

Start back at the beginning with *Used* and see how one plus one equals three when the ice queen meets her golden retriever in Book 1 of The Playground Club series.

Get your copy!

If you want to keep reading, the series continues in Book 2 with *Bound*, a spicy FFM romance with *two* plus size ladies who have the hots for each other and a cowboy who's *very* good with rope!

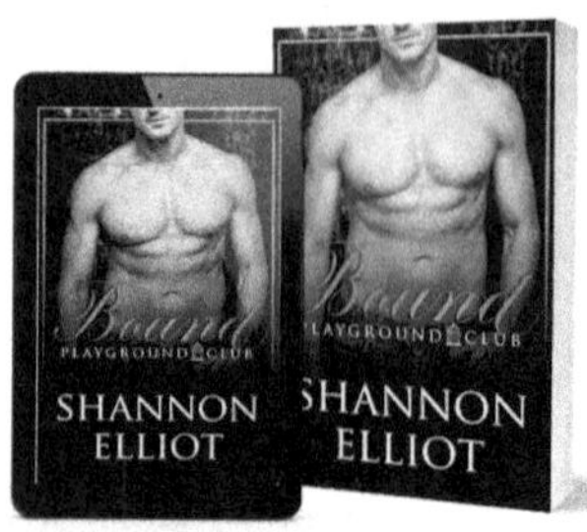

Get your copy!

To stay up to date on news, sales, and releases from Shannon Elliot, join her newsletter here:

Join the newsletter!

ACKNOWLEDGMENTS

To my friends, you're my whole world. You've been with me through everything. I wrote a love story between Selene and Gunnar, but I think more than anything this story is about us and the ways in which we love each other. I'm so grateful to each and every one of you. You're never getting rid of me at this point.

To Ashley and Becca, you're going in alphabetical order because I can't put you side by side.

Ashley, you're my soulmate in every meaning of the word. Thank you for showing up for me in every way. For giving me space to make my own mistakes and still holding me while I cry because they blew up in my face. I am a better creative because of you, but more so I'm a better person with you in my life. I will never be able to really express how much I love and adore you.

Becca, this is the first project I've written without you holding my hand the entire time and I think your absence was the best thing that could have happened to this book. Every bit of my heart got poured into this love story, because, in the end, it's a love letter to you, my wifey. It's been one hell of a year and I'm one-hundred percent on board with forgetting it ever happened. But I think we keep this one as a reminder of how much love we're capable of, now and forever.

Becky, you're truly a gift that I do not deserve. I could not have made this happen without you and your incredible contributions. You're one hell of an editor and an even better friend. Thanks for sticking with me even when I go MIA for 5 months (promise to not do that again... hopefully.) I'm so eternally grateful, thank you.

Becca Fogg, you show up for me in so many ways. Thank you for being my encouraging mother figure and accountability buddy. I will never again forget your words "You're too hot to disappoint yourself!" You're truly an icon. Love you.

Grace & Bria, besties we did it. Somehow we're making this thing happen. Thank you for your flexibility and the way you show up for me at 100% every time. Y'all keep the machine working and I couldn't do it without you.

Early readers give such an amazing insight into the stories authors tell. I cannot thank Sander, Lara, and Jennifer enough for reading through this manuscript with love and a fine tooth comb. Your insight and input into this story is what helps it feel real (and make some fucking sense.) Endless thank you's to you both!

Bullying is a necessary part of meeting a deadline and you're an angel (and maybe a little bit of a devil) for taking up the responsibility, Coletha. Thank you for reminding me that my stories need to be told. There are people waiting for this.

To my influencer and ARC teams, so many of y'all have been with me for such a long time and others are just now joining us on this adventure. I'm so grateful to everyone who shows up for me in this crazy career that I'm so honored to have.

To my family, you know the drill about reading my books, but thank you for all of your support. This is an incredible thing that you've allowed me to do and I will forever be indebted to you for all of your contributions. Love y'all.

ABOUT THE AUTHOR

Shannon Elliot resides in Texas, with her fur baby and writes romance that reflects her readers whenever she's not at the dog park or curled up with a good book. Evidenced by her background in theatre, she is drawn to story-telling and the creative process. Shannon believes that diverse and inclusive stories shouldn't be the exception, they should be the rule. Happily ever after is for everyone and she aims to write romances that reflect her readers.

www.authorshannonelliot.com/pages/links

ALSO BY SHANNON ELLIOT

The Playground Club Series

Used, Book 1

Bound, Book 2

Cherished, Book 3

Descent into Darkness Duet

Angels in the Dark, Book 1

Devil in the Dark, Book 2

Standalone Novellas

Heel